Lucilla Andrews was born in Suez, the second daughter of an English father and a Spanish mother. Her late father was then a manager in the Eastern Telegraph Company. At three she began her education in an English private girls' boarding school in Sussex and when she was eleven she wrote her first novel – an epic of love, lust and banditry in China. Unfortunately the manuscript was discovered and ended in the school incinerator.

When World War II broke out Lucilla Andrews exchanged her school uniform for that of a V.A.D. in a military hospital. After a year she entered the Nightingale Training School at St. Thomas's Hospital in London and five years later left with an S.R.N. and S.C.M. Part One. She married a doctor, had one child, and when her husband's illness necessitated that she become the family breadwinner she returned to nursing.

Her first book, THE PRINT PETTICOAT, was written while she was working as an assistant Night Sister in a small Sussex hospital. Since that time it has never been out of print.

Over the years Lucilla Andrews has established herself as one of Britain's leading popular novelists. She has created what is virtually a new genre – the hospital romance – written against an authentic and detailed medical background which is drawn from her own experience.

Readers who would like to know more about Lucilla Andrews are recommended to read her autobiography, NO TIME FOR ROMANCE, an account of her life a
wartime London.

D1300233

Also by Lucilla Andrews

THE PRINT PETTICOAT
THE SECRET ARMOUR
THE FIRST YEAR
A HOSPITAL SUMMER
MY FRIEND THE PROFESSOR
NURSE ERRANT
FLOWERS FROM THE DOCTOR
THE YOUNG DOCTORS DOWNSTAIRS
THE NEW SISTER THEATRE
THE LIGHT IN THE WARD
A HOUSE FOR SISTER MARY
HOSPITAL CIRCLES
HIGHLAND INTERLUDE
THE HEALING TIME
EDINBURGH EXCURSION
RING O' ROSES
SILENT SONG
IN STORM AND IN CALM
THE CRYSTAL GULL

Writing as Joanna Marcus
A FEW DAYS IN ENDEL

Autobiography
NO TIME FOR ROMANCE

and published by Corgi Books

Lucilla Andrews

The Quiet Wards

CORGI BOOKS
A DIVISION OF TRANSWORLD PUBLISHERS LTD

THE QUIET WARDS
A CORGI BOOK 0 552 11436 7

Originally published in Great Britain
by George G. Harrap & Co Ltd

PRINTING HISTORY
Harrap edition published 1956
Harrap edition reprinted 1956 (twice)
Harrap edition reprinted 1957
Corgi edition published 1960
Corgi edition reissued 1967
Corgi edition reissued 1980

This book is set in Plantin

Corgi Books are published by Transworld Publishers Ltd.,
Century House, 61-63 Uxbridge Road,
Ealing, London, W5 5SA
Made and printed in Great Britain by
William Collins Sons & Co Ltd, Glasgow

For
Dr. T. and Ann

Contents

1

ONE NIGHT IN ROBERT WARD

ROBERT WARD was very quiet that night, but few of the men were sleeping. Robert was a men's acute surgical ward, with twenty beds each side. All the beds were occupied, and the men watched us with troubled eyes as we moved in and out of the drawn cubicle curtains round bed number 18.

Behind those curtains Sister Robert stood still as a statue at the foot of the bed. The sleeves of her navy blue dress were rolled high above her elbows; one hand rested lightly on the metal transfusion stand attached to the bed-rail. She watched the slow, steady trickle of blood through the glass drip-connexion.

'A little faster, Nurse Snow,' she murmured. 'Put that pin in the top hole and see if gravity will do it. I've opened the screw as far as it'll go. If we can't speed it up we'll have to let Mr Dexter know.'

I moved the pin and the blood ran more quickly. Sister dropped her hand. 'That's it. Now there's nothing more we can do until he comes round. Your probationer must sit with him while I give you the rest of the report.'

I went outside the curtains and beckoned to the pro who was hovering round the cluster of empty wheel-chairs at the end of the ward.

'Stay with him, please, Nurse,' I said when she joined me, 'and don't leave him for anything, no matter who calls. I'm not sure yet how we'll manage the other men, but I'll work that out later.'

She nodded uncertainly. 'Do I—do I have to do anything for him, Nurse Snow?'

'Take his pulse every ten minutes; keep an eye on the blood, and if it slows down call me at once. Or if his pulse varies more than ten either way—it's a hundred and two now—put your head between the curtains and call me, no matter who I'm with or what I'm doing. I'll hear you and come at the double. But don't leave him. Got that?'

She nodded again. She looked terrified.

'You take over now.' I held back the curtain. 'Sister wants to finish giving me her report.'

Sister Robert pulled down her sleeves and walked to the table that was hidden behind red screens in the centre of the ward.

'Sit down, Nurse Snow, and we'll run through the others. It won't take long. Fortunately Admiral Kerry is our only ill patient.'

9

By ill she meant dangerously ill. All our men were bed patients; only seven of the forty patients had reached the stage of being lifted into wheel-chairs for afternoon tea. Robert, being an acute ward, dealt only with operation cases, and our patients were moved to a convalescent ward directly they lost their stitches. It was a pleasant and interesting ward, but it was never empty or slack.

Sister did not linger over her report. It was after 10 P.M., and officially she should have been off at nine. When she had finished I walked with her to the outer door of the ward which lay at the end of the small corridor we called 'the flat.' That was a point of etiquette.

'I'm afraid you're in for a bad night,' she said, as I held open the door for her, 'since one of you will be tied up constantly with the Admiral. I asked Matron about a spare night relief, but she said that the only spare senior nurse is specialing an accident in Charity, so I'm afraid you will just have to manage as best you can. But I'll have a private word with Night Sister on my way out and see if she can produce someone, if only for an hour or two.'

I thanked her and she left. I went straight back to bed 18. Nurse Fraser, the pro, looked round hopefully.

'Shall I get on with my routine, Nurse Snow?'

'Not just yet.' I explained what Sister Robert had just told me. 'I'll have to see to the others first and give out the sedatives before Night Sister and the men arrive. I'll be as quick as I can, but until I'm free you'll have to stay put.'

She was very young. She had a small, thin face, and her fair hair was pulled back in a tight bun. She had not yet learnt how to manage her cap, and it was sliding over one ear. She looked like a pigtailed and very frightened schoolgirl. I sympathised with her. I had been equally scared by serious illness when I started training nearly four years ago. Now it disturbed me, but did not scare me; I had been taught what I should do and what I should not do. This was the difference that training made. Pros are always scared because they think they have to do everything.

The men were as thoughtful as patients are when they suspect the presence of death in a ward. No one mentioned the man behind the drawn curtains, but their voices were compassionate.

'I'm fine, Nurse. You don't have to bother about me.'

'Let's have a couple of them tablets, duck, an' I'll not trouble you again.'

'Thanks awfully, Nurse Snow—but my dressing is grand. No, it doesn't feel as if it's sticking.'

The ward was full of merchant seamen, stevedores, shop assistants, schoolmasters, barrow boys, and West Indians, all of whom had become—Robert. Robert was a body that spoke in assorted accents but with one voice. Tonight the voice said, 'I'm O.K., Nurse. You get back to that poor old chap that's bought it behind 18.'

Half an hour later I was filling in the dangerous-drug book, when a girl called Carol Ash walked into Robert 'flat.' Carol was a plump, round-faced girl; her cheeks were pink, her hair dark brown. She looked as if she had stepped in from the country, but she was a Londoner born and thought the countryside was only tolerable when viewed from inside a closed car travelling fast. She was Night Senior Nurse in Ellen, a women's convalescent ward. I watched her hang her cloak on a fire-bucket and then walk up the ward to the table.

I looked up and smiled. 'Hello,' I said quietly. 'What goes on in Ellen?'

She leant on the back of Sister's empty chair. 'Nothing goes on in Ellen. Which is why I've come to special your Admiral.'

'Thank Heaven for that.' I beamed with relief. 'You're the best news I've had in months. But why you? Who's standing in for you?'

She sat down. 'June Pickering. Her woman in Charity died an hour ago. Night Sister said she didn't want to shove Pickering straight on to another specialing job and she knew I enjoyed it, so she asked if I should like to come.' She looked down the ward through the gap in the red screens. 'Ellen is like a tomb these nights, so I jumped at it. I hate,' she added very quietly, 'having time on my hands.'

'I can believe that.' I handed her the report book. 'Read that —and then I'll tell you all.'

I did not say any more because I knew she would not want me to say more. Carol was a good friend of mine, and what recently happened to her had happened to me during my first year in hospital. We were both only children; and now neither of us had parents. But at least I had been fortunate in having a few months between losing my father and mother. Carol had gone to Norway with her parents last June. One morning her parents had gone out for an early drive; their car had been in a head-on collision with another car, and Carol returned from that holiday alone. Matron had given me leave to go to Newcastle to meet her, and since that time our friendship had deepened.

She read the case history slowly. Then, 'Tell me the rest.'

'Not much to tell.' I was listening to the sounds of the ward as I spoke. The men were breathing quietly, but consciously. They, like us, were waiting. 'Chronic G.U. His ulcer perforated some time this afternoon when he and his wife were on a shopping spree in town. He's retired, lives in Hampshire. Joe's was

11

the nearest place, so they brought him in. There were no free private rooms, and anyway there was no time to bother much about those niceties. He went down to the theatre this evening, and the S.S.O. patched him out. He's not yet round; he's on continuous whole blood—he's a good age. See here'—I put my finger on the place in the report—'and he's mighty shocked.'

She asked after his pulse-rate and blood-pressure, and I told her what they had been fifteen minutes ago.

She nodded. 'I've got that taped. Has our John been up to see him yet?'

'Our John' was Mr Jonathan Alexander Dexter, Master of Surgery, the Senior Surgical Officer resident in the hospital.

'No. No one's been up. Sister Robert herself didn't get away until after ten, so that's just as well. And anyway the poor man didn't get back from the theatre until just before we came on duty.'

Carol raised her eyebrows. 'I thought you said he was done this evening?'

Hospital evenings start at 5 P.M.

'He went down about six. But they had to hold everything on the table and give him some blood.'

She said, 'That's quite a time. What was our John doing? He's usually pretty snappy with his knife.'

I shrugged. 'I dunno. I'm only a wretched nurse, ducks. But Sister Robert did say she had never seen a man in such a mess. She took him to the theatre herself. I suppose John took longer than usual because he had more than usual to sort out.'

She smiled rather grimly. 'I'm disappointed. I thought maybe our peerless S.S.O. might be slipping.'

I stood up. 'Our peerless S.S.O. isn't human enough to slip. But let's go and relieve that pro, or the poor kid will have a nervous breakdown.'

She did not move. 'I expect he's human,' she said, 'but I can't help wishing that once in a way he would make a mistake—only not necessarily on this miserable sailor.' She tilted her face to look at me. Her averted face was very attractive. 'You know, he reminds me of you, Gillian. You both sail around Joe's a few inches off the ground. You never touch down, do you?'

At another time I should have been fascinated to discuss any resemblance between myself and the S.S.O., but I was worrying about my Admiral.

'You could be right,' I said, 'but we'll thrash it out later. Let's just sail up the ward, shall us? My child is stiff with fear about the poor man, and I'm stiff with fear about them both.'

She stood up slowly. 'Anything you say, Gillian.'

We had nearly reached the drawn curtains when we heard the

flat door open. Night Sister and a couple of men were in the flat.

'I'll have to leave you to it,' I murmured. 'You all right?'

She looked at me. 'I'm not your pro, dearie.'

'Sorry.' I raised a hand apologetically and walked quickly away.

Night Sister and the doctors had stopped by the closed kitchen door. Night Sister was nodding to herself. She was a thin, neat Scotswoman. For some peculiar reason Night Sisters are almost invariably Scots. Miss Mackenzie was a pleasant woman in the late forties. Her face was permanently grey and her shoulders hunched from years of tiptoeing round darkened wards, but her temper was unruffled by lack of sleep and no one had ever known her to be anything but calm and thoughtful for her patients, the medical staff, or her nurses.

She said, 'I'll away, Nurse Snow. I'll be back when you are less busy.' She looked through the open doors of the ward. 'Nurse Ash has arrived?'

'She's with Admiral Kerry now, Sister, thank you.'

She nodded, and the rustle of the lace frills on her cap was louder than her voice when she spoke again.

'She will stay with you all night, Nurse Snow.'

I thanked her, and she asked quickly after the Admiral.

'Not round yet, Sister. Otherwise his condition is unchanged since we came on duty.'

She glanced up at the S.S.O., who was the taller of the two men beside her. 'I will see you later, Mr Dexter?'

He roused himself. He was still wearing his long white theatre-gown, cap, and mask. The mask had been pulled down and hung loosely round his neck. He looked very tired.

'Whenever you want me, Sister,' he said civilly. 'I'm sorry I couldn't speak to you when you rang from Charity, but I was in the middle of that last appendix. I've just come from the theatre. I suppose both those women are all right?'

'Aye,' said Sister, 'they'll do. As I do not doubt this poor man here will do, Mr Dexter.' And she disappeared from my elbow.

The S.S.O. glanced at me. 'So he's not round yet, Nurse Snow?' He used the flat tone that all trained hospital staff use at night. It is sound that carries far less than a whisper.

'The admiral had not come round a quarter of an hour ago, Mr Dexter. I have not seen him since then.'

'I see.' He felt for his pockets, discovered that he was still in a gown, and propped his knuckles on his hips. His shoulders were slightly raised, as if he was carrying a heavy weight. He made no move to go into the ward, so I stood with my hands behind my back and buttoned my sleeves under my cuffs as I waited, correctly, for the S.S.O.

The houseman who was with him had been shifting from one foot to another. Now he dodged round the S.S.O. and cleared his throat.

'Excuse me, sir—er—Nurse Snow——?'

I said, 'Yes, Mr Thanet?'

Tom Thanet was a burly young man with a broad strong-featured face and a very deep voice. He was one of the most junior house-surgeons in the hospital.

'Anything you want me for? Or shall I push off?'

Mr Dexter said coolly, 'When Nurse Snow has dealt with me, Thanet, I have no doubt she will find the time to answer your questions.' He looked at me instead of Tom as he talked, which was as well, since Tom was winking at me.

'Sorry, sir,' said Tom mildly, 'my mistake. See you later, Nurse Snow.'

'Nurse Snow,' said the S.S.O., 'are we to spend the entire night making assignations in this doorway? Or could I persuade you to allow me to see my Admiral?'

I smiled feebly. 'Shall we go now, Mr Dexter?'

'It might,' he said, 'be an idea.' He stood back and waited for me to precede him up the ward. As we walked by, the men on either side lifted their heads and then, seeing who I was with, relaxed. John Dexter might at times be short with his housemen, but he had that effect on all patients.

Carol was taking Admiral Kerry's pulse. The S.S.O. said, 'Go on, Nurse Ash,' and waited by the bed. He watched the still unconscious man in silence, then reached an arm my way for the temperature chart. When he had read all he wanted he handed it back, still in silence. He tapped the glass connexion lightly.

'This as fast as it'll go, Nurse Ash?'

'Yes, Mr Dexter.'

'I see.' He looked at the man again. 'I may have to put up a fresh drip. It'll mean a cut-down if it's necessary. I'll do it—so if you have trouble, ask Nurse Snow to get me. Right?'

Carol said, 'Yes, Mr Dexter.'

He walked closer to the bed; touched the man's pulse, his cheek, his forehead; turned back the bed-clothes and looked at the top dressing. He nodded to himself. 'He'll have to have at least another pint,' he said, 'maybe more.' Then he straightened and moved back to the foot of the bed and stood again, watching the thin, pinched face of the sick man.

At last he had seen enough. He glanced at Carol. 'Good night, Nurse Ash—thank you,' he murmured automatically, and held back the curtains for me. When we were outside them he said, 'I may as well look at the other men while I'm here. I don't like doing this ward before midnight, but this looks like

14

being a busy night, so I want to get as much done as I can before I get caught up in the theatre again.'

'Very busy, Mr Dexter?'

'The theatre has been,' he said laconically. 'I've had two perforations already this evening. I'm not a superstitious man, but I can't help feeling there'll be a third. There generally is.'

We walked to the doctors' sink on the left of the door, and I waited while he washed his hands; then we walked up one side of the ward and down the other.

The men smiled, 'Evening, Doctor. You don't get much sleep, do you?'

He said he had enough, thanks, and what were they doing awake? He never talked much to the patients, but that was not odd, since he never talked much to anyone. But the patients liked him.

'Gives you confidence, that big quiet chap,' they said; 'makes you feel safe, he does.'

He looked at the charts, sometimes the notes, always their faces. He had seen them all that morning; he would see them all again the next morning; but once every night he walked round every surgical ward in the hospital.

Nurse Fraser bustled down the ward on her way from the sluice to the linen-chute. She was carrying a closed bucket of soiled linen in each hand. We were just passing the wheelchairs, and the wide ward in that one point was narrowed by obstacles. He stood aside. 'Evening, Nurse.'

She gaped at him, and although the light was dim it was light enough for me to see the surprise in her face. She answered, 'Evening, Mr Dexter,' and in her surprise forgot to speak quietly, then remembered as she spoke and her voice trailed off in a squeal. She sounded as shaken as all juniors were by this civility from one of the two most senior resident doctors in Joe's. She was new to Robert and Mr Dexter, but like every sensible pro had accepted the fact that first-year nurses are generally considered to be beneath the notice of any doctor. I saw by the jaunty way that she now carried her buckets to the chute that she did not realise that the present S.S.O. was invariably polite to all juniors. I was not going to disillusion her. I was glad her morale was being boosted. I knew she had been very frightened over the Admiral.

When we reached the table he said, 'I won't keep you long, Nurse Snow, but I wanted to add some notes of my own to that chap Kerry's.'

I said that was quite all right, Mr Dexter, thank you, and sat down by the table, leaving Sister's chair for him.

Waiting for the S.S.O., and waiting on him when he was in the ward, was as much part of my job as Night Senior as bed-

15

making or taking temperatures. I sat beside him and waited for him to finish his notes; I wondered about his behaviour and why he was so civil, not only to the pros, but to all of us, not excluding his housemen. His irritation with Tom Thanet tonight had been so unusual as to prove his rule, and Tom had probably been as surprised as I by that irritation.

The notes were taking him a long time, and as I now no longer needed to worry about the Admiral, since the boss himself was in the ward and had taken over from me temporarily, and I knew the men were all right, I thought about Jonathan Dexter's good manners, and why he had this attribute, by no means common among doctors. And then I wondered why, despite this pleasing characteristic, I had never liked him or felt at ease with him. I decided it was because it was difficult to like a stranger. I had seen him around the hospital for years; he had been S.S.O. for the last two. And during the previous two months of this spell in Robert I had seen him nightly. But although I was now bosom pals with the house-surgeons and the surgical registrars, the S.S.O. was still a stranger. I was not alone in this. No one knew our John, and discussing him was our favourite pastime.

I folded my hands in my lap and began surreptitiously unbuttoning my sleeves under my cuffs. He could not be much longer. I did not think he had noticed what I was doing, but without looking up he said, 'I've nearly done,' and went on writing.

At length he capped his pen. 'And Nurse Ash is staying with him all night?'

I said yes.

'Good.' He leant forward on the table and propped his head on his hands. His fingers felt curiously at his theatre cap. He pulled it off, dropped it on the pile of notes in front of him, and pushed his hands through his thick black hair. When he moved his hand away some of his hair fell forward over his forehead. The table light beside him turned that bit of hair to silver. The light was false; in the daytime that streak was not silver, but white. He had a square-shaped face with a strong jaw line. His face was lined and white tonight, and his eyes were rimmed with red.

'God,' he said, 'I'm weary.'

I had noticed how tired he looked when he came in. He must have been unusually so, to admit so much human failing to one of his subordinates. He certainly looked years older than his age, which was thirty-seven.

'Was he very difficult, Mr Dexter?'

He was staring at his hands. 'Pretty.'

'Is he going to do?'

16

He went on gazing at his hands as if he had never seen them before and was surprised to find them sitting at the end of his arms.

'I wouldn't like to say, Nurse,' he said slowly, 'I wouldn't like to say. I had to do a great deal more to him than I cared to do. And he was pretty shocked before I started.' He was silent. 'There wasn't much option,' he added grimly, 'but that doesn't stop me wondering if my handiwork won't give him the final push.' He looked at me for the first time. 'And he's a nice old chap.'

I might not like him, but I could appreciate the staggering and endless responsibility that was his.

I said, 'But it's not your fault, Mr Dexter, if he's run around with an ulcer that much too long and has forced you to operate.'

He said, 'No one forces anyone to operate. I thought it was a good thing. I still think it was a good thing. But I wish to God he'd come round.'

I said I wished it too. I asked if he would like some coffee. Offering him coffee was another of my official duties.

'No thanks, Nurse. I've just had supper. And I promised his wife I'd ring her again at eleven-thirty. And also'—a ghost of a smile flickered over his face—'I could do with something stronger than coffee tonight.'

I was curious. This was probably the longest conversation I had ever had with him, and the first opportunity he had given me to see how he felt about the job. I said, 'Do these things often worry you this way?'

'Not things, people.' He rubbed his jaw. 'The ideal, of course, is to reach the state of mind where you can obliterate the human angle. You do better work that way—in theatre, that is. But every now and then you slip back. Or I do.' He locked his hands on the table top. 'I had a long talk with this old chap when he came in this evening. Like I said, he's a good chap—sensible. His wife's the same type. I had a talk with her too. I had to tell her the score.'

'What did she say?'

He glanced sideways at me. 'She said what they all say: "I leave it to you, Doctor. I know you'll do what's best." And when they say that, sometimes I wonder: have I?'

I looked down at my own hands to hide the surprise I felt. I was as shocked by the thought that the S.S.O. ever felt uncertainty as I would have been if one of the Metropolitan Police had stopped me in the street and told me he had lost his way.

When I looked up again he was still watching me.

'Tell me, Nurse Snow,' he said, 'what do you think of his chances?'

'What do I think, Mr Dexter?' I asked cautiously, wondering, unlikely though it seemed, if he was joking. British doctors, in or out of hospital, do not, as a rule, ask the professional opinions of nurses.

He nodded.

I thought a moment. 'I don't think he'll die.'

His expression was thoughtful, nothing more.

'Why not?'

'Because——' I hesitated, 'because he doesn't look like it. I've noticed,' I went on quickly to prevent the criticism I felt was bound to come, 'that when people are moribund they have a special look about them. I know that you, Sister Robert, every one, is very gloomy about him and I'm sure you're right. But I just don't think he'll die.'

'Because he doesn't look like it?' he echoed. Then he smiled properly. 'You know,' he said, 'you're right. He doesn't. He looks mighty ill, but he doesn't look as he should look. I was puzzled by that myself just now.' He tilted his head to look down through the gap in the screens to the closed curtains round 18. 'But I wish he'd come round soon. He's got a good will. I'd like to get that will consciously working on our side. That's partly why I'm hanging around here. That—and the fact that I'm too dead weary to get out of this chair.'

I half rose in my chair. 'Would you like me to see if he's come round yet?'

He said simply, 'No, thank you. Nurse Ash is there.' So I subsided obediently and wondered how I should ever catch up on my night's work, which still remained to be started, and who was the misguided person who had invented the rule that ordained that I must act as his quite superfluous shadow.

He had picked up the case notes again and was flicking through them. He reached for his pen and drew a pair of small stomachs on one of the pages, then ornamented the drawings with arrows.

'He's a good build,' he said to the drawings.

'His face is very thin,' I said. 'I thought perhaps he was too thin.'

'No'—he was shading the ucler site now—'from my point of view, you can't be too thin. And surely you've noticed the tremendous strength wiry people'—he half turned, and his eyes rested on me as if I was a candidate for his surgery—'like yourself possess. You're an apparently frail and over-tall young woman—but are you ever ill?'

I said no, I was not, thank you very much.

'While your friend Nurse Ash'—he wrote a balloon note and attached it to the first picture—'who looks as sturdy as a rock, is rather the reverse.' He blotted his work. 'Of course, it's hardly

18

surprising that she should have been knocked flat by that accident, mentally; but I gather that, physically, she's only survived her four years here by the skin of her teeth.'

I said no, it was not surprising that that accident should have upset Nurse Ash and yes, she had been off sick a good deal.

I was not surprised he knew she was a particular friend of mine; everyone in a hospital always knows everyone else's affairs, but I was surprised that he should know so much of her medical history. Then I recollected that Dr Cutler, the Senior Medical Officer and the man who looked after sick nurses, was as notoriously chatty as his opposite number was uncommunicative.

He said, 'Have you——' when we heard a small cough and Carol's voice, raised slightly to break into an anaesthetised mind.

'Just spit it out, Admiral Kerry, and take a deep breath. You'll be all right.'

Mr Dexter was out of his chair and down the ward before I had time to leave the table. He was a very big man, but despite his height he could move very lightly. He had won the inter-hospital heavyweight boxing cup for Joe's for five years in succession in his student-houseman days; and as I shot after the tail of his flowing gown I wondered irrelevantly how many middle-aged general practitioners now practising in England had broken noses which they owed to our John.

As I reached the curtains he remembered me. 'I'll manage alone, thanks, Nurse—don't you bother. I'm sure you have plenty of your own work to get on with.'

I murmured, 'Thank you, Mr Dexter,' but doubted if he heard me. I returned to the table and picked up the pulse-book and a stethoscope with which to take the very belated 10 P.M. pulses as a house-surgeon called Peter Kier came in at the flat door and, catching sight of me, raised a hand.

He waited at the ward door. 'My boss been up, Gillian?' he asked, when I joined him.

'Here now. Behind 18 with Carol Ash. Do you want him specifically, or do you want to go round?'

Nurse Fraser appeared at my elbow. 'Shall I do those for you, Nurse? I've finished the laundry.'

I remembered how much I had enjoyed wearing a stethoscope when I was a pro. It was about the one time I felt a modern, high-powered nurse, not an old-fashioned, inglorious cleaner.

'Thanks, Nurse Fraser.'

Peter grinned at her retreating back. 'Tactful little soul, that child.'

I did not tell him that I had not thought of that angle. I never disagreed with Peter. I said she was very tactful.

'How's the old salt?'

'Coming round now. Perhaps we should join that party?'

'Nightingale,' said Peter quietly, 'is your middle name, darling. Let's.'

The S.S.O. loomed ahead of us like a mammoth ghost. He nodded briefly at Peter, then jerked his head towards the curtains.

'Round,' he said; 'so I'm pushing off. Nurse Ash knows what I want doing.'

I began to follow him, but he shook his head. 'I'll see myself out, thanks. Good night, Nurse.'

'Good night, Mr Dexter.' I turned back to Peter, who was waiting for me. Peter smiled, and for an instant I forgot that I was in the middle of a long, wide, darkened ward; that it was past eleven, and I had not yet charted the ten o'clock pulses and antibiotics, or begun my first report for Night Sister. I stood and grinned at him idiotically, and then I saw that Carol was beckoning to me from outside 18's curtains.

'Jonathan D. wants him to have some morph. now, Gillian,' she said, when I reached her. 'I'd like to get it myself, because I'm getting claustrophobic, but I daren't leave him.'

I handed her the dangerous-drug cupboard keys.

'Here. I'll stay with him while you take the walk. My pro will witness for you.'

Peter drifted close to me. 'I want to talk to that chap in 26. I've seen he's still awake. Then I'll nip round *tout seul* and see you at the table later. All right?'

I nodded and went in to the Admiral.

He lay with his eyes closed, but he was not asleep. His colour was better and his jaw more firm than when I had last seen him. I touched his wrist gently, and he opened his eyes.

'Where's my little nurse?' he asked.

I explained that she would be back directly. 'She's gone to get something to make life a little easier for you.' I asked how he was feeling.

He said he really did not know. 'I feel a trifle sore, Nurse, but nothing compared to what I felt before that large fellow patched me up.'

His pulse was reasonably good. I checked his respirations, the transfusion, his dressing. Everything was going—in hospital language—as well as could be expected. He had closed his eyes again, so I sat down on his locker seat and waited for Carol's return.

I heard the man in 19 cough self-consciously, to show he was awake; and across the ward in 33, the docker with a repaired hernia began to hiccup. He often suffered from this at night, and I made a couple of mental notes concerning peppermint water and hot milk. I could feel rather than hear Peter moving round the ward, but intentionally I did not think of Peter. I made a point of not thinking of him on duty. It is difficult to concentrate on your job when your bones feel as if they have turned to water. Peter had had that effect on me since the first evening he took me out two years back.

We had met in the theatre. I had been taking my first case and Peter was then a senior dresser. That morning I had scrubbed my hands and put on sterile gloves, then realised that in my nervousness I had forgotten to open the unsterile lid of a certain tin. Since I could not touch it myself, I had asked the nearest dresser, Peter.

'Delighted to be of service, Nurse'—the operation had not yet started, and the dressers were ambling round the technically empty theatre—'if you will come to the movies with me to-night?'

I had been annoyed with him for the first and last time.

'Please don't be absurd.' I hoped I sounded like Sister Theatre, and I had turned to the other dressers. 'Will one of you open my tin, please?'

The remaining quartet of young men chanted, 'Not unless you go to the movies with our Mr Kier.'

I had to have my tin opened, so I agreed, meaning to stand him up, but I had nothing to do that evening and my feet were hurting, so I thought I might as well enjoy a free movie. I enjoyed the movie and rested my feet; I also fell in love.

I was never certain what, if anything, Peter felt for me; I did know that he liked having me around and always took me out on the rare occasions when our off-duty periods coincided. I was fairly happy at the way our affair was going. At least it was still going, and there was no hurry. Peter was twenty-six and I twenty-one. Intelligent housemen do not marry while they are housemen; Peter Kier was an intelligent young man.

Carol returned with the hypodermic syringe in a small dish, the drug-book, and a box of morphine ampoules.

'Your pro has vanished. I thought we could cope here.'

'Right.' I checked the dose, then filed the top of one of the quarter-grain ampoules. Admiral Kerry watched interestedly. Carol disappeared to wash, then returned with dripping hands and fitted the syringe together. She moved to his side.

'Just let your arm go loose, Admiral.'

When it was over he said, 'That didn't hurt. How much blood have I had?'

I left her explaining his treatment to him and took the empty syringe, book, and box of drugs with me. I stopped at the centre table to fill my name and the time in the D.D. book and began to count the number of ampoules remaining in the box, to check

21

them with the number written beside the previous injection. Then I discovered Night Sister was at my elbow.

'I'm sorry, Sister. I did not know you were in the ward.'

She said she was not, officially. 'I only want to borrow a grain of morphia for Charity. Can you spare four ampoules?'

I showed her the box. 'Easily, Sister. This is nearly full.'

I watched her take four, made a note in the D.D. book, and passed it to her to sign; then I tucked the box under my arm and walked out of the ward with her.

'How is that poor man Kerry now, Nurse Snow?'

'Round, Sister, and fairly comfortable.'

'Aye,' she said, 'I never doubted that he'd do. Mr Dexter is a grand surgeon.'

I said Mr Dexter had seemed very worried tonight.

Sister blinked. 'He would not be a good surgeon if he did not worry, Nurse. Sister Theatre was telling me a while back that she had not seen the like of that abdomen.'

The Sisters all adored the S.S.O.; and since I liked a quiet life, and the way to a quiet life in hospital is to agree with Sisters, I said Mr Dexter was a splendid surgeon, and nearly added, worried or happy.

Peter had finished his round and was waiting by the kitchen door. He overheard my last words, and a corner of his mouth lifted. 'What does on, darling?' he asked when Sister had gone. 'Wherefore this build-up for our John?'

I said it was a beautiful friendship that had blossomed and died tonight.

He smiled. 'You had me worried, love.'

I smiled back. 'No call for that. John had just had a surfeit of perforations, so for once he broke down and almost talked like a human.'

'He did, eh? The old devil. I'll thank him not to act human when you're around, Gillian—and if he wasn't my boss, or such a ruddy Goliath, I'd tell him so myself. But I ain't no David. Don't even own a catapult.'

'Peter'—I shook my head—'you'll have to excuse me. I haven't done anything tonight yet. I must get on. And that reminds me—I must rustle up hot milk and aqua menthe. pip. for Bracey. He's hiccuping.'

He said, 'Not now he isn't. Uncle Peter beat you to it—with your pro!'

'Bless you,' I was going to walk round him, but he blocked my way.

'Aren't you going to offer me some coffee, darling?'

'You can have a gallon,' I said, 'if you help yourself. It'll be on the stove in the kitchen.'

He grimaced. 'I can't drink alone. Fatal thing. Turn into a

secret drinker while you watch. I'll get you a cup. After all,' he added, as I was about to protest, 'you've got to keep your strength up—and think of the morale of the resident staff. I look forward to my nightly drink in Robert all day—that's why I leave this ward till the end. To that—and seeing you. How do you like being the carrot to my donkey, sweetie?'

I liked it very much, but I was not going to say so here.

'Look,' I suggested, 'I'll nip round and then go and write my first report beside the Admiral, and send Carol to drink with you. She's low tonight and needs boosting.'

'Doesn't she care for Admirals?'

'Peter! It's about her parents. You remember.'

'Darling,' he murmured, 'I have a head like a sieve for stocky brunettes. What about them?'

I explained, and he grew serious.

'You can't have told me, Gillian,' he said. 'I wouldn't have forgotten that.'

'Of course . . .' I remembered that it had happened when he had been on holiday himself, and then when he returned he had vanished to our sector hospital immediately and had only been back in London for the last few weeks. 'And you wouldn't have seen the English papers in Italy, I suppose?'

'Why did it rate the papers?' he asked curiously.

'Ashton Ash,' I said quickly. 'He was always news.'

His rather long jaw dropped. 'Did you say Ashton Ash? My dear Gillian, you are not seriously telling me she is that Ash? The daughter of the man who made all those machines?'

'Yes. Only daughter. Only child. That's what's made it so awful.'

He said, 'I never realised that.'

'Surely I told you years ago? I thought everyone knew. Most people do.'

He shook his head. 'No. I didn't. Well,' he sighed, 'haste to your errand of mercy, love, and leave your little friend to Uncle Peter! Morale-raising is my forte. But,' he smiled, 'I'd much rather talk to you.'

'I'll send her,' I said, and tore back into the ward. When I reached the table I realised I was still carrying the morphia, so I took the D.D. book and box back to the medicine cupboard and relocked it safely before I went round the patients. Once I looked back to the corridor. Peter had not gone into the kitchen, but was still standing where I had left him. The light was on his face, and his expression was unusually serious. I thought how nice he was, to be so concerned about Carol.

Night Sister came for her official round; the general Surgical Registrar and a couple more housemen arrived for theirs; and then the night settled, and by five o'clock Nurse Fraser and I had caught up with all the dressing-making, book-ruling, laundry-folding, report-writing, bread-and-butter cutting, and trolley-laying that constituted our regular nightly routine, apart from the care of our forty patients.

Carol came in to the duty-room at ten minutes to eight, when I was changing my apron.

'Mind if I go, Gillian? He's sleeping and the blood's all right. That last bottle is still half full. I think I had better get back to Ellen. Sister Ellen will create if I'm not there to explain my absence in person, and I don't want to be late off as it means missing my train.'

I had forgotten that she had the next two nights off.

'You go,' I said, 'and enjoy yourself as an Old Girl.'

She said she did not really know why she had said she would go back to the speech day of her old school. 'I suppose one must do these things.'

'One must,' I agreed. 'I hope it isn't too bad.'

She looked at me in silence; it was a queer look, as if I was a stranger. Then she smiled slightly. 'Thanks. I hope so too. Have fun while I'm gone.'

My mind was on the verbatim report on my forty men which I was due to deliver to Sister Robert and all the day nurses in seven minutes' time. 'I'll have a splendid time,' I said absently; 'never a dull moment in Robert.'

She said, 'So I've gathered. How nice it must be for you, dearie. Well, if you'll explain to Sister Robert I'll nip off.'

'I'll explain.' I fixed the buckle of my belt. 'She'll understand. Sister Robert is a honey.'

Sister Robert was perfectly amicable about Carol's absence. She was a large, placid woman, only annoyed by the sight of faded flowers. She would greet disaster calmly, but a withered leaf roused her to fury.

'I expect you'll be glad to be off yourself, Nurse Snow,' she said kindly, when my report was over. 'Sleep well.'

I did not sleep well. At half-past eleven that morning Home Sister woke me; and when I got back to bed two hours later I had a couple of good reasons for not sleeping. Neither of them was pleasant.

2

A VISIT TO MATRON

HOME Sister said, 'I'm sorry to disturb you, Nurse Snow, but I am afraid you must come to the telephone. Sister Robert is very anxious to talk to you.'

I fought the sleep that filled every corner of my brain and ran down the corridor, tying my dressing-gown as I went. I did not know what I had left undone, but I knew it was something serious. Ward Sisters, these days, do not rouse night nurses for trivialities.

It was no triviality. Sister Robert asked if I had checked the morphia that morning.

That was it. I remembered instantly. I had put the box back in the cupboard meaning to check it later. I had not gone back.

I closed my eyes, although I had lost all desire for sleep.

'No, Sister. I'm sorry. I'm afraid I forgot.'

Sister spoke quietly, 'That was very reprehensible of you, Nurse Snow, but I should not have woken you for that. I find we are a grain short. Four ampoules are missing.'

In a glorious wave of relief I remembered about Charity Ward.

'Night Sister borrowed four ampoules for Charity, Sister.'

'I know that, Nurse—it's in the drug-book. We are still four short. Where have they gone, Nurse?'

My hand slipped on the receiver; I changed hands, and wiped my palm on my dressing-gown.

'I'm afraid I don't know, Sister.'

She was silent a moment; then I heard her sigh.

'I'm sorry, Nurse,' she added, 'but you have apparently mislaid a grain of morphia. I'm very sorry'—she sounded it—'but I am left with no option but to go to Matron. I think you had better get dressed and come over to the hospital and apologise to her at once. She will want to see you.'

'Yes, Sister; thank you, Sister,' I said mechanically.

Home Sister was waiting anxiously outside my room. She was not surprised that I had to dress. Sister Robert had already spoken to her.

'Think hard, Nurse, dear. Where can they have gone?'

I shook my head. 'I don't know, Sister.'

'Perhaps you made a miscalculation somewhere? I expect that is what has happened.'

'I hope you are right, Sister.'

I was pretty sure that she was not. A miscalculation over a quarter of a grain injection might occur—it was unlikely and I had never heard of it happening, but it was just possible—but there was no possibility of four doses being overlooked. A quarter of a grain of morphia is a good dose. We seldom gave more.

As I dressed I went over the night mentally. Carol was the only person besides myself to have been to the drug cupboard; she had brought the whole box into the ward, and I had opened it and taken out the one ampoule.

It was inconceivable that she would have taken any out before

25

reaching me. Nurses do not pocket ampoules of morphia lightly; even the lowest pro is aware that to touch a dangerous drug illicitly is probably the most serious crime a nurse can commit and would certainly result in dismissal and possibly, if you were State Registered, in being removed from the register.

No, there was no question of Carol's having anything to do with this. Apart from any other reason, there would be no point in her taking them. Carol was an intelligent young woman and far more thoughtful than myself. She never made a foolish mistake. There was a lot of her father in her. Ashton Ash was a self-educated and brilliant man who had learnt his engineering at night schools and from his colleagues in the workshops, and then built the best aeroplane engines any country had yet produced. He not only had the skill; he had the brains to make money, and a great name and business for himself, from his engines. Carol was her father's daughter physically; and from the little I had seen of him in our holidays together, I should have said that she was like him mentally. She was not the type to drop morphine ampoules around a ward without noticing it.

But if they were not lost, where were they? The only alternative was that they had been taken. And the drug keys had been in my possession all night from that one time. I had handed them back to Sister Robert on handing over the ward this morning. As Night Senior, the keys and the contents of the drug cupboard were my sole responsibility when I was on duty.

I put down my brush and stared at my reflection in the glass. It was possible that I might lose my job over this.

Matron folded her hands on the desk in front of her and looked at her spotless white organdie cuffs. When she raised her head her eyes were cold, and her lips were set in a thin line of displeasure.

'Where have they gone, Nurse Snow?' she asked for the second time.

And for the second time I repeated, 'I am sorry, Matron. I am afraid I don't know.'

She said quietly, 'But you should know. You were the nurse in charge of the ward. And you are sure you gave the keys to no one but Nurse Ash? Did you leave them on the table at any time? Could someone else have picked them up and used them?'

I hesitated. I could remember having the keys in my hand for a brief period after we gave that injection, but I was not sure now if I had repinned them on myself immediately afterwards or not. I must have done that at some time, as they were there when I felt for them this morning before the report. There was a slight possibility, I now realised, that I had left them under the report book when I was talking to Night Sister about the drugs for Ellen. I had done that before when I had been rushed. I could have left them there unconsciously and picked them up again, equally unconsciously.

I said, 'I don't think I did, Matron.'

She was on to that at once.

'You should know. Think now.'

I tried to concentrate, but I was too cold for thought. So I told her what had been in my mind.

She shook her head at me, and the lace in her cap frills rustled disapprovingly.

'Nurse Snow, you know that that is forbidden. Those should never leave your possession, and no one, not even your fellow senior nurses, should go to your drug cupboard. It was remiss of you to hand over the keys to Nurse Ash, but I can understand that. I cannot understand your criminal carelessness in leaving the keys lying on the table in the centre of the ward. Do you realise,' she went on, 'that, due to you, someone may be walking round this hospital with a near-lethal dose of morphia in their possession?'

I realised all right. 'Yes, Matron.'

'Who,' she asked pertinently, 'was in the ward around that period?'

I did not have to hesitate over this. I had been over this in my room. 'Mr Dexter had just left, and if he returned I did not see him. Mr Kier was going round by himself. Nurse Ash was with Admiral Kerry. Night Sister was with me during that time. Nurse Fraser was mostly in the sluice-room and the laundry.'

Matron's voice was dry. 'Presumably she was also attending to the patients, Nurse?'

'Yes, Matron.'

'Then she must have been in and out of the ward also. I shall have to ask Home Sister to waken Nurse Fraser and speak to her.' She picked up a pencil and fiddled with it. 'No dressers were there?'

'No, Matron.' For some reason there had been no students in the ward the previous night. I was glad of this; it let the boys out. The doctors were beyond suspicion, since there was no point in any doctor's helping himself to something for which he could quite legally file a prescription at the nearest chemist.

Matron tapped the desk with her pencil. 'We must take it that that is what you have done, Nurse. And that while the keys were on the desk someone used them to take the drugs and replace them under the report book again.' She sighed and asked if I knew where Carol had gone for her nights off. 'It is highly improbable that Nurse Ash will be able to help us, but we must overlook no eventuality. She may have noticed the number of ampoules in the box when she brought it to you.'

I said, 'I don't think she did, Matron, as I opened the box. She had just tucked it under her arm and brought it along.'

Matron said, 'I will telephone to the school before we decide that point.' She glanced through her hospital report book. 'You have no patients in Robert at the moment who are capable of getting out of bed without assistance?'

'No, Matron. No one with their stitches out.'

She nodded. 'Wait outside please, Nurse, while I call Nurse Ash.'

The next fifteen minutes dragged by more slowly than many a month I had known. Then Matron opened her office door.

'Come in, Nurse Snow.'

She said Carol had not reached the school yet, and that she had left a message asking Carol to ring the hospital immediately she did arrive. She said I had better return to my room.

'Can I go back to duty in Robert tonight, Matron?'

Her pale brown eyebrows met in a straight line; she glanced at the list of night nurses at present working in the hospital that was propped on the desk beside her and pursed her lips. She did not answer my question directly.

'Night Sister has a spare senior relief tonight,' she said, 'and she may take over Robert tonight. That will give me time to consider this matter carefully, and also to discuss it with the Committee. I am afraid there can be no question of your returning to duty until that is done.'

I said quickly, 'But I did not take the morphia, Matron.'

'If I thought for one moment that you had, Nurse Snow,' she replied sharply, 'I should dismiss you at once. As I feel you have been guilty of criminal carelessness, I am willing to discuss the matter with the Committee. But I cannot countenance your working, or being in charge, in a ward. I have never'—she looked up at me—'permitted any nurse I could not trust to work in the wards of this hospital.'

I said, 'Yes, Matron.'

'Your conduct and work until this episode,' she went on, 'have been unexceptionable. I am taking that into account now. But, Nurse'—she suddenly seemed much older and quite human—'how could you let me down in this way?'

I said, 'I am very sorry, Matron, that this has happened.'

Matron said, 'I do not doubt that you are, Nurse. That will be all.'

I did not go back to my room immediately. I could not face the silent Night Nurses' Home. I was shivering with the cold all night workers feel in the day-time, so I decided to have some cocoa in the canteen.

The canteen was milling with hungry students, a few nurses, several physiotherapists, and half the medical staff. I saw a good many people with whom I was acquainted, but no one whom I knew well. In a large hospital you are frequently among strangers, even in your fourth year. Our hospital was very large. There were over five hundred nurses on the staff, and over that number of students in the medical school. I never discovered the size of the physiotherapy school, but it was one of the biggest in London, nor was I ever able to count how many resident doctors there were connected with all the various departments, but it must have been somewhere around sixty.

I collected my cocoa and carried it to one of the small red-covered tables against the far wall. I drank the cocoa absently, thinking over my interview with Matron, those wretched drugs, and how I hated leaving Robert. I loved that ward; I loved the men and the work; I liked my nice pro and Sister Robert. I wondered about Admiral Kerry, and Toms, my favourite patient, an antique but active stevedore, who was not, as he frequently admitted, 'a one for changes.' And I thought again about the missing grain of morphia.

A white coat stopped in front of my table. 'You're up late, Nurse Snow.'

I saw who it was and stood up. 'Yes, Mr Dexter.'

He said quickly, 'Please don't move, I'm just passing.' I sat down again, but he did not move. Instead he said, 'I'm glad Admiral Kerry had a good night. Let's hope he repeats the performance tonight.'

'Yes, Mr Dexter.' I did not tell him I should not be there to see how anyone in Robert slept. He was on the Committee. He would hear what had happened soon enough from Matron. I was quite relieved that she, and not I, would have to tell him. He was not a man to whom I would care to admit a mistake.

He said, 'You ought to be in bed. The second night,' he added to remove any misapprehension that he was concerned with my personal welfare, 'is often far heavier than the first. And I'm doing two more men from Robert this afternoon.'

I said, 'Yes, Mr Dexter,' again, but as he still lingered, obviously expecting a further explanation, I went on lamely, 'I had to get up, and thought I'd have some cocoa before I went to bed. It's a cold morning.'

The canteen door opened, and Peter and Tom Thanet came in together. Tom saw me and touched Peter's arm. Peter glanced round and waved.

The S.S.O. was watching the two housemen. He said, 'It is cold for September—I'm just going to raise some hot coffee for myself,' and moved away towards the counter.

Peter threaded his way through the crowded tables, put down

29

his cup and saucer, and dropped into the chair beside me.

'Hi, darling! What are you doing up at this hour?'

'I had to see Matron.' Now that he was here I knew that subconsciously it was the hope of seeing him that had brought me to the canteen. I wanted to talk to someone on my own side. I wanted him to help me get rid of the worry that was nagging, like toothache, in my brain.

He smiled. 'Poor Gillian. What hadn't you done? Forgotten to order the milk? Mislaid one of the chaps in Robert?'

Tom called from the next table, 'Burning the midday oil, Nurse Snow?'

'Just about.' I grinned feebly, then turned to Peter. 'Peter, something grim has happened. Someone swiped a grain of morph. in Robert last night.'

'Someone swiped what? Don't tell me we've an addict in our midst! It isn't me, miss, I swears it isn't me. Always stick to coke, I do!'

'Look,' I said, 'this is serious.' I told him everything.

He was silent for a short while after I had finished.

'Of course,' he shrugged, 'someone can't count. That's what's happened.'

'It isn't.' He knew as well as I that the dangerous drugs were checked by the dispenser on issue, and rechecked by the sisters when they arrived in each ward. 'Sister Robert had a new lot in yesterday morning, which was why she spotted something wrong the moment she had occasion to open the box. I had reported all we gave in the night. Ward Sisters don't make mistakes over the D.D. cupboard.'

He lit a cigarette. 'You say your pal Carol went to the cupboard. How about her?'

'I don't think she even opened the box. It was under her arm, and her hands were occupied with the hypodermic dish. Also— why should she? I know Carol—she's no fool—and apart from all moral aspects, only a complete goon would run such a risk. It was bound to be discovered. Every nurse in Joe's knows that.'

'How about your pro? Or is she too bright too?'

I was getting desperate. 'Peter. It's something we have dinned into us from the moment we set foot in the P.T.S. Pros never even lay a hand on the D.D. keys. They're hot.'

He said mildly. 'Well, someone has, darling—so why not one of the girls?'

'But why should they?'

'My sweet,' he said, 'you do ask stupid questions. It's not "why" that matters, but who. But all right. If you rule out your girls how about the chaps?'

'In Robert? None of them are capable of even walking.'

He laughed. 'Can't you just see that old Kerry nipping across craftily, clasping his bottle of blood in one hand and the packet of morph. in the other?'

'Peter—do be serious.'

He said he was grimly serious. 'My middle name is Dexter. But you aren't giving me much help with my sleuthing. Or do you think it was me? Or old Garth? Or Tom?' Garth was his name for Dexter. He glanced round. 'Let's ask old Tom how he slept last night? Sweet opium dreams?'

'Not now. Please.'

'Anything you say, love.' He relaxed. 'I quite agree. Let's leave it to rest. You are brooding overmuch. We'll talk of other things.'

He had misunderstood my reason for not wishing to question Tom yet, but I let it pass. I did not bother to explain that I wanted to put off the moment when I should have to face the curiosity and sympathy of my friends. The hospital would hear all about my missing drugs only too soon. The grapevine in any hospital is as efficient as a radar set. I was thinking this over and wondering what the general reaction would be when I realised that he was still talking and I only caught the end of what he was saying.

'—so I said that I knew it would be fine with you as you haven't got the right nights off. She said she'd be happy to save me from the horrors of a partnerless evening and the possibility of having to dance with the Sisters.'

'Sorry, Peter. What was all that?'

'Darling, you're out on your two feet. I was only telling you I've asked your pal Carol to the rugger dance as you aren't off. I was being a Girl Scout—as per your instructions.'

I wondered sleepily why Carol had not mentioned this. Then I remembered how she had had to hurry off this morning and how busy we had been in the night. There had been no time for light chatter.

'That was nice of you,' I said. 'But you know what? If I haven't been chucked out I'll probably be free after all. I very much doubt whether Matron will let me go back as Night Senior anywhere. That's the pick of all our jobs.'

He whistled quietly, 'Bad as that?'

'I expect so. I did tell you that this would be going to the Committee.'

He looked sober. 'So you did. Well, well, well.'

I waited for him to tell me how sorry he was that this had happened to me; that the drugs would turn up; that at least it was not as serious as I imagined. Peter was good at getting things in proportion, and he was good at making me laugh. I wanted badly to be able to laugh at something now.

He said nothing for several seconds, and his eyes narrowed as if he was calculating it all. 'Your job,' he said eventually, 'is somewhat in the air, eh?'

I nodded.

'Do you really think she'll give you the bird?'

I thought over my interview again. Thought was becoming very difficult. My brain was clouded with my desire to sleep. 'Maybe not. But, whatever happens, my nursing reputation here has gone for six.'

'I see.' He looked at me reflectively. 'I suppose you haven't any conceivable notion where——'

I interrupted him. 'Peter. If you or anyone else asks me where again, I shall burst into womanly tears.'

'Darling,' he said coolly, 'don't do that. While on the subject of reputation, I beg you to consider mine at this minute, if at no other.'

The meaning of his words took a little time to penetrate the haze that was between me and normal people who go to bed at night.

I said, 'I won't weep on you, Peter. I'm not really the little woman type. I'm just suffering from night nurse's blues.' And those, I thought, are two of the biggest lies I have ever told.

He gazed across the canteen, as if the queue at the counter fascinated him. 'I always said you were a sensible girl, Gillian,' he murmured. 'The thing to do is to go on being sensible. Don't let this business get you down. Matrons have to get tough—they wouldn't be Matrons if they weren't tough! ' He pushed back his chair. 'And if the worst comes to the worst—well, you are State Registered, and there are dozens of jobs going in the provinces. Who wants to stick at old Joe's indefinitely?'

I fiddled with my empty cup. 'Who indeed?'

'I'll have to push off.' He stood up. 'My boss has been giving me dirty looks for the past ten minutes. If I dally any longer— much as I'd like to—old man Garth will probably heave me bodily through the door.' He grinned and leant over the back of his chair. 'Do you suppose it was him after all? Perhaps he chews it instead of shag? Perhaps that's why he's so ruddy big?'

I smiled weakly. 'Could be. Glass and all. Stimulates the pituitary no end.'

He said he must try it some time and I really was a splendid soul, darling, and he hated to leave me, but—— 'Be seeing you, Gillian. And remember, any time you want your own or anyone else's morale boosted, send for Uncle Peter.'

'I'll do that.' I pretended to be oblivious of his anxiety to get away. There was no reason why I should not have left the canteen with him as we usually did—no reason beyond the fact that he did not desire my presence any further.

32

I sat on for some time longer, staring at my empty cup and thinking of nothing. Once I felt someone looking at me. I glanced round. John Dexter was talking to a man in the doorway and watching me. His expression was unusually anxious, and I wondered if anything had gone wrong in the theatre. The man to whom he was talking was the Resident Anaesthetist. The S.S.O. caught my eye and looked straight through me. That did not worry me. He and I had never been on smiling terms. I looked through him.

The canteen cleared; it was midday, and the hungry students were off to lunch. The voluntary workers collected the stray cups from the tables and wiped the plastic table covers. One elderly woman flapped her dish-cloth over my table, then hesitated.

'Off duty, Nurse?'

I smiled. My smile was a reflex action now, requiring no effort from me. 'Nights.'

She clucked like a kindly hen.

'You should be in bed, dear. You look ever so tired.'

'I'm just going,' I assured her.

She shook her head. 'I don't like to see a young girl like you looking so tired. Mrs Symonds—that's the lady with the tea urn, dear—and I were just talking about you. That poor dark nurse in the corner, we said, looks really ill. We were wondering if anything was the matter.' She twisted her dish-cloth anxiously. 'I'm so glad to hear it's only tiredness—Mrs Symonds will be too.'

I stood up. 'It is very kind of you both. Thank you so much. I'm sorry you should have been worried.'

I went back to my room, undressed, and got into bed, but I was too tired to sleep. I lay and thought about Peter and how clearly he had shown me that he wanted no part of my problems or my future. I was a 'sensible girl' who was good for an evening at the movies, or as a partner at hospital dances, but that was all. And then I thought, in fairness, why blame him? He had always been most careful in our relationship. He had never once hinted that he felt for me as he must have guessed I felt for him. And I could have refused his many invitations and so have prevented him from monopolising my off-duty. I wondered now if he would give me many more opportunities to refuse his invitations? Whatever happened over this affair in Robert, as I had told him, a certain amount of mud would stick to me. 'Gill Snow? Oh yes. The girl who was mixed up when that dope was missing in Robert. Nasty thing to happen.'

Very nasty.

Peter was an ambitious young man. I knew he saw himself as a future S.S.O. at Joe's. Young doctors who wish to get on do not get involved in scandals. I was the centre of a glorious scandal. Peter would certainly not wish to be involved with me any longer.

I smiled wryly at the ceiling. Poor Peter. He was probably as strung up as I was today, wondering how much this was going to affect him. Then I smiled properly as I realised that, in my panic over the possibility of losing him, I had forgotten the drugs and my job in Robert. I had never had much faith in counter-irritants before; now I began to wonder if they might not be a very good thing.

Home Sister sent for me after supper that night.

'Matron wishes you to have two nights off, Nurse dear, while she decides what is to be done about you.'

The 'Nurse dear,' showed that Home Sister was on my side.

'Do you think I'll ever get back to Robert, Sister?'

Her old, creased face grew some more lines. 'I'm afraid it is unlikely, Nurse Snow.' She went on to say that Matron had contacted Carol, who, as I had expected, knew nothing of any spare morphia. 'Matron will send for you, Nurse, when she has reached a conclusion.'

I asked if she knew anything of my Admiral?

'Sister Robert was fairly sanguine about him at supper to-night.' Her myopic eyes peered through her thick spectacles. 'You liked working in Robert, did you not, Nurse?'

'Very much, Sister.'

She sighed, then smiled. 'I liked Robert too,' she said conspiratorially, 'I did so like all those seamen and dockers.'

We had a pleasant quarter of an hour exchanging stories about the men in Robert. I forgot my own problems, and I think old Home Sister forgot her arthritic knees and the fact that she had not nursed in a general ward since before I was born. Nursing was our job and our hobby, and when you are lucky enough to have work which is that, you have to pay for it with painful joints or set-backs over drug cupboards.

Home Sister laughed reminiscently, 'You know those weighing machines, Nurse—the wheel-barrow type? Well, when I was in my third year—during the first world war, that was—we had a very difficult gastric patient in Robert. It was both surgical and medical in those days. He so disliked being weighed it was quite a business to get him on the scales. One night he was so difficult that I said, "Mr Yeo, if you let me weigh you—you may weigh me!" Sister pulled at her cuffs primly. 'Of course, I never dreamed he would say yes. But he did.'

I was enchanted. 'What happened, Sister?'

She sighed, but not unhappily as she had done earlier, 'I was rather plump in those days, Nurse—and the machine was in the middle of the ward. Mr Yeo had to put on all the weights as I went over eleven stone! The men were all laughing, and then suddenly there was silence.' She blinked through her glasses. 'Sister Robert and Dr Greet—he became Sir Gaston Greet—had come in. Sister,' she said, with simple pride, 'was furious and sent me to Matron. But Dr Greet told his houseman—who told me—that I had made a new man of Mr Yeo, and he thought I ought to weigh all his gastric patients.' She straightened her old, well-corseted back, and came back to the present. 'You had better go back to bed, now, Nurse. You will look very tired. Did you sleep at all?'

'Not very much, Sister.' I thanked her for telling me of her time in Robert.

She coloured slightly, but did not comment on her burst of reminiscences. 'Good night, Nurse.'

The girls in my set came to visit me; the day staff that night, the night staff next morning.

'Poor old Gillian. What rotten luck! Let's hope the miserable bod. who pinched it is suffering from acute deprivation symptoms!'

Kirsty Forbes, the girl who had taken my place in Robert, was doubly sympathetic. 'I'm not surprised you mislaid a grain, Gill. After one night in Robert I'm surprised you didn't lose the lot! What a ward! I've not been off my feet all night!'

I asked after Admiral Kerry and my favourite, Toms.

'All doing nicely and ever so sorry to hear their Nurse Snow is poorly. That's the official gen on you—via Matron. But you've a lovely ward, Gil. Not a difficult type among them.'

'There never is. Robert men are always honies.'

Kirsty wondered why it was that only pleasant men appeared to suffer from perforated appendices or strangulated hernias.

'Must be Sister Robert,' I said. 'After all, a Sister makes or breaks a ward.'

'That's so.' Kirsty looked thoughtful. 'She had a little chat with me last night, and, reading between the lines, I got the impression that she wanted me to tell you not to fret too much, that she knew it had nothing whatsoever to do with you—apart from your leaving your keys around, of course.' She took off her shoes and tucked them under her arm. 'And, you know, I've got a sort of feeling this is someone's idea of a joke.'

I said drily, 'I'm killing myself with laughter.'

'I don't doubt it.' Her expression was very kind. 'But seriously, Gill, it has to be a joke. It's such a wee dose.'

'Kirsty! It's near-lethal.'

'Och,' she said, 'it's not enough to bump off anyone but a child—and who ever heard of even a maniac using that on a kid? No. I consider this is one of those daft students, either

35

taking it for a bet or for some stupid experiment on himself. You know what fools medical students are! They'll try anything. And only a daftie, not on the staff, would not have known the immediate bust-up that would follow. All the staff know they are checked constantly. But the student boys have no conception how we check and recheck. They just think we rush round shoving in needles, regardless.'

'I never thought of that,' I said slowly.

'Nor did I, until I caught one of the lads helping himself to some milk in Robert kitchen last night. Fraser was in the sluice, and it was pure chance that I caught him. He was very civil and said he hadn't bothered to ask as he knew we had masses and were busy and so on; but it put a whole lot of ideas into my head. If milk can disappear unnoticed they're daft enough to think drugs can do likewise. And anyone finding the drug keys need have no doubts about which keys they are, since they have that whacking great red plastic label with "D.D. Keys" stamped on it for all to see. It's too easy.' She yawned. 'I must get to bed. But I'll keep my eyes skinned tonight for stray visitors, and for as long as I'm in Robert. I doubt that I'll be there long. You'll be back after your nights off.'

The other girls were as kind as Kirsty, and most of them admitted leaving their keys on the table at various times.

'Might have happened to any of us, Gill. Wretched that it had to be you.'

In the middle of the next afternoon Carol returned to the hospital. She came up to my room.

'I've just met Peter. He said you were off nights, and he thought warded in your own room. What goes? Are you really ill?'

She looked ill herself and not at all as if she had had a night in bed. Her round face was pale and haggard, and her skin hung in soft, fleshy folds.

I said I was not ill. 'How were the Old Girls?'

'Ghastly. Too hearty to bear. I wish I had stayed here and slept all yesterday, instead.' She flopped on to the foot of my bed. 'Matron rang me yesterday, and I had to call her back. Did you hear? She was in a state about how much we had given the Admiral that first night. I said a quarter and only a quarter. What's wrong? Is he supposed to have had an overdose?'

'No. Didn't Peter tell you?'

She shook her head. 'We didn't really discuss you—beyond him telling me you were proper poorly. No,' she said again, 'we didn't discuss you. He was being rather nice about my father. He said he had only just heard who Daddy was.' She turned to look at me as I sat sewing in the armchair at the opposite side of the room. 'I'm beginning to alter my opinion of your young man,' she added slowly. 'I could never quite see what you saw in him. I do now. For all his gay chatter, he is rather kind, isn't he?'

I said yes, I was fond of Carol. I saw no reason why she should be disillusioned about Peter.

'But you still haven't told me what the flap was about?'

I told her.

She gaped. 'Oh, no! Gillian! You couldn't!'

'I certainly didn't take it myself, if that's what you mean.'

She said it was not. 'What's shaken me is your making a mistake. You're the bright girl of the set—don't forget you're in running for the Gold Medal. You aren't the type to drop your keys around for anyone to pick up!'

'You couldn't be more wrong, ducks. I did just that. I've had that medal. I've very nearly had my job. Matron calls it criminal carelessness. She won't be pinning a medal on me after this. But what I could do'—I snapped the thread with which I was sewing, in my sudden fury—'with the fiend who's helped himself to my drug cupboard is nobody's business.'

She said softly, 'Poor old Gillian.' She lay back on my bed and closed her eyes. 'But who?'

'Search me.' I told her Kirsty's theory, but she thought little of it. 'The boys may be nuts, but they aren't as nutty as that.'

'Then who?'

She was silent; then, 'How about the S.S.O.?' she suggested.

'John Dexter?' I put down my sewing. 'Why ever him? He doesn't have to pinch the stuff. He can get it for the signing any time he wants.'

She said she had not meant that he had taken it for his own use, but to teach me a sharp lesson. 'Perhaps he saw the keys around and thought you needed a jolt to show you how dangerous that was.'

'But, Carol—I was his little shadow. He didn't have a chance.'

She said pertinently, 'You weren't his shadow when he came back to watch Kerry coming round. And he wandered off alone to wash his hands at the far sink before he left, because I heard him. Weren't you nattering to Peter in the doorway? I thought I saw you down there through a crack in the curtains?'

I was worried. 'Yes, I was.'

She said, 'John D. was drifting round Robert alone, and he's mighty quiet for all he's so big. He might easily have got at the cupboard.'

Something was wrong here, and I knew it was not only her idea about the S.S.O.

'I'm in a complete muddle,' I said, 'but I do think you're wrong. I can't say I go for that man—never have—but I must

37

admit that the boys all say that he's a good type. He might have lectured me to hell for leaving my keys around, but I don't see him as a petty thief.'

'Maybe you're right.' She did not sound at all certain. 'Only I wouldn't underestimate him. I'd say he was rather thuggish under his smooth surgical exterior.'

'Thuggish no doubt, but not mean! This is such a mean thing to have done! The S.S.O.'s too big to be mean. Haven't you noticed how it's always a small person's line?'

She grunted without answering. A few seconds later she sat up, 'Which reminds me. If you are really off nights there's something we have to settle.'

I guessed what she was about to say and said it for her.

'We don't have to settle a thing about the rugger dance, honey.'

'Of course we do. I meant to tell you he'd asked me before I went away, but I forgot. I wouldn't dream of going with him now.'

'You might just as well. Peter won't want to take me now.'

She looked at me curiously. 'He won't? Nonsense. He always takes you if you're free.'

I grimaced. 'Them days is past.' I explained what had been his attitude yesterday in the canteen.

She said, 'I never thought of that.'

'Why should you? Nor did I.' And so much, I thought, for my noble resolutions about not disillusioning Carol. But it was a relief to have told her.

'Gill dear,' she said gently, 'I am sorry. How miserable of him.'

She looked very upset about all this, and I was touched by her concern. I was glad that she was back in the hospital; I felt stronger and more able to manage my problems now Carol was again on hand to listen to my worries but the situation was not without irony. Our normal relationship had become reversed. Usually I was the one to lend the shoulder or the ear. I was very grateful for the comfort of her presence.

She got off my bed and offered more tangible assistance.

'Want any books? Cigarettes?'

'No, thanks. I've got all I want. This is a homely gaol. No bars. I can come and go as I like. Only thing I can't do is nurse again until Matron and the Committee decide that I'm fit to be let loose among the patients. The snag is,' I added, 'that I can't blame her, or them. Those drugs were my baby.'

She seemed very preoccupied with the S.S.O. 'I wonder what our John will say about it all?'

'Probably suggest bread and water,' I said gloomily.

She tidied her hair at my dressing-table. 'Have you thought,' she asked quietly, 'that it might have been me? I went to your cupboard.'

I smiled. 'It might indeed! Or Peter. Or Tom Thanet disguised as an oxygen cylinder. Only snag is, none of you dope. Your pupils are all too big! Pity, but there it is!'

She giggled, 'You are a goon!'

'Only crafty. Don't forget I've worked in Matthew and Mark. After four months' hard among assorted alcohol, morph., coke, and heroin addicts, I can recognise them in my sleep. You don't forget Matthew and Mark in a hurry,' I added grimly.

'That's true.' She fiddled with my brush and comb. 'Listen, Gillian—perhaps it'll all blow over. Perhaps Matron doesn't take quite the serious view you think. In a week or so you'll find you've come out of the cloud and gone back to square one.'

I shook my head. 'She takes a serious view, all right, and she's got to. This is a pretty serious thing. Of course, if she doesn't give me the bird the cloud will move off eventually; the sun will rise; the birds will sing; the patients will burst their appendices and chop themselves into little pieces; but it won't be back to square one for me.'

'Are you talking from Matron's angle, or Peter's?'

'Both. But mostly from Peter's.'

She left me after that, I sat on sewing for some time, then decided I must get out of the hospital if only for half an hour. It was tea-time, but I could not face any more sympathy or any more questions from my friends, so I took myself out to tea.

It had rained that morning, but the September afternoon was golden. In the park the chrysanthemums and Michaelmas daisies blazed in the flower-beds; the grass was thick with yellow leaves, prematurely torn off by the gales of the last week. The trees were still green and heavy with soaking leaves from the rain this morning. The afternoon sun turned the raindrops to topaz. There were more leaves floating in the lake. I stopped on the wooden bridge and leant over. The scent of wet grass and soaking wood filled me with nostalgia and a sadness I had hoped forgotten; but in my new despondency that old unhappiness returned, and I remembered my home and how my father's land had smelt at this time of the year.

I thought of the birds on the marshes, and of the floods that would already be out after a wet summer such as this last one; I remembered how the men cursed the water and how they all worked overtime on the pumps. My father's land had been reclaimed centuries ago, but it still needed frequent pumping and drainage to save it from the hungry sea that thundered against the sea-wall only a couple of miles away. I closed my eyes momentarily and caught a faint tang of salt in the breeze that drifted parkward from the river; at home the wind tore inland over the dykes, and when you licked your lips, your tongue tasted fresh sea-salt.

I turned from the bridge and walked on slowly.

The restaurant was very full, and the food was very expensive. I did not expect to see anyone I knew, so I did not bother to look at anyone but my immediate neighbours. Later I wished I had been more curious. As I was leaving I recognised the voice of a man behind me.

'Sorry I can't join you at that show,' he was saying, 'but I only arranged for Henderson to stand in for me a couple of hours.'

I longed to be able to look round and see to whom it was John Dexter was talking, but since I could hardly do this I pretended to be engrossed in one of the display counters, and hoped to see them when they had passed me.

This was not a good scheme. An assistant came up to me at once. 'Can I get madam anything?'

I asked for some chocolates, then looked round quickly, but I was too late. The S.S.O. and his companion were outside the glass front door, and he was handing her into a taxi. I saw only a small black feather hat and a wing of gold hair. It was an attractive hat, and that hair was a glorious colour. I mentally reviewed the entire nursing staff at Joe's. Who had hair that colour? Or had I stumbled by chance on John's secret love-life?

The assistant broke into my thoughts by asking if I wanted all soft centres.

'Yes, please.'

While she weighed them I glanced back at the front door, and was pleased to see that John had vanished. He had probably taken a second taxi and was already half-way back to Bill Henderson (the senior surgical registrar at Joe's). Good. I had come out to get away from the hospital. I should be back soon enough.

'Good afternoon, Miss Snow.'

My head jerked sideways and upward. I was so surprised to find that I had somehow missed John's large, dark, grey figure that all I said was 'Oh.'

He smiled. 'I apologise for my intrusion. I wanted to buy some of these chaps.' He touched a glass jar filled with gold-papered chocolate coins as the assistant handed me my parcel.

'Yes, sir?'

He bought a pound. 'Bribery,' he murmured to me.

'Bribery, Mr Dexter?'

'I'm teaching in Christian [the children's ward] in the morning.'

40

'I see.' I smiled, I hoped civilly, and added that I was just leaving. 'Good-bye.'

The assistant was a quick worker, and she had dealt with his parcel and change before I reached the door. He caught up with me and held it back for me. 'Do you want to drive back?' he asked.

I gathered from this that he had his car and was offering me a lift. I thanked him, but said that as it was such a lovely day I thought I would walk.

He looked down at me calmly, 'I was going to walk back myself. May I join you?'

I wished I had the courage to refuse. I did not want to talk to him or anyone else. If he had been any other man I might have been able to think up some fairly civil excuse, but in his case I could not do it. I should as soon have told Matron that I should prefer to dispense with her company. I said, 'Please do.' He thanked me, and we walked away from the restaurant together.

3

A WALK IN THE PARK WITH THE S.S.O.

WE talked about the weather.

'It must have been a grim summer for farmers,' I said.

'But surely they always complain that there isn't sufficient rain?'

'Depends just when it rains. This year they can't have had time to cut their hay, much less dry it. And the wind will have ruined the fruit.'

He said curiously, 'Wasn't haymaking over weeks ago?'

'Should have been, but I expect it went on into August because of the rain—and that does no one any good but the game.'

'Why the game?'

'The young partridges and pheasants don't get disturbed so early when the hay is late and that gives the birds a chance to grow bigger.'

'You are very up in all this, Miss Snow. Is your father a farmer?'

'Was.'

He nodded. 'What part of the world do you come from?'

'The south-east coast.' I told him about our marshes. 'It's a pleasant part of the coast and the birds are wonderful.'

He said he could believe that. 'I'm afraid Kent is not a county I know well. What's your nearest town?'

I told him. 'It hardly rates as a town. No chain-stores, not even a weekly market—but it's an attractive place.'

41

He glanced at my face. 'It sounds it.'

We fell silent again; then, for something to say, I asked where he came from?

He raised his stick and pointed in the direction of the hospital. 'My father had one of those houses that front on the river—the hospital bought it and uses it as flats for the married staff.'

'Was your father a Joe's man, Mr Dexter?'

He smiled slightly. 'And his father before him. My father used to take me on his Sunday rounds of the hospital when I was a small boy. My grandfather always took him, so he decided to carry on the family tradition. It served its purpose. It broke me in early.'

'Yes.' I did not ask the obvious question, and we were silent again.

This time he broke it by asking if I was in a hurry to get back. 'Or would you mind if we sat down on one of those benches for a few minutes. There's something I want to discuss with you.'

I groaned inwardly. Once more. I should have guessed he had not chosen to accompany me because he wanted a walk in the sun. I had not the courage to invent an excuse so I said I was in no hurry and walked meekly over to the nearest bench.

He took off his hat and put it on the bench beside his stick.

'I am exceedingly sorry about all this, Nurse Snow,' he said.

'Thank you.'

He frowned at his stick, as if he disapproved of the way in which it was behaving. 'I'm not throwing platitudes about, Nurse Snow, for the pleasure of hearing my own voice. I'm very sorry that a sensible young woman like yourself should have run into this mess.'

The Committee had obviously met. I wondered what conclusion they had reached. I knew he was not going to break down and tell me that: that I would hear from Matron in her own time. I was pretty sure that his soothing opening was merely his technique to show quite how inexcusable my behaviour was. To forestall him I said:

'It was my own fault. I should have hung on to those keys.'

'You should indeed,' he said casually. 'Who do you think used them?'

'I can't imagine. I only know it wasn't myself.'

He leaned on his stick with his hands clasped on the handle. His hands were the only small things about him, despite his boxing past—if boxing enlarges hands! All good surgeons have small hands and not, as is popularly supposed, long, thin, tapering ones. John's were very small for his height, broad and incredibly strong. In the theatre I had seen him lift a man off the table without apparent effort, and as easily as I could pick up a baby.

He said, 'Clearly it wasn't you, since you are carrying the can. Who was in the ward with you that night?'

He must have known my list as well as I did. Matron would have told the Committee. I repeated it again.

He told me he had seen the keys on the desk when he was writing his notes. 'I was just about to remind you of them when you picked them up and pinned them on yourself.'

'So I did leave them there earlier.' I explained how I had not been certain. 'I'm always doing it.'

He said casually, 'Most of you nurses do. Foolish young women, aren't you? Oh, well, you won't do it again. I've often thought of mentioning it, but then I felt it was rather a nursing point, and I can't say I like getting involved in that side of things.' He glanced sideways at me. 'I rather wish I had now. It would have saved a good deal of bother.'

I agreed that it would. I was thinking of what Carol had suggested, and how wrong she had been.

'You don't sound very certain?' He looked my face over coolly. He had brown eyes. I had never bothered to notice the colour previously. I was surprised to see that his brown eyes could look as cold as Matron's pale blue ones. 'Was I'—he spun out the words as if he had all eternity in which to complete his sentence—'on your list of suspects? Did you think I took the stuff?'

He said, 'I might have done it to give you a fright. Was that what you thought?'

'Look,' I said sharply, 'I've thought of everything. I've had nothing else to do since yesterday morning.' I had never spoken to him like that before, but then I had never discussed anything but patients with him before, apart from his slight lapse in Robert the other night. 'I'm sorry,' I went on, 'I don't mean to be impertinent, but do we have to go into all this? It's happened, and there doesn't seem to be anything anyone can do about it. It's just one of those things.'

He said quietly, 'Don't be childish, Nurse Snow. It is not one of those things. Morphia doesn't get up and walk away from the drug cupboards as a routine occurrence. And at the risk of being really trite, of course one can do something about it. One can always do something—although not necessarily the right thing.' He moved his hands, propped his stick carefully against the seat, and took out a cigarette packet. 'Will you?'

I kept forgetting that I was in mufti on a park bench. I refused automatically. He held the packet in front of my face. 'I should if I were you,' was all he said, so I fell back into routine and did as he said.

His expression reminded me of something Peter once said: 'You girls suffer under constant delusions concerning old Garth. He may be mighty quiet, but he's rousable all right. And roused he's quite something. Personally I'd sooner cope single-handed with an H-bomb explosion. Easier to put out.'

He might not be roused now, but it would be easier to hold up an oncoming bulldozer with one hand than stop this cross-examination. I gave up trying.

'Now,' he said, 'you didn't take that dope, and I didn't. But someone has.'

'Why should they?'

He said that was precisely why he wanted to talk to me. 'I wanted to ask if you thought there was anyone who might want to get you in a spot.'

'Me? In a spot?' I dropped my cigarette.

He bent down and picked it off the grass. 'You—in a spot.' He handed me the cigarette. 'That may sound farcical, but this is hardly an amusing situation for you, is it?'

But it might be amusing someone else, I thought. I did not like to mention Kirsty's theory of the students. John was too closely connected with them, and if I told him he might start an investigation.

I might as well have spoken, since he went on to tell me that he wondered if any of the men had done it for a bet. 'But if they had I'd have heard. I hear most things. And a bet requires two people to give it any point.' He shook his head. 'It's unlikely, although not impossible.'

A duck stepped out of the lake and came across the grass towards us rolling like an old sailor. We watched the duck, as if we expected to see four ampoules of morphia hanging round its neck. He said, 'It's such an extraordinary dose to take. Too much for a joke—a quarter would have proved any bet—too little for an addict. People don't just feel the need for one grain. The stuff would have been vanishing all over the place if we had an addict on the staff. And you can't hide that sort of thing, not in a hospital. Apart from the checking, it's something we all know about. And God knows'—he pushed his hand through his hair—'we all know just about everything about each other. No'—the duck was by our feet now and seemed as fascinated by us as we were by her—'it doesn't add up.'

'Nothing adds up,' I said, 'nothing at all. What good can it do anyone to get me out of Robert—or the other wards?'

He said, 'So you know that?'

'Matron told me yesterday.'

'Do you mind very much?'

'Having no patients? Yes, I do. I mind a lot.'

He said, 'Of course you wouldn't be a nurse if you didn't feel

44

that way. But there are other departments in a hospital that are just as important as the wards.'

I had purposefully avoided considering my immediate future. I could postpone that thought no longer. I wondered where Matron would send me. To help in the dining-room? Home Sister? The Diet Kitchen? I loathed the prospect of any of them.

'Someone has to work away from the wards,' he said drily, as if I had spoken.

I was getting annoyed with his thought-reading. 'I'd rather that someone wasn't me. Unless you've been a nurse, that may be hard to understand, but it's a fact. Nurses detest working in departments; they need patients quite as much, if not more, than the patients need them. I like flapping round sick-beds and people; I like people, and doing things for them. Not from any altruistic motives, but because I just like doing that. I am just not the admin. type, Mr Dexter; and if I've to face the future as acting unpaid Sister Dining-Room or checking over the laundry in the Home with Sister'—I was really worked up—'then I feel I may as well resign here and now, and go somewhere else and start all over again.'

So help me, I thought, I'm going to cry! I was thinking of Peter and how empty life was going to be without him; and of Robert when the night rounds were over, and the ward was mine until daylight. My throat pricked and my eyes were smarting. The duck had wandered off, and the lake was empty. I stared at the water and held my breath.

He said, 'Stop dramatising, Nurse Snow.' He sounded bored. I was so surprised that I lost all desire to cry.

'Me?'

'Yes. You're well away in a cloud of self-pity and having a wonderful wallow.' He looked me over coolly. 'I suggest you come down to earth and remember that everyone of us makes a cracking mistake once in a whole. There's nothing strange about that. But you have, through your carelessness, caused a considerable commotion and a great deal of inconvenience. And you've allowed someone to get unlawful possession of a mighty dangerous drug. And not the least inconvenience is to those chaps in Robert. You know how all patients dislike changes of staff. All right.' He picked up his hat and stick. 'You made a mistake; now you're having to pay for it. That's the usual form. That's all. And you can thank Heaven that it's no worse. Supposing one of the patients had got hold of that stuff—they might have pushed themselves out. A grain could do that to a weak heart. Think of what might have happened then—and what might still happen—and how you'd feel.' He stood up. 'Now, I'm afraid I must get back. Are you coming, or do you

45

care to sit here and watch the ducks?'

I felt about two inches high and eight years old. I also felt rather ashamed of myself. I said I would watch the ducks, thank you.

'As you wish,' he murmured. 'Afternoon, Nurse.'

'Mr Dexter——' He turned back. 'I'm sorry—but there's something I've been meaning to ask you since I met you. How's the Admiral? Is he going to do?'

He took off his hat, stroked his hair with the same hand, and put his hat back on again. 'Still early days,' he said, 'but I think he'll make it. He's all right.' Which in hospital language meant out of danger. He waited in case I had anything else to say; but I had not, so he nodded briefly and walked away.

I stayed on the bench until he disappeared from sight. I concentrated on the Admiral. That at least was a cheering thought. Then I picked up my chocolates and walked slowly back to the hospital.

Home Sister was waiting for me. 'Matron wants you to move back to the day nurses' home this evening, Nurse Snow.'

I did not ask her where Matron was going to send me; Home Sister was a clam where Matron was concerned. She was still worrying about my lack of colour.

'I'm probably a bit cold, Sister. I've been sitting in the park, and now the sun has gone it is chilly.' That was not true, it had been perfectly warm in the park, but I was not going to explain that I was white because I was angry. John Dexter had been quite right, but that only made me more angry. And when in a rage I lose what little colour I possess.

Next morning I saw Matron.

'There can be no question of your returning to Robert yet, Nurse Snow.' She said she had discussed my case with the Committee, and that they had agreed to leave me to her. 'I intended sending you to help Sister Dining-room with the meals,' she explained, 'but it has been suggested to me this morning that you might be more useful—and could do no harm—in one of the Out-Patient departments.'

So I had been right if only about that. I wondered who my friend on the staff might be; I suspected Night Sister or Sister Robert. Whoever it was, I was very grateful to them.

Matron was still talking. 'I know you have already had your period of training in that department, but the extra experience will be useful. And since you have recently worked in Christian, I want you to work in the Children's Room.' She looked hard at me. 'I am relying on you, Nurse; so kindly remember that. I must admit that I agree with——' She hesitated, then changed her mind and went on. 'I must agree,' she repeated, 'that it would be a waste of a young and healthy trained nurse if I sent

46

you, even temporarily, to some domestic sinecure. This hospital, like all hospitals, needs every nurse it possesses.'

I said fervently, 'Thank you very much, Matron.'

She said, 'I am not taking this step solely because it has been suggested to me. I am considering your past conduct. I feel that you should know that. You may go and report to Sister Out-Patients immediately.'

I thanked her again, and she dismissed me.

I walked quickly to Out-Patients thinking gratefully not of Sister Robert, but of Sister Christian. Perhaps it was she who had suggested this, I had worked in Christian before going to Robert; Sister Christian and I had become good friends, and she had suggested that when I completed my training I should return, with Matron's permission, to Christian as a Staff Nurse.

As soon as I was free I would go up to Christian to thank her. I would also thank Sister Robert, who had sent me a private message via Home Sister yesterday, to say that whenever Matron considered it suitable, she, Sister Robert, would be pleased to have me back as her Night Senior.

Sister Out-Patients was not at all pleased to see me. She was new to the hospital and had not been in Out-Patients during the four months I spent there the previous year. She came from St Martha's, a rival hospital, with the reputation of being the best-looking girl at Martha's and the possessor of that hospital's gold medal for nurses. I had heard about Sister Out-Patients from my colleagues, but until now had never seen her.

Her name was Miss Mack. She was a young woman in the late twenties or early thirties. She was the same height as myself, but whereas I was thin, she was slim. She appeared to have no bones at all. Her face, even to another woman, was breath-takingly lovely, and I wondered at the effect she was having on the boys and why I had not heard about this. Her hair was the gold of a Victorian sovereign. My grandfather left me three, so I know the colour. Her eyes were more violet than dark blue, her lashes improbably, but obviously naturally, black. Her skin was perfect, and there was nothing wrong with any of her other features.

I had heard a good deal about Sister Out-Patients from my junior in Robert, but what I had heard did not tally with her appearance. Nurse Fraser said that Sister O.P.s was now the most unpopular sister in the hospital, from the probationer's point of view.

Looking at her, it was hard to see why she should be so tough with the girls; with looks like hers, she had no cause to feel put out by the presence of so many younger women around her. Yet, according to Nurse Fraser, the whole first year quaked at the suggestion of working in Out-Patients and longed to be transferred to the neighbouring care of fierce old Sister Casualty, who barked like a sergeant-major most of the time but was always impeccably fair in her attitude to pros. This particular aspect of life in O.P.s did not trouble me now, as it would have done had I been in my first year. I had passed the stage when an unpleasant Sister can ruin your working life.

There comes a time in every nurse's career, usually towards the end of the third year, when she discovers that Sisters are merely young women slightly older than herself, in navy blue dresses and frilly caps, and that their feet still hurt, and their backs still ache as her own does; only since they are older, their feet and backs possibly hurt and ache even more than her own.

Sister Out-Patients frowned at me as I stood in front of the desk in her small office, my hands correctly behind me. Her lovely eyes were empty of everything but displeasure.

'I cannot conceive,' she said, 'why Matron should consider you suitable to work in my department, Nurse Snow. I was not consulted; if I had been, you would not be here now.'

'I'm sorry, Sister.'

She sniffed. 'Apparently you are to work in the Children's Room.'

'Yes, Sister.'

She clearly did not approve of my agreeing with her. 'At least,' she said coldly, 'there are no drug cupboards and no keys in that room. I suppose I will just have to make the best of it.'

I did not like to say 'Yes, Sister,' and could scarcely say 'No, Sister,' so I smiled weakly. I was not surprised that she reminded me of the lost drugs; I was fairly certain that I was in for a good many such reminders.

The Out-Patients nurses did not follow Sister's lead. The Staff Nurse, a fat, cheerful girl called Blakelock, who had once been my senior when I was a night pro, welcomed me warmly.

'Between ourselves I'm more than glad to see you back, Snow. We can always use an extra trained nurse in this dive. We've got even more clinics than we had last year, and you know what it was like then!' She said the business in Robert had been a bad show. 'Nasty thing to happen when you're in charge. Could have happened to me dozens of times—thank goodness it never did. I always dumped my keys in the mending box on the desk when I was having a panic!'

Lisa Smith, the other senior nurse in O.P.s and a member of my own set, greeted me with open arms. 'It'll be bliss having one of us girls to work with again.' We called our set 'us girls.' 'But I'm afraid you are in for a tough time with our luscious Sister, dear girl.'

I said I had heard that toughness was routine in O.P.s nowadays.

'But, Lisa, why is she so tough, with that face? And what were the Martha's men doing letting her go? She's really beautiful.'

Lisa said grimly that the Martha's men had more sense than she had previously credited them with, after seeing their behaviour at the last finals of the rugger cup. 'But seriously, Gillian, this is more than her usual line. I'm so used to that by now that I take for granted the fact that all the pros will be in tears each morning before we open. I always bring a couple of dozen extra handkerchiefs. No. This concerns you. She's been up the wall about you for the past hour. I wouldn't mention it if I did not think you ought to be warned.'

'You mean she takes life—and crime—seriously? Maybe you have to if you win a gold medal. And maybe Martha's Sisters are not so human as ours. Sister Robert's been a honey, and old Home Sister has been clucking round me like a kind old hen, and saying, "There, there, Nurse dear, we all make mistakes, and after all no one seems to have come to any harm yet." '

'Dear girl,' said Lisa, 'this has nothing to do with her gold medal—or the fact that she comes from the rival firm. You could personally have rifled every drug cupboard in the hospital as far as she was concerned. I'm certain of that, because, like the whole hospital, we've been talking drugs for the past two days. When we described you to her she said she knew which was Nurse Snow, and you looked one of those insipidly pretty, frail girls, who would do an insipidly frail thing like leaving your keys around. And that, did you but know it, is open-hearted charity from dear Sister Out-Patients.'

I asked, 'Then what's got into her?'

We were cleaning the Children's Room. Lisa dropped her duster, and stared at me.

'Dear girl, is it possible you don't know?'

'Don't know what?'

She retrieved her duster and polished the arms of a wheelchair furiously. 'Of course—you've been buried on nights and this has only been going on for the past couple of weeks.'

'What has been going on? Get to the point, Lisa,' I begged.

'Sister and our John.' She grinned. 'That's it, Gill. True love has blossomed at last. Or rather—we are all hoping and praying that it has, as it makes Sister so much happier.'

'Sister and John Dexter? That's who it was!' I suddenly remembered the hair I had glimpsed under that black hat. 'No wonder I did not recognise it.' And I told her about yesterday afternoon.

'You don't tell me!' She laughed. 'My, my! So he takes her out to tea! That's big stuff from John. I hate to admit it, loathing her guts as I do, but I've got to hand it to her. No Joe's

49

girl has ever rated so much as a stroll in the park with our John.'

I did not want to contradict her, so I asked instead if she was sure it was a big thing. 'I can't believe John has fallen at last.'

'To be truthful, that I couldn't say. Who can say what John D. thinks about anything? But I'm certain about her. Life in the department is almost bearable when he's around. Sister turns into a little woman. All smiles and charm. Wonderful sight.'

I said I was delighted to hear it. 'They'll make a good pair.'

'Dear girl,' said Lisa seriously, 'you can't really wish her on John? He's a sweetie, even if he isn't susceptible to our charms. Besides, he's got nice manners and that fascinating white streak. I think John's a dear.'

'I still think they'll make a good pair. All right,' I added quickly, as I saw she was about to protest again, 'I'll grant he's always civil. I'm just allergic to giants. But, anyway, what's all this got to do with me?'

She dropped the tin of polish this time. 'You really don't know?'

'All I know is that Matron wants me to work in this department.'

Lisa said I had better hold on to something. 'The reason you are here and not lost in the outer darkness of the dining-room is because the dear S.S.O. asked Matron how she dared complain of being short-staffed when she went around wasting her trained staff in sinecures! He actually said that. Matron was so shaken that she told Sister O.P.s all; Sister was so shaken she told Blakelock, who told me. So you are here, dear Gill, by courtesy of the S.S.O., and dear Sister O.P.s is out for your blood!'

4

A MORNING WITH THE CHILDREN

I HAD no time that morning to consider what Lisa had said, nor was I anxious to consider it; the last sensation I cared to feel towards John Dexter was gratitude. The thought that I should be very grateful to him made me even more annoyed with him.

Sister Out-Patients frowned each time she passed the open door of the Children's Room. Her frown did not trouble me. I knew she would shortly discover what little cause she had for anxiety about my relationship with the S.S.O., and that eventually she and I would get along all right. I was sanguine about this because I was used to getting along with Sisters. Falling in with their little ways is something you learn in a general nursing training. I felt mildly sorry for her; she must be very taken with him, if she could seriously imagine that he had designs on me. She and I might not have met before, but she must have heard from the other Sisters of his general attitude to the nurses, and she knew enough about hospitals to appreciate the glorious gossip that would follow if he so much as glanced, unprofessionally, at a nurse in training.

There was an unwritten code which was rigidly followed in such matters. A student and a pro might smile at each other unremarked; a senior nurse and a houseman; a staff nurse and a registrar. But let a registrar look at a pro or the S.S.O. or S.M.O. glance mildly at any nurse, and the hospital would rub its hands and lick its lips in happily scandalised anticipation. Sisters were reckoned to be above and beyond such affairs; every nurse in training knew they were not. Every Sister had her pet Consultant, and most Consultants—married or single—their pet Sister. This was a pleasant scheme, since it ensured that the ward sisters were in a good mood at least twice a week, when their chosen Consultants did a teaching round. The S.M.O. and S.S.O., being only one step below the Consultants, were considered Sisters' territory. They were also generally married. Dr Cutler, the medical officer, had three children and was charming to everyone; Mr Dexter, being a bachelor, was polite to all but charming to no one—with the new exception, apparently, of Sister O.P.s.

He never so much as glanced my way when he walked into Out-Patients half-way through that morning. Sister, who was seated at a small table in the corridor directing patients, rose with a smile of welcome that was only temporarily dimmed when she saw me standing, quite officially, in the doorway, talking to the departing mother of one of the many infants I was shepherding out of my room.

Half an hour later Mr Rufford, the orthopaedic specialist, smiled at the small Australian boy I had just wheeled into his office.

'Mr Dexter in the department, Nurse Snow?'

'He's taking Mr Makin's [the general surgeon's] clinic next door, Mr Rufford.'

Mr Rufford got up from his chair. 'I'd like a word with him in a moment. I want him to look at young Randy here.'

Young Randy looked up at us. 'More docs, Doc?'

'More docs, chum,' said Mr Rufford. 'But you'll know this one. Just let's have you on that couch and we'll see what we can do about those legs.'

He beckoned to Mrs Durant, Randy's mother. She came over from the front bench and hesitated at the door of the glass-fronted office. She was a thin, tired-looking young woman, with a lined, sun-burnt face.

'Come in, Mother,' said Mr Rufford, 'and take a chair. I want you to tell me how your boy has been since we discharged him? How's he been in himself? Better than he was those last two years when you had him in that pram? Before I put this new plaster on?'

'Oh, my word, Doctor,' she said, 'he's been real good. And hungry. Eats like a horse.'

'I see.' He made a few notes, asked a few more questions. 'I had another letter from your doctor in Australia. I wrote and told him what I had done. He sent you his regards.' He found the letter among the notes. 'From Masonville. That your home town?'

She said no. 'Randy was in hospital there, Doctor, but we live in the out-back.' She mentioned the place. 'Randy had to fly there, he did, and I got in often to see him. They treated him real good. That so, son?'

Randy said, 'Too right, it was.'

'But he wasn't getting any better, Doctor,' she said urgently, 'so his Dad and I decided he ought to come home.'

Mr Rufford nodded. He had heard all this from her before, but he was a patient man, and he listened carefully as if it was news to him.

'Have you been out there long, Mrs Durant?'

'Oh, my word, Doctor. I was born out there. My grandparents settled in Australia sixty years back. But we always call this home. And Doctor Mally—that's our Doctor out in Masonville —he told us about you. He said you were the best man for legs in the world, he reckoned. So I brought him here,' she added simply.

Mr Rufford was a small man for an orthopaedic surgeon. His line of surgery was one which required considerable physical strength in a surgeon and the majority were built on the lines of the S.S.O. Mr Rufford was small but square; his face was pink and cherubic. He looked suddenly older, as if he found Mrs Durant's faith a great responsibility. He looked down at the notes on his desk.

'It's a long way to come,' he said.

'Oh, my word, Doctor,' she said again. 'I'd have brought him twice as far, if need be. He's our only kid.'

'I see.' He smiled—a shy smile. 'Well'—he scribbled something on a fresh sheet of paper—'we've done all we can to get him on his legs again'—he glanced up—'you've seen he's been having all that massage, haven't you?' She nodded, and he folded the sheet of paper and handed it to me. 'Take that to Mr

Dexter, please, Nurse. My compliments and I'd be obliged if he can spare a moment.'

Sister leapt at me as soon as I was outside the door.

'Why are you not in your room, Nurse Snow?'

I explained and tentatively offered her the note.

'And what makes you think I have the time to spare to deliver letters, Nurse?' she demanded. 'Get on at once and don't keep Mr Rufford waiting! He's a very busy man!'

'Yes, Sister.' I walked round her and into the next room.

Lisa was presiding there. She glided up the aisle between the benches of waiting patients, with raised eyebrows.

'Wanting something?'

I said Mr Dexter. Her eyebrows rose even higher. 'Does Sister know, Nurse?'

I said Sister did indeed. 'Mr Rufford wants him.'

She sighed. 'Oh dear. Another hold-up. He's alone in the office—I was just going to shepherd in the next patient, but you'd better have him first.'

'Thanks, pal,' I murmured, and walked on.

The general room had no glass office. I knocked at the wooden door. Mr Dexter called, 'Come in,' and when I went in, said, 'Good morning, Nurse Snow,' to the wall behind my head.

I told him why I had come, and handed him the note. He read it, then smiled faintly. 'I'll come now.' As he came round the desk, he asked if I knew what was in the note.

'No, Mr Dexter.'

'Take a look.' He held it in front of me.

It read: 'I've got a worried mum here who thinks I'm a miracle worker. The subject is Randy Durant. I think I'm justified in providing a little drama, but I'd like a second opinion first. Toppling off a pedestal can be an unnerving experience.'

We went back to the Children's Room office. Mrs Durant smiled uncertainly as Mr Rufford introduced John. 'You know this Doctor, eh, Randy?' said Mr Rufford. Randy said fair dinkum he did. 'Hi, Doc.'

'Hi, Randy,' said John gravely.

They looked at the old Australian X-rays, at the pictures taken when Randy first arrived, at the pictures of the operation, and at the wet plates taken this morning. They looked at Randy, who grinned back at them; they avoided looking at Mrs Durant; then they looked at each other.

Mr Rufford screwed up his face and resembled an elderly puck as he said, slowly, 'I think—off.'

Mrs Durant started, then sat forward on the edge of her chair, Randy's face altered from a child's to an adult's.

'You going to take me—me legs off, Doc?'

'Not your legs, son,' said Mr Rufford, 'your plasters.'

Randy hesitated. 'I expect,' he said, 'I'll need new ones, will I, Doc?'

'Why?' asked Mr Rufford. 'Think you'll be cold without 'em?' He turned to Mrs Durant. 'When did you last see him on his feet?'

She told him the exact date. I think she could have given the hour and minute had he asked for them. Her voice was unsteady. 'It seems ever such a long time, Doctor.'

He smiled at her. 'I'll bet it does. Too long.' His round eyes moved upward, 'Eh, Mr Dexter?'

John said, 'Too long. This chap's'—he jerked a thumb at the boy—'getting fat and lazy. Thoroughly pampered brat, aren't you, Randy?'

Randy beamed. 'Too right, Doc.'

'Well,' said Mr Rufford firmly, 'what are you waiting for, Nurse Snow? Get the plaster shears off that trolley. Come along.'

I handed him the waiting shears, saw John was removing his white coat, so I offered him another pair.

Mr Rufford said, 'You got the time to do this, John?'

John said, 'No,' and went on with what he was doing.

Mr Rufford said it beat him that's what it did, and the trouble with this hospital was the fact that the senior residents had too much time on their hands; and when he was a senior resident he never had time to put on a plaster, much less cut it off, which should be done by the registrar and housemen anyway.

'And will you kindly tell me, Nurse Snow,' he demanded, 'just where my houseman has got to, and why, because my registrar has an examination this morning, my house-surgeon considers I am well able to dispense with his services at this clinic?'

I had been wondering this myself. I was about to say that I was afraid I had no idea but would ask Sister, when John answered for me.

'Gilroy [the orthopaedic house-surgeon] is on the sick-list. Tonsils, or something equally infantile. Thanet is meant to be standing in for him, but he had to assist Mr Smith with the urological list first, and I'm afraid he must have been held up.'

Mr Rufford snorted. 'Trust Smith!' I was cheered by his sudden transformation into an irate Consultant. That meant he was satisfied. Mr Rufford prided himself on his bark; he liked to think we all trembled whenever he opened his mouth. On the contrary we much enjoyed his outbursts, they were never serious and were a sure sign that he was happy. When Mr Rufford was worried, he became the quietest and most civil of men.

It did not take them long to cut off that plaster: in a very few minutes John carefully lifted off the twin shells.

Randy twisted his ankles. 'Feels real good.' The poor child tried to sound casual, but his voice cracked. 'Do I have to have another lot on right away?'

'Oh, I don't know,' said Mr Rufford. 'Let's see you walk first.'

Mrs Durant jumped up. John had his back to her, but he felt her moving, caught my eye, and shook his head slightly. I stepped back and put my hand on her arm.

'Sit down,' I said very quietly, 'and don't say anything.'

She dropped back in her chair, her lips pressed firmly together, her back straight. Cautiously she reached for my hand that was still on her shoulder, and gripped it momentarily.

'Slippers, Nurse,' said Mr Rufford.

We had an assortment of slippers waiting on the bottom layer of the clinic trolley. I looked at Randy's feet, guessed threes, and fitted that size on him.

'How's that, Randy?' I asked.

'That's great, Nurse.'

'Come along, come along,' said Mr Rufford, 'who do you think you are young fellow? Cinderella? Up you get.'

Randy stared, 'Up? Right now?'

'Right now. Up on to those two feet. And see here.' Mr Rufford opened the office door wide. 'See that girl over there? The one with red bows? Well, you just walk over to her and ask her to give you one. Dessay she won't—but you ask her.'

'I'm to walk?' Randy propped himself forward, and touched John, whom he knew well from his sojourn in Christian. 'I can? Really, mister?'

John said gently, 'Really, chum. Your legs are mended now and you've always had two good feet. You just try. You can do it.'

Randy looked from one man to the other, uncertainly. Then he turned to his mother. 'Mum—did you hear what they tell me?'

Mrs Durant raised her head and smiled. 'I heard,' she said, 'I heard. Good news, Randy. Think what your dad'll have to say about this. He's going to be pleased.'

She was wonderful, that woman. She was white with anxiety, but she answered him as calmly as if he had asked her what time it was.

Mr Rufford half turned away from Randy, and picked a blank history sheet off the desk. 'What do you think of this, John?'

John looked closely at the sheet of paper. 'That's interesting.'

Randy watched them, but as they were not apparently paying

any attention to him, he decided he might as well get up. He sat forward, pushed aside the shawl that had been covering him, and climbed alone off the couch. The two men were very close to him, but they did not touch him. I was holding my hands behind my back, and I found I was gripping my own wrist in my effort to keep my hands where they were.

Mrs Durant was holding her handbag in her lap. I saw her knuckles were white, but she never moved or uttered a sound. She sat there quietly as if it was the most normal thing in the world for a child to walk after all that time in plaster. And that child was her son.

Randy was on his feet. He swayed only once, and glanced again at the surgeons as he steadied himself on the side of the couch; but the men were not bothering with him, they were engrossed by their piece of paper; his mother was now searching for something in her bag, and I was apparently watching the rows of waiting children on the benches outside the glass wall. Randy nodded to himself, experimented with one foot, tried the other, then grinned swiftly. Of course walking must be dead easy; why fuss? The docs had said he could walk, hadn't they? So he walked.

As he left the office our four heads jerked upward as if we were puppets and someone had pulled our strings. We saw him walk slowly but steadily across the long room, heard him shout 'Hi, Red Bow,' to Red Bow, heard the triumph in his voice, and saw the increased confidence in his dressing-gowned figure as he returned, more quickly this time, to the office. He stood in the doorway, scarlet with effort and pleasure. 'It feels great!'

Mr Rufford frowned awesomely, 'Where's my red bow?'

'Oh, gee,' said the boy apologetically, 'I forgot, mister. Shall I go back and ask her?'

Mr Rufford relaxed, 'You go back, son, but don't bother to ask her. I was just teasing you. But you take another walk.'

Randy was gone before he finished speaking.

John said, 'I'll have to leave you.' He shook hands with Mrs Durant. 'Good-bye and good luck.'

'Oh, my word, Doctor,' she said, 'I don't know what to say or how to thank you.'

He smiled. 'I haven't done anything; it's Mr Rufford here who's done it all—and that boy of yours. He's a good boy, that, but I expect you know that already.'

She said, 'I do, Doctor, but thanks, thanks all the same.'

Mr Rufford got out of the doorway, 'Thanks, John—do the same for you one day.'

John smiled at him without answering, then walked quickly across the room, waved at Randy, and disappeared through the open door.

Mrs Durant stood up. 'I can't begin to say what I feel, Dr Rufford——'

'Then don't say anything, Mother,' he said briskly, 'just sit down again and listen to what you must do. You'll have to take your boy along to the physiotherapist again this morning and give her the note I'll write now. Then keep on with those appointments and the exercises I told you before; come back and see me in three weeks, and maybe I can hand you back to your doctor in Australia.'

She sat down and controlled her face with an effort.

'He won't have to go back to being in a chair? He'll be all right? Really?'

'He will. But you mustn't let him overdo things, so don't throw away the chair yet. He's got his confidence back, which is what we are aiming at this morning, so you'll have your hands full in that direction, I'm afraid! My goodness, young woman! Here's a fine time to cry after sitting there good as gold the way you did just now! You dry those tears and stop worrying. You've had more than your share,' he added kindly. 'You write and tell your husband that you'll both be back for the New Year and tell him from me that he's got a splendid young woman for a wife. Now then,' he swung round and glared at me as I was re-dressing Randy after having caught him with considerable difficulty, 'now then, Nurse, don't dawdle! Send young Randy on his way with Mrs Durant.' He shook hands all round. 'Good-bye, Randy—see you once more, maybe twice—good-bye, Mrs Durant; don't bother to thank me, thank you for coming. Nurse Snow! I can't hang around all day waiting for my next patient! Who's next? Red Bow? Or Dorothy?'

'Dorothy Bland.' I had pushed the protesting Randy back into his wheel-chair with the promise that it was only for the ride to the massage department, and was handing Mrs Durant the mass of forms and notes that she would need to give the physiotherapist and the Out-Patient almoner. Mrs Durant tucked the notes under her arm.

'You know, Nurse,' she said softly, 'I've thought I've been happy before. But until now I didn't know what happiness was.' She sailed away, pushing the wheel-chair in front of her, and the children on the benches turned their heads to smile at her, and even her back seemed to glow with relief and wonder.

Mr Rufford said, 'Ask Mrs Bland to come in with Dorothy, please, Nurse.'

Mrs Bland was surprised at my request that she should accompany her eight-year-old daughter, who sat straight as a guardsman in her spinal jacket.

'Me too, dear? Ta, Nurse, I'm sure.'

It must have been Dorothy's first follow-up clinic, or Mrs

Bland would have known that Mr Rufford insisted on the mothers of his child patients being present when he looked at their children. Not all our doctors agreed with him on this point, but he was adamant, and had explained his outlook to us in his lectures.

'When I send a child home,' he had said, 'I hand over the case to the mother. If that mother isn't working with me, then I've wasted a good deal of work and time. So I just treat the Mums as normal intelligent human beings, and you'd be surprised how many of them are that! I tell 'em what I want done and why. In ninety-nine cases out of a hundred it works. Works very well.'

Mr Rufford's patients did very well. Certainly orthopaedic surgery is a branch in which a hundred per cent. cures are cures and not limited to a five-year period; but even among orthopaedic surgeons Mr Rufford and his statistics were considered outstanding. We often wondered how much of this was due, not only to his skill, but to his sympathetic personality. He was also an unconscious mimic. He could talk pure Elephant and Castle, straight Geordie, or assume a Dublin accent automatically, depending on where his patients hailed from. The patients were invariably delighted and at ease.

'Lass,' one Yorkshire mother said, 'it's a real treat to meet a lad like 'yon. Home-like.'

Mr Rufford was born and raised in Wimbledon.

At ten minutes to one Sister's head came round the door.

'Nurse Snow, you should have gone to twelve-thirty lunch.' I went over to her. 'I'm sorry, Sister—I didn't realise that.'

She tapped her foot. 'If you are to work in my department you will kindly understand that I do not expect to have to chase senior nurses to meals. Surely you can read the notice on the wall in my office?'

I did not like to remonstrate again with the explanation that I had had no time to read any notices since I had come on duty; I apologised once more, and said there were still three children waiting to be seen.

Sister frowned, 'Your room should be cleared by now. I shall have to send a probationer to finish off for you, which will be most inconvenient.'

'I'm sorry, Sister.' I was sounding like a gramophone record.

A few seconds later a harassed pro scuttled into my room; I told her what remained to be done, excused myself to Mr Rufford, and crossed the corridor to collect my cloak from our changing-room.

The S.S.O. had come out of his room when I got back to the corridor. He was talking to Sister; his back was to the changing-room door.

'I won't be back until after three this afternoon, Sister,' I heard him say. 'I have to be on Mr Marcus' round in Robert.'

Sister was in the way, and I had to wait. I heard her answer clearly. 'Something,' she said, 'always seems to be going on in Robert these days. I wonder why?'

John noticed me, and side-stepped for me to pass. He was looking at her as I glanced up to see how he was taking this. I learnt nothing; his expression was as non-committal as hers. 'I've no idea, Sister.'

I told Lisa about this at lunch. 'But really, that silly young woman needn't flap! Our John never notices me. Often, when he's around, I wonder if I'm there at all. If Sister could have seen the way he never looked at me in Robert—or this morning when I had to haul him out for old Rufford—she'd be a new woman.'

Lisa reached for the salt. 'I wish you'd say that again, dear girl, when she can overhear you. She was quite insufferable when he vanished with you. The pros have been having nervous breakdowns all morning; she came in and gave me the once over while I was waiting for him to come back, and I nearly burst into tears myself! Not sorrow—blind rage. Blast!' She had half-emptied the salt-cellar in her preoccupation with Sister O.P.s. 'She found fault with every miserable thing I had done, and made me look an absolute fool in front of the patients. They were sweet—as always—but that only made it worse. I sniffed round the benches like a first-year.' She sighed. 'You know something, Gillian: if you are going to affect her thus, fond as I am of you, dear girl, I can't help wishing you had kept your hands on those darned keys.'

'You don't wish it any more than I do,' I said gloomily, thinking of Peter.

She was instantly remorseful. 'Dear girl, I am sorry. Why can't I keep my big mouth shut? I know it's wretched for you. And sad bad luck your buddy Carol Ash isn't on days to cheer you up.'

I agreed. 'I miss Carol. She and I could generally raise a laugh in the old days.'

Lisa said, 'Poor kid, she's had a packet too. That was a bad do she had.'

'Bad as they come. Hardly surprising if she's a bit subdued now.'

Lisa murmured sympathetically. She did not say anything specific, but the sound was kind. A few minutes later she said, 'Still, there's always Peter Kier, isn't there? Don't,' she added quickly, 'think I'm prying, dear girl. I'm just a busy little bee combing the horizons for silver linings.'

I said I had not thought she was prying. 'I'm all for a silver lining, Lisa. Tell me if you find one.'

She smiled. She had a very attractive smile—it illuminated her whole face, as smiles are meant to, but seldom do. She was not pretty; her features were too irregular, her eyes too small and deep-set, her mouth too wide, yet the general effect was attractive and lively. Lisa was the most mobile person I have ever seen. She was never still, mentally or physically; even her hair was mobile. It was light brown, and stood out from her head as if electrified, which at times indeed it was. Lisa combing her hair could put any near-by wireless out of action. It was one of her parlour tricks which we had discovered accidentally years ago in the Preliminary Training School. My set were all very proud of Lisa's hair, if slightly scared of her forthright tongue.

'Now do tell me,' she said, 'if you two are engaged yet? I know you've been inseparable for the past year and I've wondered——'

'No call to wonder,' I said, 'we aren't. We are just——'

She broke in. 'Let me guess—good friends?'

I nearly said old acquaintances, then decided against it. I was not yet ready to have a hearty girlish laugh at my late friendship with Peter. 'Something like that.'

'One thing I like about this hospital,' said Lisa complacently, 'is the number of Good Friendships that exist. Why do you think it is? Our hearts wrapped up in our work?'

'Our feet hurt too much?'

'Could be, dear girl. Of course, there's always the ugly fact that none of us have any money. You can't set up house on a houseman's pay—if you'll excuse the horrible pun! Not unless you are someone like your pal Carol.' She wagged her head at me. 'We ought to be heiresses, Gill, you and I. Then we'd knock 'em cold.'

'Heiresses?'

She nodded, and her cap nearly took off from her wiry hair. 'Yes. Like your pal Carol.' She said she got quite a kick out of having all that cash in our set.

'But Carol's not all that wealthy?' I protested.

'Dear girl,' she said, 'don't be dumb. Open any aeroplane bonnet—if aeroplanes have bonnets—and what do you find? One of her old man's machines. He must have made a packet, and she's the one and only, isn't she?' I said yes. 'Well, ducks, she must have most of it, less death duties, tax, and what have you. I wonder the boys aren't queueing up.'

I said I had wondered that too. 'Not because of her cash. Funnily, I've never connected her with much cash—she's a good soul, doesn't throw it around. That's one of the nicest things about Carol. Just shows,' I went on thoughtfully, 'how nice. There am I, her best friend here, and I had forgotten all about it. But to get back to the boys—I've often wondered why she's never run around with them. I've come to the conclusion that it's because she's just not interested in them; which is a pity, because Carol's a honey, and ought to have had a lot of fun all these years.'

I expected Lisa to echo this, but all she said was, 'I don't really know Carol at all for all that she is one of us girls. You know how it is in a place this size if you've never worked together. But I know she's a great buddy of yours, so she must be nice.'

I laughed. 'I am staggered and touched. To think I never even knew you cared!'

'Dear girl,' she said sententiously, 'I am undemonstrative but I feel deeply.' Then she laughed too. 'Hang it, Gill, you and I have sweated over the sick together a lot. Remember our dark days as co-juniors in Luke and John?'

'Don't remind me.' I closed my eyes. 'Draw a veil. I don't think we stopped laughing or collecting rockets from Sister L. and J. the whole four months. Wasn't she a horror?'

Lisa admitted that Sister L. and J. was sheer murder.

'But reasonable murder, Gill—I mean she was just hell-minded to one and all, regardless of sex and rank. She's not like this glamorous so-and-so in O.P.s. Wait till you see her with the student men! She's pure syrup.'

I was still thinking of Sister Luke and John. 'Remember that time we both wanted the same off-day to go to the ball? And Sister asked if we thought this was a hospital or a palais de danse, and reminded us that in her young days probationers had never heard of dances!'

'Wasn't she ghastly!' said Lisa with simple pride. 'But she gave us the evening off all the same! Which reminds me—I suppose, now you're off nights, you and Peter will be joining the merry rugger throng?'

'No.' I took a piece of bread I did not want. 'No, we won't.'

'Why not, for goodness sake? You both love dancing. You're surely not going into purdah because someone has swiped some morph.?'

'No,' I said again, 'not that. He's taking Carol for a change.'

She put down her knife and fork and gaped at me. 'He's doing what? Dear girl, why?'

'He asked her.'

Lisa's hair was positively vibrant. 'Dear girl, do you mind?'

I was going to lie, when I changed my mind. I like Lisa and disliked lying to my friends, or come to that, my enemies.

'Life's not exactly an untrammelled song at the moment, so what's one more snag? Only don't get this wrong—it's got nothing to do with Carol.'

'Then why is she going with him?'

I explained.

'I see.' She looked down at her plate for several seconds. Then she said, 'I suppose you know what you're doing—and certainly Peter Kier gives one the impression that he eats out of your hand—but if I were you, I'd be careful.'

'What do you mean?'

'Well,' she said slowly, 'I'm all for kindness to dumb animals and children, but I think there should be a limit to altruism. And me, I think handing over your young man even to a bosom pal, goes beyond that limit. Tricky. Dead risky. Still,' she brightened, 'I'm sure you know what you're doing.'

'That's where you're wrong,' I said. 'I don't. I am in the dark.'

She said I was in bad company. 'With you in the dark is our respected Miss Mack. She's like the proverbial cat on hot bricks with our John. The only fun I get these days is watching her watching him.'

I was so relieved to drop the subject of Peter that I was happy to discuss the chances of this—to me—novel affair.

'Maybe she's secretly knocked him for six?'

Lisa snorted. 'Not her. And not him. Nothing short of a bulldozer—and a dirty great bulldozer at that—could make any impression on dear Mr Dexter.'

I said I did not see why not. 'She is quite lovely, Lisa—and don't forget he takes her out to tea. That's purple passion for John.'

'Phooey,' said Lisa, 'she hasn't got what it takes! No—don't laugh—she hasn't—truthfully. I've watched the other young men with her, and for all her golden hair and coives, they run like stags in the opposite direction. Notwithstanding the syrup. No sex appeal.' She smiled up at the maid who was collecting our plates, 'Don't pretend to be shocked, Agnes. You know all about sex appeal.'

Agnes giggled and said, 'Get along there, Nurses; really, Nurse Smith, the things you say!'

Lisa watched Agnes' swaying back-view reflectively. 'If only that man is really casting lingering, longing looks at Sister, how happy we will be in the department.'

'But I thought you said he was too good for her?'

'So he is, but who am I to wish our John ill? I'm fond of him. I think he's sweet'—she talked as if he was her pet teddy-bear—'and I find I can't bear to think of his pining away under that granite exterior. I also can't bear to think of life in O.P. as it was this morning. One degree lower than slave-labour. So if he'll only take her off our hands, I'll give him my blessing and even raise a subscription among the O.P. girls for a wedding present!'

'Oh, my goodness!' I had seen the clock. 'Lisa, it's twenty-five past! She'll kill us if we don't get back on time.'

We stood up quickly, and left the dining-room. Lisa glanced round casually, and said, 'Bother—I've left my pen in there,' and ducked back through the glass doors as Peter came out of the men's dining-room, which lay opposite to our own.

'Hallo, Peter—be seeing you,' she called over her shoulder.

Peter caught me up. 'Gillian! Where are you working?'

I forgot my desire to return to duty punctually, and stopped. 'Hallo. O.P.s. *Pro tem.*'

'That must be nice for O.P.s, darling.' He did not look as if he thought it at all nice for anyone. Then he pulled himself together, and said he was glad I was back in circulation again.

'Makes a change,' I agreed.

'Look here,' he smiled suddenly, 'are you off? Can we chat?'

'On.' I told him about Sister. 'If I'm not back in three minutes I really will be out on my ear.'

He dug his hands in his pockets. 'Like that, is it? Too bad. I wish,' he hesitated. 'I wish you weren't in such a panic.'

'You do?'

He was not much taller than I, and our eyes were nearly level. As so often happened when we met, we seemed to be carrying on two conversations at the same time. I was certain that he had heard as little of what my voice had said as I had of his.

He shook his head. 'When are you off?'

'Six.'

He said, 'That's good.'

'Is it?'

'Darling,' he said impatiently, 'you do ask the damnedest questions. Of course it is. You've been buried in Robert for months. Long time no see.'

One of us, I thought, must clearly be up the wall.

I reminded him that we had met a couple of days ago in the canteen.

'Oh—that.' He waved the scene away with one hand. 'You were all strung up then, sweetie, too grim and earnest. But you know quite well what I mean. It's months since we've seen each other in a bright light—and months since I've seen you without that covering layer of white starch. I was just wondering if I couldn't bribe old Tom to stand in for me tonight, and maybe we could eat something somewhere and talk of this and that.'

I did not understand this change of attitude, nor did I bother to understand it; it was too pleasant. I was also far too busy holding my breath—in case I woke up and found that this was not happening and that it was all wishful thinking on my

63

part—to trouble about even a minor analysis of his words.

I said I thought it would be a splendid idea if Tom Thanet was open to bribery.

'I can fix Tom,' he said easily, 'and the boss should be all right. He's pretty co-operative if there's no crisis brewing. I'll see what I can do.' He rocked on his heels. 'Will you mind if I leave things in the air until this evening? I'll ring you and let you know—or drop in chez O.P.s. All right?'

I did not mind anything or anybody. I said that would be quite all right, and I would enjoy an evening out. And with that miracle of understatement I suddenly recalled Sister O.P.s, and rushed down the broad main hospital corridor to Out-Patients so quickly that I reached it before Lisa, who had been walking there by way of the basement stairs and corridor all the time I had been talking to Peter.

'Haemorrhage or fire, dear Nurse?' she asked as she caught me up.

I said neither; I was just a keen type, and couldn't wait to get my hands on my lamp again. We reported back to Sister Out-Patients, who looked at us coldly, and said that at St Martha's hospital the senior nurses were expected to be punctual.

As she spoke, the clock in the hospital tower struck the half-hour. Lisa and I stood with our hands behind our backs and chanted smugly, 'Yessister, sorrysister.'

5

AN INVITATION FROM THE WRONG MAN

SISTER was off duty from two until five that afternoon; the department was as busy as it had been all morning, but there was an atmosphere of calm in the corridor and waiting rooms. Nurse Blakelock had been a staff nurse for two years and had a placid nature. She was also extremely efficient, and remained unperturbed by anything from the premature birth of a baby in the corridor to a coloured seaman going berserk with a plaster knife in the orthopaedic room, both of which incidents had occurred while she was in charge when I was last in O.P.s.

'Never a dull moment, Snow,' she murmured as she hauled me from the security of my children to the skin clinic, and then sent me to chaperone for a stray cardiac who had wandered up on the wrong day for her clinic, and had to be seen by some physician immediately. 'I'll rustle up a medical registrar from somewhere,' she promised, 'but for Pete's sake stand by with the oxygen. That poor old girl is as blue as they come. And crazy! Imagine coming up on the underground with that heart!' She warned me not to let Matron see me. 'Put on a mask—and if she

64

asks what you're doing out of the kids' room say you're borrowing something. I can't leave my old Mrs Jenks with a pro.'

At three she sent Lisa to relieve me. 'E.N.T. kids for you now, dear girl,' said Lisa, 'and surprise—who do you think is taking little Ears, Noses, and Throats this afternoon? Dear John.'

'Oh, no! What's wrong with Mr Dulain?'

'In St Martha's hospital, Nurse Snow,' she said sternly, 'senior nurses never mention a doctor's name without curtseying. Let us have a little more respect around this establishment!'

Mrs Jenks, who seemed to be an old friend of Lisa's, shook with laughter, and said that Nurse Smith was a proper caution the way she carried on.

'Talk about laugh—Nurse!'

Lisa said she was known as the Sunshine of St Joseph's. 'But how are the legs, Mrs Jenks? Still letting you run races on the underground, I hear.'

I excused myself and went back to my room, which was now almost full. I had just time to take over from the pro who had been organising the ranks, when the S.S.O. arrived and comparative peace settled in the large room.

The children, unlike the adults in the neighbouring room, felt no inhibitions at the sight of our uniforms, the men's white coats, or the scent of ether and wet plaster that always hung around O.P.s. They had all been patients in Christian or Margaret—the other large children's ward—and regarded their follow-up clinics as a social occasion. They hailed each other and us in loud voices, exchanged comic papers and sweets, talked, laughed, and often fought, with a total disregard of their admonishing mammas. 'Hush now, Janet—whatever'll the Nurse think of you——?' They were also expert at recognising the different professional stratas. 'She's not a staff nurse, Mum —she wears a blue belt, 'cause she's fourth-year!'

'Nah—he's not a proper doctor—the proper doctors wear long white coats! He's just a houseman.'

Adult patients often had difficulty over the different uniforms and grades, but the children had us all taped. I knew several of them from my own period in Christian. There, very obviously, I had been nicknamed.

To the shame of their mammas my old patients greeted me with shrieks of 'Hi-ya, Snowwhite! Ain't you got no dwarfs yet?'

My lack of attendant dwarfs had been a constant and unflagging joke. They screamed with joy now, as they had done in Christian when they lost their tonsils, adenoids, or mastoid processes.

I had been too busy this morning to be miserable, now I was too busy to think of this evening, but I beamed happily round the children and the noise worried me not at all. Occasionally I wondered how much was penetrating the glass walls of the office; but John seemed impervious to it, so I did not give it any serious thought.

Once, inadvertently, I found myself beaming at him, then realised what I was doing, and caught the eye of the serious little girl whose throat he was examining.

'Wider please, Marion,' he said, 'that's it. Now a big Ah.'

'Ah!' she bellowed obediently, her round eyes on my face. 'Ah! Ah! Ah!'

'Hey!' he smiled at her, 'that's plenty. You'll do. You're cured, young woman.' He turned in his chair to talk to her mother, and as he did so he glanced momentarily at me.

'You needn't bring Marion up again, Mrs Forbes—unless you have any more trouble. But I doubt if you will.'

'There now,' said Mrs Forbes contentedly. 'Hear what the doctor says, lovey? You don't have to come up to the hospital no more.'

Marion's small face was scarlet. She was one of my old patients, and, like her mother, I knew what that colour foretold.

We spoke together, 'There, there,' pleaded Mrs Forbes.

I said quickly, 'You must come back to our Christmas party.'

We were too late. Marion's face appeared to distintegrate. 'But I don't want not to come up to the hospital no more,' she wailed, 'I like hospital!'

John said, 'I'm glad of that, Marion. Because you can do something for me.'

She was so interested that she stopped crying immediately, and the forgotten tears dripped off her cheeks and on to the small velvet collar of her blue coat.

'Go on,' she said, 'I can?'

'Yes. You. You're quite a big girl, aren't you—six? And you understand all about hospitals, don't you?'

She nodded so violently that her hair slide flew off.

'Now, see here,' he said, 'there's a girl out there'—he jerked his head towards the waiting-room—'who's not as lucky as you. She doesn't know about hospitals, and she's got to come in— same as you—and have the same thing as you did.' He spoke very seriously, as if he was talking to the Professor or the Dean. 'Will you go and have a chat with her? Tell her what it's like. She'll like to know—and she's around your age, I should say.'

Marion scrubbed her face absently with the handkerchief her mother had pushed into her hand.

'What's her name?'

'Joan Devon,' he said. 'Nurse Snow will show you which she is. So will you do that for me as you go out?'

Marion said, 'Is she a big six? Like me?'

He looked her up and down. 'No. I should say she's rather a middle-sized six.'

Marion sighed with pleasure. 'All right,' she said and made for the door.

I took her over to Joan Devon, wondering if he was clairvoyant. I could find no other explanation to account for his knowing how a child he had not yet seen felt about hospitalisation. When I went back to the office he explained.

'I heard what you were saying to her when I came in, and saw that hers was the only new name on the list. But what's she doing here? She shouldn't be at a follow-up.'

'Nurse Blakelock said that Mr Dulain arranged for her to come up this afternoon. Her doctor is a friend of his.'

'Has she got a letter?'

'Yes.' I took her notes off the file and gave them to him.

He glanced through them. 'Right.' He handed them back. 'Thanks, Nurse.' He told me Mr Dulain was away on holiday. 'Fishing. Which is a pity. I'm quite happy to see his private patients for him, but they aren't always so happy to see me.'

I said, 'I'm sorry. I didn't realise she was a private patient.'

He smiled slightly, 'Officially she isn't. But her father is an old Joe's man and her mother an ex-Joe's nurse—that's in the letter. What else does that make her?' He went back to his seat and the desk. 'Well, Nurse, can I have the next, please?'

The last infant was in the office by four-thirty. A pro came to relieve me and I went to tea. Lisa had already eaten and gone, so I sat alone and thought about Peter and wondered if I was being a fool, and what was wrong with folly?

When I got back to O.P.s the waiting-room was empty and the pro busy tidying the chairs and benches.

'I'll take over,' I said, 'if there is anything to take over?'

She glanced at the closed office door, through which we could see John at the desk.

'The S.S.O. is just writing a letter about that boy with a chronic sinus, so I'm afraid I've not been able to tidy in there.'

'I'll do that when he goes. Thanks.'

She looked at the office again, then came nearer to me. 'Mr Kier was in a few minutes ago. He asked for you, Nurse. I said you were at tea but off at six. Was that all right?'

I smiled. 'Fine. Thanks again.'

She smiled back and I saw my own reflection in her eyes. My cap was a white halo on my head. By her expression it was obvious that she had mistaken it for that. She was very junior and very young, and the hospital to her was a terrifying place and not just the place where she worked, and where healthy people tried to make less healthy people more comfortable.

I could remember treading that same harassed, Sister-ridden path, where nothing made much sense and the only thing that mattered was the time. And where even the race against the clock hands was unreal, because of the nightmare quality of the eternal, 'Hurry, Nurse!' 'Get on, Nurse!' 'Haven't you finished that sluice—or laundry—or kitchen yet?' 'Come along, Nurse— you must learn to be quick as well as thorough!'

I guessed that temporarily I had broken into her private nightmare and turned it into a dream.

The senior nurses had all been sympathetic to me over this affair, because they felt 'There but for the Grace of God go I.' The pros reacted kindly or indifferently, for other reasons. As they were far from the stage of being left in charge of wards, they could not visualise themselves in my position or guess at the snags that come with responsibility. And to some of them, this child among them, I was mystery, romance, and a pathetic heroine rolled into one. I could see by the way she was gaping at me that she had decided that one day she too would mislay a shot of morphia, and have attractive house-surgeons asking for her, beautiful sisters making unkind remarks, and the most senior surgeon in the place intervening for her for some inexplicable reason.

Only his reason would not be inexplicable. He would naturally be pining with unrequited love, and unconcerned with such mundane details as the shortage of trained nurses in Out-Patients.

I said, 'You'd better go to tea, Nurse. Sister Dining-room creates if you girls are late.'

She blinked, smiled dreamily, and drifted out to the changing-room. I thought I must have looked very much like that all this afternoon.

I carried the last two chairs to their places against the wall, and picked a yellow hair-ribbon off the floor behind the radiator. John came out of the office.

'Sister back yet, Nurse Snow?'

I said she was off until five.

'Oh.' He juggled the notes he was holding like giant playing cards, then found what he was looking for. 'Would you give this to Sister?' He handed me an envelope. 'It's about that Devon child.'

I tucked the letter in my apron bib. 'Yes, Mr Dexter.'

He looked round the empty room. 'What was going on in here this afternoon? A riot?'

I said, 'I'm sorry, Mr Dexter. I'm afraid they were a bit noisy.'

He said it had not bothered him much. 'I don't have to use my ears when I look down a throat. But'—he looked at his feet—'you know you ought to keep 'em quieter. I don't know how you can do it, but you should.' He told the floor that it was possibly a good thing Sister was off-duty.

I said, 'Yes, Mr Dexter,' and longed to ask if he had heard whether the Out-Patient nurses at St Martha's hospital used gags or open ether in the Children's Room.

He asked what kind of a day I had had.

'Busy, thank you, Mr Dexter.'

He looked up, 'I was aware of that.'

I was full of charity to all my fellow men at that moment, and since that necessarily included him I thought I might as well take the opportunity to thank him for suggesting to Matron that I should be sent to work here. I said it was very kind of him.

'It was not at all kind of me,' he said calmly; 'I only suggested this because I dislike waste. I knew how busy this place is now—remember, since the new regime last year they are working with only one staff nurse—and the staff here have far too much to do. I could not see that you were necessary in the dining-room, but I could see that a spare trained nurse was essential here. I merely pointed that out to Matron and she agreed.'

'I see.' I did indeed. All this song and dance about wasting nurses in domestic sinecures was merely a rationalisation of his desire to help Sister O.P.s. I wondered if he had explained this to her. Life would be very much more pleasant for us all if he did, but I doubted if he would. He was not given to explaining his actions, and was only telling me this to prevent my having any ideas that it might have been for my personal benefit. I was quite pleased. It stopped me having to feel grateful.

He tucked the sheaf of notes under his arm. 'I won't,' he said pointedly, 'keep you any longer, Nurse. I'm sure you are anxious to get on.'

All nurses are always anxious to get on, and that hour of the afternoon, off. I said correctly, 'Yes, Mr Dexter, thank you, Mr Dexter,' as Sister Tutor had long taught us always to answer and thank any senior, for anything.

At six I went off duty by way of Matron's office, in case there was a note or dictated telephone message waiting in my pigeon hole. There was none, so I walked slowly back to the nurses' home. I did not meet Peter in the hospital corridor or the grounds. It began to rain when I was half-way across the park that separated our home from the main building. The doctors' house overlooked that corner of the park; I strolled past their house, pretending to be lost in thought and ignoring the rain. I hoped he might see me from a window and come down. I achieved nothing but a ruined cap and wet feet.

There was no message waiting in the Home either. I wondered if he had forgotten. I was back in the Day Nurses' Home and walked across to the Night Nurses' house to look in the 'S's' pigeon hole there. It was empty.

I went back to my new room and decided to have a bath while I was waiting. I left the door ajar while the water was running, and only turned the taps half on, so that I should hear the telephone if it rang. It did not ring.

I reminded myself that he had warned me it was only in the air, that this silence merely meant he was held up and unable to contact me. I was fairly content with my explanations; only fairly, since all nurses are well aware that any doctor at any time can get a message to anyone, if he really wants to do so.

Next morning he smiled at me as he rushed past the Children's Room on his way to Casualty, then stopped and came back to the doorway. 'Sorry I couldn't make last night,' he whispered, and vanished again.

He went on smiling at me for the next couple of weeks but we never met for more than a few minutes in the corridors, or did more than glimpse each other across the canteen. He made no more attempts to speak to me or contact me in any way, and I began to wonder if I had met him outside the dining-room at all, or simply imagined it.

'But why,' I asked Lisa, who now seemed to know most of my affairs, 'why did he have to say anything about taking me out? He didn't have to take me out. Why pretend?'

Lisa hesitated, 'Perhaps,' she said slowly, 'he couldn't really help himself.'

'I don't follow you.'

She looked at me. 'I see you don't, dear girl.' She smiled, not unkindly, 'For all that you're an S.R.N. you are a little green about the facts of life, aren't you?'

I smiled back. 'I could be at that. Tell me, Grandmama.'

'Right.' Her eyes danced. 'Listen hard. You have a thing for Peter, and Peter has a thing for you. I know—I know—he handed you the frozen mitt in the canteen, and I know he's been avoiding you like the plague recently because he does not want any of the mud of this affair to rub off on him, but——' she drew a deep breath, 'he's still got a thing for you. When you are around, he can't take his eyes off you, and I suspect he has a hard time keeping his hands off you. I don't think it's true love, alas, but I do think that physically, where he's concerned, you hit the spot. Only since he isn't a purely physical type, his head rules his heart, to coin a corny phrase, and not the other way about.'

'He certainly had things under control that morning in the canteen,' I said dryly.

She said, 'Dear girl, Peter's had things—and, forgive my saying it, you—under control for the past couple of years. He's managed it all very neatly. That invite the other evening was one of his rare slip-ups. But once he got away and thought it over, he decided the only thing to do was to give you the air, from his own angle, quite as much as your own. Mind you,' she added, 'this is only guess work. Your guess is as good as mine.'

I shook my head. 'My guesses are out. Haven't got any about anyone. So you are probably right.'

She said gently, 'I hope I'm not, Gill—but I've a nasty feeling I am. I can see no future for you—or any other working girl—with that young man.' She was silent for a short while, then, 'Has he got any money?'

'Peter? Only what he earns.'

She grimaced. 'I thought so. In view of which, it's just as well, dear girl, that Carol Ash is your greatest friend.'

'Carol? What's she got to do with it?'

Lisa said, 'Well—you did fix up about the rugger dance, didn't you? If that isn't throwing them together, I don't know what is. And Carol is the one girl at Joe's who would be more than an asset to a rising young doctor. A rich wife,' she reminded me, 'is a splendid thing if you want to hang around waiting for the good jobs. The waiting takes years.'

'I suppose it does.' I felt very bleak.

'Don't let it get you down too much,' she said. 'Heaven knows I could be all wrong. It'll probably all blow over in a month or so when this missing-dope business blows over. After all, no one seems to have taken it, and no harm been done, so it may be a dispenser's mistake, regardless of what they say.'

'I wish I could believe you. I can't say I do. I find it hard to credit that Peter ever liked me at all.'

'Phooey! This I'm certain—as long as you are around Joe's, Peter will have to be around you. He may not like it, but he can't help his hormones. They act for him.' She turned to me, 'Gill, I hope I haven't hurt you with this girlish frankness? I feel I've been opening my big mouth too wide.'

She looked really worried, and since I had grown very fond of Lisa lately, and disliked having to upset her, I said, 'No. I haven't enjoyed it, but you haven't hurt me. Subconsciously I've known that was the set-up. I pretended to myself that I didn't, but I did.' I sighed. 'Of course, I should have had more pride and what-have-you than to stick around with him, but where Peter is concerned, my pride goes out of the window.'

I thought she would laugh, but all she said was, 'Dear girl,

71

how well I know that sensation.'

'You do?' I was surprised. Lisa was on dining-out terms with half the resident staff. I had never heard or suspected that she took any of her many young men seriously.

'I do.' She coloured slightly. 'Just another Lonely Heart am I.' Then she laughed. 'Lonely Hearts are legion in this hospital —and boring! In my particular case, he doesn't know I'm around—rather like you and John Dexter, with the difference that while you couldn't care less if John sees you or not, I, alas'—she smiled self-deprecatingly—'care no end. I'm only un-burdening now, dear girl, to show you that you aren't the only mug at Joe's.'

I was curious to know who he was, but she did not say, and I did not want to force her confidence.

'You shake me, Lisa. I hadn't a notion.'

'I know that. Nor has he. Which gives me a good laugh, in a bitter way, from time to time. I'll tell you all one of these fine days. But thanks for not asking leading questions.'

I thought over Lisa's words during the next few days. She had been very shrewd about Peter and the more, or rather the less, I saw of him, the more I realised how right she was. I knew I was not good at judging people's reactions or behaviour, but I tried to discover whom it was that Lisa had been discussing.

It was something to do, and something else to think about in place of Peter and what Matron was ultimately going to do with me after this spell in O.P.s. I was not successful, although I turned into the perfect little watch-bird watching the young men watching Lisa. I was no better with Lisa's affairs than I had been with my own. The only thing I discovered from my watching was that John Dexter appeared to spend far more time walking through Out-Patients than he had done when I was last here, and that when he walked through Out-Patients he always found it necessary to talk to Sister.

One of the most consoling features in any nurse's life is the necessity for speed. That speed, which was the terror of all first-year pros, once acquired, is a great defence. You move so quickly, there is so much work to be done in any appointed time, and that time is never sufficient, but has to be made sufficient, with the obvious result that during your working life you have no time for any other problem but will you beat the clock? And when you are doing that from seven-thirty in the morning to nine P.M., for six days a week, even allowing for three hours of that time off duty—three hours that always in-clude a meal, and into which you have to fit your whole private life, so that consequently you are racing against time then also—the night becomes solely the time for sleeping. Nurses in train-ing do not suffer from insomnia. I always meant to worry about the future when I got into bed, but I never remembered to do more than switch off my light.

I fell back into the routine of the department as if I had never left it. And although Sister still frowned on me when we met, even she was so occupied with patients, almoners, Consultants, forms, and training the junior pros, that she was only able to spare the occasional moment in which to criticise what I was doing and inform me that at St Martha's Hospital, London, such behaviour would not have been tolerated. I decided that John must have stilled some of her fears by his constant presence, and total and habitual disregard of myself, because she now distributed her displeasure equally between Lisa and myself, and we automatically chanted, 'Yes, Sister, sorry, Sister' whenever she approached us.

The days were filled with endless clinics, clinics that inevitably overflowed into each other, while the patients grumbled, not unreasonably, and the men fingered their collars, and thanked Heaven and the hospital committee that there were no sterilisers in Out-Patients as there were in every room in Casualty. Consequently Out-Patients, when full, fell slightly short of the inferno that Casualty could become.

My children arrived with lollypops—iced and sugared—bags of toffees, and boiled sweets; some of them cried, some of them were sick, but the majority seemed alarmingly healthy and not in need of any medical care; their spirits were constantly high. There was nothing wrong with any of their lungs either, whatever their notes might say.

They continued to bellow, 'Hi, Snowwhite,' and roar with goblin laughter at my lack of dwarfs. 'Garn, Snowwhite, ain't you never going to get none?'

Sister disapproved of these unprofessional welcomes, and her lips would tighten to a thin line whenever she overheard one.

One afternoon she beckoned me to her table. 'Nurse Snow, this must stop. You will kindly take steps to see you are not addressed in that undignified manner in my department again.'

I apologised, and returned to the latest arrival to my clinic, who was grinning at me from the doorway.

'Listen, Joy,' I whispered, 'you heard what the Sister said. Now be an angel child and don't call me that again or I'll get into trouble.'

'O.K. Sno——' She swallowed obediently and started again. 'O.K., Nurse.'

I explained that the room was full up. 'Would you and your mum just sit by the door for a few minutes? I'll shift them up the benches, and then you can move forward.'

Joy was an intelligent eight-year-old. She had broken her leg in a street accident, and had been admitted to Christian in my

73

first month there. Her leg had been badly broken and there was a small sinus still to heal which necessitated her coming back frequently for treatment.

'But you know what,' she went on thoughtfully, as I began unwinding the crêpe bandage that covered the gauze bandage on her leg, 'I got a book at home with pictures, see—the real thing sort of, what they had in that picture me mum told me about'— she turned to her mum—'didn't you, Mum?'

Her mother was busy with her knitting. 'That's right, ducks,' she said encouragingly.

Joy said again, 'And you know what, Snowwhite?'

'What, honey?' I looked up from the bandage.

Joy bent forward and touched my cap. 'You look just like that picture, see, with that white hat an' your black hair. Ever so black ain't it, Sn——' she remembered this time, 'Nurse?'

'It isn't.' I smiled up at her. 'I wish it was, but it's not. It's just dark brown.'

' 'Sblack,' said Joy stubbornly. 'Truly.'

The bandage was off. I stood up, leaving the under-bandage until she was ready to be seen. 'Have it your own way, honey. The patient is always right.'

A voice murmured, 'An admirable sentiment, Nurse Snow.' Tom Thanet was standing beside me. I had not seen him since I left Robert. 'Hallo,' he said, 'how goes it, Nurse Snow? When did they let you out? I heard you were behind bars in the Nurses Home.'

I said I was on parole. 'Something I can do for you, Mr Thanet?'

He said he wanted Sister. 'Or rather I hear she wants me.' His eyes creased with amusement. 'Think I ought to stay or run?'

'She was at her table a few seconds ago.' I put my head out of the door but there was no one at the table. 'You'd better hang around.'

Tom said that whatever he did was bound to be wrong, so he might as well stay. 'Somehow I appear to lack the technique of the house-surgeons in St Martha's Hospital, London,' he added sadly, 'but then what can you expect of poor old Joe's?'

I said '*Et tu?* I thought you men were all splendid.'

Tom said he was far too junior to be splendid yet. 'Just a simple Conjoint man, Nurse. Very low.'

Joy tugged at my apron. 'Ask the doctor what colour it is.'

'Ask him what, duckie?' I had forgotten my hair.

'Always happy to oblige,' said Tom helpfully; 'something I can do?'

Joy began, 'Well——' and sucked in her breath, 'you see——'

'Excuse me——' I leapt across the room and caught the arm

of the anxious-faced elderly man who had rushed by me, and was already half-seated on the children on the front bench.

'Now then, you lads,' he was saying, 'move over.'

I smiled, 'Good afternoon. Can I help you?'

'Oh, Nurse,' he said, 'ta.' He handed me an envelope. 'I got a letter from me doctor,' he announced proudly. 'To see the doctor, like.'

The envelope was addressed to the House-surgeon in charge of Out-Patients, St Joseph's Hospital. That meant the S.S.O. in Casualty. No one as junior as a house-surgeon ever saw a patient who arrived with a letter from a doctor. And only very rarely, by special arrangement or string pulling, were new patients seen in Out-Patients.

I asked if he could tell me what was wrong with him?

He was pained. 'That's what I wants the doctor to tell me, miss.'

I looked at the long lines in his cheeks, his thin face, tired eyes, and general air of gloom, and guessed, not altogether wildly. The medical wards were full of men looking like him. 'Your stomach worrying you?'

He brightened. 'That's it, miss. Worries me! Murder, that's what it is an' all. Sheer murder. Can't keep a thing down—and the pain! Cruel it is!'

I said I was sure it was, which was true. 'And if you'll just come with me, I'll show you the way to the Casualty department, and you must give your letter to the Sister there.'

He twitched the envelope from my hands. 'I got to give it to the House-surgeon, miss. Like it says.'

This was not the time to go into hospital procedure, so I agreed on that point, 'Sister Casualty will see that he gets it.'

He nodded uncertainly, but did not move from the seat, and the squashed children beside him watched him with interest.

'I ain't no casualty, miss, I'm a patient—an out-patient like what it says on that notice outside the big door.'

I explained that in Out-Patients we saw only old patients, and that all new patients were first seen in Casualty. I left out the exceptions so as not to confuse him.

He was not at all happy at my explanations, and for a few seconds seemed determined to remain among the rows of en-thralled infants, but he finally allowed that I might be right at that, and let me lead him to a porter.

Tims, one of the six O.O. porters, was a paternal young man. 'You just come along of me, Dad,' he said comfortingly, 'like the nurse tells you. You'll see your House-surgeon, don't you worry.'

The poor man had a fresh anxiety. 'Will he give me some more of them powders, Nurse?' He clutched my hand. 'Won't

75

tell me as I has to do without 'em, will he?'

I said I was sure he would not.

Tims took the old man's arm. 'You come along of me, Dad,' he said again. 'I'll see you gets your powders. You just leave the nurse to her parcel of nippers—got her hands full an' all she has—and you and me'll go and find your House-surgeon.'

The waiting mothers smiled sympathetically as I tried to restore order among the children who were now quite out of hand, and swapping places and sweeties with a total disregard of my appointments list.

'Don't get much chance to get fat, you girls,' said one lady; 'what a life for you!'

'That's right,' agreed another, 'and I think I'm busy with my four! Talk about on your feet! Rather you than me, duck, that's what I say!'

The first mother said that was a fact, and I left them happily comparing hospital experiences and shaking their two heads over a nurse's lot. 'But you got to be born to it,' they reckoned, 'you got to be born to it.'

Were they right? I often wondered and generally doubted. Perhaps. I certainly had always wanted to be a nurse; but nursing, when I discovered what it was, bore no relation to what I had imagined nursing to be. Not that that made me want to change jobs. This was the only job I ever wanted to do and I still felt that way. There was only one thing I wanted more, and that was to marry Peter.

I settled the back benches in reasonable order, then crossed the room at the double, and caught a small boy who was swinging on his crutches. 'Johnny Brandon, if you do that on this polished floor you'll probably break your other leg. Be a good boy and sit down and read your comic.'

'Finished it,' he said laconically, and went on swinging under my hands.

'If I find you a new one will you sit down?'

'Spaceman stuff?'

I nodded. 'Dan Dare?'

'O.K., Snowwhite.' He subsided obediently, and I went to the cupboard for fresh literature. I handed these to Johnny and Johnny's friends, who had promptly begun to slide on the floor, and the room was quiet again.

Tom was still chatting with Joy. 'We've agreed you're black, Nurse Snow,' he announced when I returned to my official stand by the door.

'Anything you say, Doctor.' I counted the heads and checked them with the list in my hand. 'Where has Mr Rufford got to?'

Tom said he had left his temporary boss looking at wet plates in the darkroom. 'He said he was starting in here any minute. Shouldn't be more than another hour.'

'Nurse,' said one of the mothers, 'will it be all right if I slip along to the canteen? Ever so dry I am.'

I promised to keep her and her son's places, and then two-thirds of the room developed acute thirsts, so the trip to the canteen became an official exodus, each bench going in rotation.

Tom peered down the corridor. 'Where is that wretched woman?'

'Search me.' I was counting heads again. 'I wish you could see these kids for me. There'll be murder done if the clinic doesn't start soon.'

He nodded. 'Wish I could at that. Still, Rufford will soothe 'em when he comes. He's a good chap. Expect those plates were washouts, and he's waiting for fresh pictures of that last woman we had across the way. Conscientious bloke, Rufford. He'll only hurry when it doesn't matter.' He asked how long I was to be in O.P.s.

'I don't know. Nobody tells me anything.'

He swung his stethoscope. 'They don't tell me much either,' he said casually, 'but I keep my ear to the ground. I hear one or two things.'

A fight broke out on the front bench. I broke it up, smiled artificially at the mothers concerned, who said placidly, really, Nurse, they didn't know how I did it, they just wouldn't heed a word they had said.

'The uniform,' I suggested, and retired to the door again.

Tom was talking to Joy. He glanced round. 'Strong arm stuff, eh, Nurse?'

'More or less.' I asked if he heard interesting things.

Tom, who, like all hospital employees, was more than capable of carrying on two conversations at the same time, said 'I liked him very much as Hans Christian Andersen,' to Joy, and, 'Sometimes. I did hear you might not be booked for the rugger dance tomorrow night,' to me.

I had forgotten it was tomorrow. 'No, I'm not.'

He handed Joy his stethoscope. 'You hear the noise through this bit—it works like a microphone,' then turned to me. 'No time like a quiet afternoon with the nippers to make a date. I suppose you wouldn't care to come with me? I realise it's late notice—but you know how time flies.'

'I do indeed.' I did not answer his invitation directly, because although I liked Tom, I did not much want to go to a dance with him, or anyone but Peter.

He noticed my hesitation. 'Or maybe you're booked by the big boss?' He leered horribly. 'I understand he is taking an interest in your welfare.'

I smiled. 'My welfare nothing. He sees me as a pair of hands and moderately good feet. Can you see him breaking down and asking a nurse in training to gallivant with him?'

Tom said, 'Frankly, no.'

Sister rustled into the room. 'Nurse Snow, perhaps when you have finished gossiping with Mr Thanet you will be good enough to attend to your clinic.' She looked at Tom. 'I would like to speak to you, Mr Thanet.'

Tom said meekly, 'Yes, Sister, certainly, Sister,' and clicked his heels.

Sister looked at him and then back to me. His face was expressionless, and I knew that mine was the same. Mr Rufford roared into the room. 'Terribly sorry—got held up! I hate to have kept you all waiting this way, but we'll get things moving now. All right, Nurse Snow! Let's have the first pair. Mothers with their children, please!'

Sister drew Tom out into the corridor and said whatever it was she had to say to him. Then John appeared at her elbow, and she dismissed Tom with a belated smile, 'Thank you, Mr Thanet. So sorry you had to wait.' She turned back to John and smiled even more charmingly. I could not hear what she said to him, but I saw him glance my way.

'Really?' he inquired disinterestedly.

Lisa, who was standing in the opposite doorway, rolled her eyes at me, and then composed her face quickly as Sister looked round.

Later, as we sat at tea, Lisa said, 'Gillian, what's all this I hear about you and Tom Thanet?'

'Me and Tom?'

'Yes.' She buttered her bread thoughtfully, 'I heard Sister telling our John that she hardly dared let you loose among the housemen, or words to that effect. Really, dear girl, I had no idea you were such hot stuff.'

'Was that it?' I laughed. 'Poor Tom has obviously been stood up by some girl and got two tickets to spend.'

She smiled, but there was something wrong with her smile. She said she had not known that Tom and I were buddies.

'We aren't. We only met in Robert. I'm as surprised at his asking me as you are, but he's a pleasant type, and I suppose he's between girl-friends. Who was his last, do you know?'

She said she had simply no conception. Her voice was as unnatural as her smile had been.

'I thought Tom was an old pal of yours, Lisa?'

'Dear girl,' she said airily, 'Tom Thanet and I are as one. We have been for years. We came from the same home town—didn't you know? We almost grew up in each other's back yards, only we hadn't any back yards as we both lived in flats.'

I suddenly realised why she was behaving so oddly. I said, 'I think Peter probably asked him to take me.'

'You do?' Her eagerness proved my secret point.

'Yes.' I had not thought of this before, but now I wondered if unconsciously I had hit on the truth. Tom and I were casual professional acquaintances, nothing more. But he was a friend of Peter's and he was also a kind young man. He was the sort of man who would ask a girl to a dance to oblige another man. I told Lisa this, and she beamed.

'He is rather nice,' she said carefully, 'isn't he?'

I assumed the expression of utter imbecility which I always used when talking to Sister O.P.s, and agreed that Tom Thanet was a credit to the medical profession and a pearl among housemen.

6

TOM THANET GETS FRATERNAL

PETER came into the department that evening. Sister and Lisa were off duty, and I was helping the Staff Nurse with the end of the diabetic clinic.

Blakelock tucked a wisp of hair under her cap and cursed quietly.

'Do you think we'll ever finish tonight, Snow? It's ten-past seven and O.P.s officially closed at six.'

I looked down the corridor. 'I doubt it, Nurse. There are still eight to be seen.'

She sighed. 'The poor dears. They've been here hours, but what can we do? They all take so long, and old MacGill is slowing down. There just aren't the men to go round.'

'Short of a man, Nurse Blakelock?' Peter was beside her. 'Can I fall into step?'

She shook her head. 'No good, Mr Kier—thanks. What I want,' she said grimly, 'is another high-powered physician.' She handed me the list. 'Keep them in the right order, Snow. I'm going to see if I can't hurry things up in the office.'

The patients on the bench shook their heads as she went by. One of them said something, and I saw she had not heard, so I walked over to them. 'I'm sorry you've had to wait so long. But you should all be home soon.'

'It's not good enough, Nurse,' said one middle-aged woman irritably, 'not good enough at all. I know you girls are doing your best, but there shouldn't be all this hanging around. Can't that doctor over there see us?'

'I'm afraid not.' I explained that Peter was a surgeon. 'And you want to see the diabetic specialist, don't you?'

She said, 'I've been waiting two and a half hours, Nurse. I don't mind who I see.'

I could understand her annoyance, but I could also understand why Dr MacGill was slowing down. He had been in that office since two-thirty this afternoon and had not even come out for tea, but had had a cup of tea and a cake sent up from the canteen. I explained this, and she seemed slightly placated. 'But if that young doctor over there is doing nothing, Nurse, why can't he help?'

I wished Peter anywhere but in O.P.s at that moment.

'Look,' I said desperately, 'if you break an electric fire, you don't take it to the grocer's to be mended, do you?'

She asked what that had to do with it. The man beside her nodded wisely. 'I see what you're getting at, Nurse. A hospital's split up into different departments like everything else. That young chap over there doesn't deal with diabetics.'

'Oh, dear.' I smiled. 'This is difficult. He can treat diabetics, because he's a qualified doctor, but he doesn't here, because in a hospital of this size the various complaints have to be divided up. He's a surgeon and you want a physician—do you see?'

They said they did—sort of—and they knew we nurses were doing what we could, but still it wasn't right. But they were more cheerful now they were arguing the ethics of modern medicine, so I went back to the small note-littered table at the end of the corridor.

Peter raised his eyebrows. 'Mutiny quelled?'

'I hope so.' I looked back at the patients. 'The awful thing is I do so agree with them; it isn't right, but what can we do? We're running a twenty-four-hour service with a twelve-hour medical staff—and so is every other hospital in the country. Something should be done about it.'

He said lightly, 'You'd better climb off that soap-box, darling, and save it for the Committee. You talk to them and get them to double the resident staff. Then maybe the clinics will finish on time.'

'Well, somebody ought to do something about it,' I repeated; 'those people over there are good and mad. And they think you are wasting time. But if I told them the hours you worked—what is it——?'

He murmured, 'One hundred and four a week, darling—where's my union!'

'Is that what one half-day a week and every other week-end from Saturday midday to Sunday night come to?'

'That's what it comes to—with luck! And don't forget the night calls, my love! Each and every night!' He grinned. 'Why do we do it? It's a wicked life.'

'I dunno.' I suddenly remembered that he must have come

80

for something to be still hanging around. I asked what he wanted.

'You.' His voice was serious but his eyes laughed. 'I thought you'd be clearing up and I wanted to talk to you.'

Blakelock had come out of the office and sent the next patient in. The remaining seven shifted up the bench more cheerfully.

'You still here, Mr Kier? Something we can do for you?'

He bowed. 'Helpful little bunch, you O.P.s nurses. Actually, I'm here for purely social reasons, Nurse. I wanted to give Nurse Snow a message. But she's been reading the Riot Act to your family on the bench and I've not had the opportunity to deliver same yet.'

Her pleasant, fat face stiffened. 'You've done what, Nurse Snow?' she demanded, turning instantly from a good-humoured young woman to a dignified St Joseph's staff nurse.

Peter said smoothly, 'My little joke, Nurse. Nurse Snow was merely commiserating with the unhappy octet.'

'I see.' She smiled slightly, but she did not seem very re-assured with his words. That was understandable. The staff in our hospital were not encouraged to lecture the patients; Sister Tutor's maxim, 'the patient is always right—to his or her face,' was certainly engraved on the classroom walls if not on all our brows.

She said Peter had better go into Sister's office and give me his message there. 'Sister does not encourage stray housemen in this department, Mr Kier.'

I said, 'Thank you, Nurse,' and followed Peter into the office.

'Completely crushed,' he observed and shut the door.

'For the love of Mike, open that door,' I said quickly, 'or the fat will be in the fire! And you really shouldn't have said that to Blakelock—luckily she's a nice girl. If Sister had been on, she would have slain us both.'

He half opened the door. 'You take too much notice of these tiresome women, darling,' he said nonchalantly, 'but listen—I just came to tell you how sorry I am about all this nonsense tomorrow. I wish you hadn't got me into this, as I would far rather take you, but I can't very well leave your little friend out in the cold—so I'll have to go with her. I haven't had any chance to say this to you, but I wanted to make sure that you'd understand.'

I said of course I understood and I thought it very civil of him. I did not point out that he and I had been working in the same building for the past three weeks, and any time he had wanted to see me he had only to do what he had done tonight and walk along the corridor.

He frowned. 'I'm going to miss you, sweetie. I like dancing with you.'

'You may manage it yet. Tom Thanet's asked me to go with him. Perhaps we can meet in a jolly Paul Jones.'

'Tom has?' he asked sharply. 'When?'

I told him. I was suddenly very happy to see him so obviously annoyed.

'Damn. Gillian'—he shook his head—'you really are the darnedest girl. This is going to be a wicked party. Me with that Ash girl and you with Tom? Why in the devil did you have to do it?'

'Well——' I smiled helplessly, 'Peter, it's all got out of hand. I thought I'd be on nights.'

He said, 'Why the heck didn't you keep your hands on those keys, darling? You've made everything so complicated. I loathe the thought of you dancing with someone else.'

My heart felt as if it had turned over. I forgot everything but his last words and the way he was looking at me.

'Really, Peter?'

He did not answer immediately. Then he said softly, 'I wish——' But he had no time to tell me what he wished. Nurse Blakelock was at the door talking to someone over her shoulder.

'Mr Kier is in here,' she said. 'I'll get him for you.'

John's voice said, 'I'll do that for myself, thanks, Nurse. Don't bother.' He opened the door. 'Oh, there you are, Kier. I've been ringing round for you. Have you seen the new girl in Martha?'

Peter said, 'Yes, sir. I saw her when she came in. I'm going back after supper to write her up.'

John said pleasantly, 'No, you aren't—you're going back now. I've just been up there myself, and she said she had seen the doctor, but I discovered her notes were blank. How do you expect the nursing staff to treat her if she has no notes and no treatment ordered?'

Peter said he was very sorry. 'I'll nip up there now, sir.'

John said he was sorry too. 'I want my own supper and instead I've had a wild-goose chase looking for you.' He appeared to have just noticed me. 'Evening, Nurse Snow.' He did not wait for my reply, but sauntered away after Blakelock.

'Darling,' murmured Peter, 'I'll have to git. And snappy.' He smiled. 'I'd clean forgotten about those notes—trust old Garth to check up! Ruddy man never misses a thing. Be seeing you!' He disappeared from the office and down the corridor towards the stairs and Martha.

Nurse Blakelock had only five patients still to be seen. She told me to go into supper. 'This is my party, so I'll finish here and eat with the pros at eight. There's no need for you to be late as well.' John was standing a couple of yards away reading the list of the next day's clinics that hung on the notice board. She glanced at him and lowered her voice.

'Sorry I snapped at you just now, Snow. I didn't seriously think you'd be ticking off my patients, but that young man gets in my hair. I cannot stand conceited young men.'

'Mr Kier?' I was surprised. I thought everyone liked Peter.

'Mmmm,' she was unusually vehement, 'Kier. Thinks he's the answer to a nurse's prayer. Oh Lord!' she grinned apologetically, 'Snow, I do beg your pardon. I clean forgot he was a pal of yours. I'm verging on a diabetic coma myself after this afternoon—do forgive me.'

I said I did not blame her and would she like me to stand by with the insulin?

She smiled again. 'Mightn't be a bad idea. I missed tea, and my blood sugar must be down to zero. I'm starving, but I can't leave, so off you go and don't forget to tell Sister Dining-room that I'm going to be late.'

John overtook me when I was half-way to the dining-room.

'Dr MacGill seems to have taken residence in Out-Patients tonight,' he said.

'It was an extra large clinic, I believe.' I asked if the theatres were busy.

'Moderately. We've finished the day's lists in time, but we're starting again in an hour.' He walked with his hands in his pockets and his shoulders hunched as all doctors walk in hospital. I thought again about those irate diabetic patients and wondered if they had any conception of the hours worked by the resident staff, and what the reactions of an ordinary citizen would be if he were told at the end of a twelve-hour day to start work again at night, and still be expected to do his normal day's quota of hours the following day, with no question of overtime or even thanks.

I said suddenly, 'Don't you get very tired, Mr Dexter?'

He looked at me curiously. 'Don't I——? Why?'

I told him what was in my mind.

He half smiled. 'They do get so cross, don't they? Yes, of course I get tired—we all do—including the nurses.'

'But we do go to bed at night,' I said. 'I hate to admit this, because, like all nurses, I think no one in any job works as hard as nurses when on the job, but I'm talking of hours. At least when we're off, we're off.'

'Nurse Snow,' he said gravely, 'you astonish me. Don't tell me you are going to start a campaign for the rights of the medical profession?'

I said, 'Not a campaign. I just don't think it's right.'

He raised an eyebrow. 'That the patients should get cross or we should keep 'em waiting?'

'Both,' I said thoughtfully. 'There are so many of them—so

many thousands of people flocking into hospital all the time. All this illness going on like a factory-belt. There's never any let-up.'

He said, 'I'm not sure that one particularly wants a let-up. I don't mean from the patients' angle, but from our own. We none of us have to be here, we're here because we like it—factory-belt notwithstanding.'

I was becoming so used to having him around these days that, temporarily, I forgot he was not just one of the boys. 'Doesn't the responsibility get you down? You and Dr Cutler carry the hospital between you. Isn't it a dreadful strain?'

He said, 'No. Not at our stage. You get used to it, as you get used to anything. Cutler and I have been at this a good many years.' He pushed his hand through his hair, and his white streak fell forward. 'I've been qualified fifteen years. Those years make a deal of difference to one's outlook.'

I said I supposed they did. 'I know how my own attitude to illness has altered in the past three-and-a-half years.'

We had come to the end of the half-mile main corridor and were outside our respective dining-rooms. He stopped and stood with his hands locked behind him.

'What,' he asked curiously, 'did you think of it all at first?'

'There wasn't time to think.' I smiled at the query. 'I was far too scared of Sisters and in too much of a hurry to do anything so constructive. And when I did reach the stage of doing things for the patients I was plain terrified.'

His eyes were amused. 'But now you take Sisters in your stride?'

I said, 'As you've just said, Mr Dexter, you can get used to anything.' And I wondered whether I had over-stepped his dividing line. Apparently I had not.

'Touché,' he murmured. He looked at me for a few seconds in silence, and I was about to excuse myself and go into supper, when he spoke again.

'I don't,' he said, 'much like giving advice, and I very much dislike giving my advice on anything, unasked. But I'm going to do that now.'

I said, 'Yes, Mr Dexter?' and waited, curious.

'Don't think that I'm criticising yourself or Nurse Blakelock,' he said slowly, 'because I've no wish to do that. But don't you think you'd be wiser to keep your private life out of the hospital? You know,' his voice was extraordinarily kind, 'you're still skating on somewhat thin professional ice. It's not entirely your fault, but it's a fact. So for God's sake don't play the fool on duty, or the balloon will go up properly.'

I knew he was right, as I knew what he was alluding to. If Matron or Sister O.P.s had found me alone in that office with

Peter there would have been the father and mother of rows. I was a little surprised to find that this time I did not mind John being right. It was probably because I was more used to him.

I said, 'I'm sorry about that. I didn't think. I know that's no excuse, just an explanation. But thank you.'

He did not answer; he looked at me and through me as if I was not there at all, and then I saw he really was not seeing me, but was smiling at someone over my head. I turned as Sister O.P.s came out of our dining-room. She was in mufti.

She looked me over. 'You are very late for supper, Nurse Snow.'

'Yes, Sister.' I held open the door for her, then went in myself, but not before I heard him say, 'I'm glad I've run into you, Sister. There's something I wanted to ask you.'

I apologised for being late to Sister Dining-room, told her about Blakelock, and sat down at the fourth-year table. I remembered I had forgotten to say good night to John, but that did not matter as he had forgotten to say it to me. I remembered the dirty look Sister O.P.s had given me and was intensely pleased by the memory.

None of my set were at supper, and I ate in solitary silence. I was glad of the opportunity to think about Peter and whether I would go with Tom tomorrow night or not. I wanted to work this out on my own before I got back to the girls in the Home tonight. I did not reach any conclusion; I was too occupied with thinking about Sister O.P.s. She was having a humanising effect on John, and for that I had particular cause to be grateful. He had been very civil tonight, when he could well have been very nasty. I hoped he would humanise her in return. She could do with it. And then I thought, does she need anything else? Really? With that wonderful hair, her face, and figure—and now John Dexter thrown in? I decided that Frances Mack was a very fortunate young woman. I wished I could talk to Carol about this.

I had not seen Carol for over two weeks. The chasm that divides the day and night staff is a very wide one. The night nurses live in a separate home, eat at different hours, and only synchronise with the day girls at lectures. Our own lecture years were over, so we did not even meet in Sister Tutor's classroom, and Carol had had no nights off since her visit to her old school.

She came into the bedroom the following evening, as I was finishing the hem of the stole I had decided to make to boost my one evening dress and sagging morale.

'Gillian, I wish you were going with Peter.'

'Don't be daft, honey.' I looked for my scissors, but they had vanished, so I bit the thread. 'It's all worked out according to

85

schedule and Tom Thanet, and we're all going to have a jolly evening—I hope.'

She said gloomily that Peter had told her I was going with Tom.

I shook out the scarlet stole. 'This'll need ironing, which is a bore.' I looked up at her. 'Have you seen him today?' I had only accepted Tom that morning.

She said she had not seen Peter for a few nights. 'I thought he told me on Monday—but I might be wrong. You know how it is at night. You never know which day it is.'

I agreed that I knew how it was. I thought how right my wild suggestion to Lisa had been. Peter had briefed Tom, and all that talk last night was just so much talk. Peter was having his cake and eating it.

'How's Ellen? Busy?'

'No. Pretty quiet. There's been nothing much to do but be sociable lately.' She said Peter had taken to having coffee with her. 'Now that you've left Robert I imagine he feels lonely. Kirsty is hardly the coffee-drinking type.'

'Poor Peter. But Kirsty is a future Night Sister whatever else she isn't. She's a good girl and, for my bet, the best nurse Joe's has turned out in years.'

Carol was not interested in Kirsty's future. She fingered my stole. 'It'll need a lot of ironing. Pity. It's lovely material but I'm afraid it'll crush badly.'

'It shouldn't, according to the shop.' I draped it over my uniform and moved to the mirror. We stared at my reflection critically. 'I think it's just my manhandling,' I said at last. 'After all, I've only thrown it together in the last hour. Maybe' —I fingered it smugly—'maybe I was wrong to panic about messing up my missing life. I'd have done all right if I had been thrown on the cold hard world with my needle.'

Carol, being a night nurse, took me seriously. Life is a grim affair after a couple of months of night work. She shook her head.

'There's a packet of difference between a good amateur and a professional dressmaker.'

'Don't disillusion my girlish hopes,' I said. 'I was just thinking I might risk it. At least I'd be clear of Matrons and Sister O.P.s.'

She smiled. 'Sister O.P.s being difficult?'

'That,' I said, 'Is a miracle of understatement. But you've got the general idea.'

She sat in my armchair and swung her legs over the side. 'What's all this I hear about our John fixing you up in O.P.s? Is it really true?'

'Yes. Unlikely though it sounds. But don't get any ideas

86

about me and our John. He only did it to oblige his beauteous young woman.'

She said she had heard that rumour too.

'No rumour. I am the horse and I am telling you. Straight from my mouth.'

'You mean he's so far gone that he cast caution to the winds and went to Matron—for her benefit?'

'He certainly went to Matron. And I'd say he's certainly got it badly. But to be fair to our John, I don't honestly think he was solely thinking of it from her angle. That man takes the job seriously.'

She said she supposed so. 'But what's all this about you wanting to be fair to our John, Gill? You've never cared about being fair to him before.'

I said I was a changed woman and growing old before my time. 'This affair with my dope has made me tolerant and kind.'

Carol said it was all most unnerving.

'I'll tell you something that'll unnerve you still more, honey. John thinks that whoever took that dope was plotting my downfall and that it was all intentional—or I think he thinks that.'

She yawned and closed her eyes. 'Dear! I'm sleepy! Why does he think that? And how do you know?'

I told her about my walk in the park.

'Gill.' She opened her eyes. 'Did you ask if he had taken it?'

'Didn't have to. He guessed.'

She stretched. 'Did he guess who it was?'

'No. Or if he has he didn't say. And I don't think he has,' I tried on the stole again, 'because the only conclusion he reached was that it did not add up and it was high time I took a grip and stopped feeling sorry for myself. Dramatising was the word.' I saw she was smiling, and smiled back. 'I suppose it is rather funny.'

She said apologetically, 'Sorry, ducks, but I can't help thinking that last bit is, knowing what you think of that man. You must have been livid. I should have been. I would have hit him over the head with my handbag.'

'You wouldn't,' I told her, 'not at all. I'm bigger than you and I only reach his shoulder. You don't hit men of his size lightly. Particularly in this decadent age, when the chances are the little gentlemen will hit back and hard.'

My next-door neighbour banged on the wall at that moment.

'Snow,' she yelled, 'I've finished with the iron. Want it?'

'Please,' I bellowed. 'See you later, Carol—enjoy yourself.'

Carol said she could hardly wait, and she could also hardly

keep awake. 'I can't think why I ever agreed to this dance. I'd far rather go to bed.'

The Medical School ballroom was crowded; the floor was jammed with couples, and the couches against the walls were as full as the Out-Patient benches on any weekly morning. The Rugger Club had always printed and sold too many tickets. The Rugger Club was the one financially solvent club in Joe's. No one ever appeared to object to the fact that dancing was consequently an athletic feat, or that the lack of sitting-out accommodation was inconvenient; and the general reaction was that since so many people had turned up it must be a darned good party, and after all what does it matter if a girl's feet do get trodden on? Most of the girls present were senior nurses or staff nurses, and by that stage their feet were so tough that even the full weight of one of the first fifteen's backs coming down smartly on an evening sandal meant nothing but a torn nylon.

Tom Thanet was a good dancer. He was fairly tall, being just over six feet in height. Had we not had John as a standard against which to measure all the young men, we should possibly have considered Tom very tall. John stood six feet five and a half inches, and was proportionately broad. Tom was thin, and beside the S.S.O. looked a frail youth.

I enjoyed dancing with him, and in a detached fashion was deciding that the evening might be bearable after all, when I saw Peter and Carol come into the room. A few seconds later they had joined the crush on the floor; I saw the back of Peter's head and then the line of his cheekbone as he turned his head and bent to say something to Carol. I saw the way she smiled up at him. I had never seen Carol smile like that in all the years I had known her. She was wearing a grey chiffon dress. It was a beautiful dress, and the colour suited her. I lost my detachment and wondered whether I ought to have my head examined. Carol was certainly my greatest friend, but I recalled what Lisa had said about there being a limit to altruism. The recollection did not improve my morale.

Tom's arm tightened round me.

'The name is Thanet,' he murmured, 'and you're dancing with me. Just in case you forgot.'

I tilted my head back to look at him. 'Do tell me, Mr Thanet —are you a doctor?'

'If you promise not to tell anyone—yes, I am.' He glanced over his shoulder. 'I do hope nobody heard me. It's such a responsibility being a doctor—I mean if anything should happen everyone, but everyone, will turn to me.'

I said I thought doctors were wonderful. 'So noble.'

'It's a vocation, Miss Snow. Just that. Don't praise me; I

88

know how you feel about me—I overwhelm you—let it pass.'

'And to think,' I said, 'that if there was an accident—if someone was suddenly taken ill—you would know just what to do!'

He nodded gravely. 'I certainly would. I'd run like hell in the opposite direction.'

I laughed. 'Tom, you are a fool.'

He smiled. 'There's quite a percentage in folly, it seems—there is also a percentage in dancing with ghosts.'

'Ghosts?'

'Uh-huh. You were one just now. But I don't mind,' he said mildly, 'if the specific ghost looks as good in black as you do.'

'That's nice of you, Tom.'

He said he was a splendid type.

In fact that was just what he was. I had known that before from my professional acquaintance with him, but I thought him doubly pleasant to be so civil when he was merely obliging a friend.

John danced by with Sister O.P.s. I had noticed them earlier, but now I had a better look at her dress. It had a halter neckline and was made of violet faille. Her eyes tonight were the exact shade of that dress. She looked incredibly lovely.

I said quietly, 'I think she's the best-looking young woman I've ever come across.'

Tom reversed to get a good view. 'Personally,' he said, 'I find perfection excessively boring. Imagine seeing that face at the breakfast table every morning. She'd never have a hair out of place and one would feel indecent if one hadn't used brilliantine or something. And how could you kiss a girl like that before you'd shaved?'

I said, 'Our John doesn't appear to agree with you.'

'My dear girl—not he! The man's a perfectionist himself—and he probably has an electric razor.'

The music stopped. I saw Peter lead Carol quickly to one of the overcrowded sofas.

Tom said, 'It's too hot in here, Gillian. Let's find a quiet spot, rest our feet, slake our thirsts, and cool off.'

I was looking at Peter. 'Anything you say.'

He took my arm. 'I say, yes.'

Peter was talking to Carol and making her laugh; neither of them glanced at us as we walked across the floor. On a sofa near the door Frances Mack was smiling at John Dexter. He said something and pushed his hand through his hair, then smoothed it mechanically. Tom was looking at them too. 'Now what,' he said when we had passed them, 'is worrying the boss? He only pulls his hair out in handfuls that way when something's in it, if you follow me.'

'Is that why he does it? I thought it was just a line.'

Tom said no, indeed. 'Poor chap has the most ghastly time when he's worried in the theatre and can't touch his hair. But it's no line, fact. Sure sign something's wrong somewhere. You watch out, next time you see him at it. There'll be a snag handy.' He opened the door of one of the small offices that lay off the hall. 'I think these are always available at these do's.'

I hesitated. 'Tom, isn't this the Dean's?'

He walked in, switched on the desk light, and flopped on to the small sofa that stood beside the empty fireplace.

'His secretary's, I think—but who cares? Relax, girl.' I was still hovering, and he held out a hand. 'The Dean isn't Matron. He was young once. No'—I had reached for the switch by the door—'don't put that on. It's nicer like this. Come on,' he waggled his hand again, 'come and sit down.'

I sat down, warily. I was in no mood for sitting on sofas in the gloaming. 'What about that cool drink you promised me?'

He sighed. 'I thought the operative word was rest.'

I said I was thirsty.

'Right.' He heaved himself to his feet. 'Chivalry, you will note, is not dead. It has merely taken refuge in St Joseph's Hospital. London.'

'Not even St Martha's?'

'God help you,' he said, 'if you ever sit out with a Martha's man. Now they are real men.'

He was back in a few minutes. He put the glasses on the floor beside us and sat down again.

'Bless you, Tom.' I raised my glass.

He nodded amicably and touched a fold of my net overskirt. 'This is pretty,' he said, 'and it goes well with that red scarf thing. You don't really have to worry about our mutual girl friend, the flower of Martha's. You look all right—more than all right.'

'Bless you again. But I'm not really worried about her.'

'Only by her?' he suggested, and we laughed.

'Not off duty. I'm a big girl now—fourth year and all. I take off my working problems with my uniform.'

He sipped his drink. 'Wise girl. Of course, if you were even wiser, you'd have no problems.' He turned sideways to look at me. 'You aren't still upset about that bust-up in Robert?'

'Well—it was a bit of a bust-up.'

'So what? My good girl, who doesn't run into a sticky patch once in a while? Happens to everyone. But it blows over. These things have a way of straightening themselves out.'

'Peter said that too,' I said thoughtfully.

He twisted his glass. 'He did, eh?' He put the glass back on the floor and produced a cigarette case. 'Have one?'

I accepted, and decided I had much maligned him by the

90

thoughts I had entertained when he brought me into this room. He obviously only intended that we should do as he had suggested: rest our feet and cool off. I thought this was a good opportunity to thank him for helping Peter.

I said, 'Tom, it was really very kind of you to ask me tonight.'

He raised one eyebrow. 'Gillian—this is so sudden. But what are you talking about? What's so kind about my asking a pretty girl to a dance?'

'Look,' I said, 'you don't have to pretend all that much. I know this wasn't an ordinary invitation—that you were just doing it to oblige.'

He sat back in his corner. 'I don't doubt that I'm very dense, but I'm not with you. Of course I'm doing this to oblige—myself.'

'Didn't Peter ask you to bring me?'

'Peter Kier?' He shook his head slowly. 'Where did you get that bright idea?'

I hesitated. Certainly Carol had not said this in so many words, yet I was sure of her meaning, and how else could she and Peter have known of this invitation when I had not known it myself? 'I just wondered——' I said lamely.

'Then don't wonder. No one tells me whom I'm to take to dances. I asked you because I heard you were free and thought it might be fun. No subtlety. But what's all this about Peter? Did you seriously think he fixed this up for you because he was booked himself?'

I shrugged. 'I got it wrong, that's all.'

He smiled. 'You definitely have got things very wrong if you don't yet know Peter well enough to know that this would be about the last thing he'd do.'

'What do you mean?'

He folded his arms and stretched his legs. 'Peter,' he said carefully, 'is a splendid type and a splendid man on a party, but he's not exactly a philanthropist. He rather looks on you—rightly or wrongly—as his private property. If it interests you, he wasn't at all happy last night when he heard I had asked you. Took a poor view, he did, and told me so. A stern warning, it was.'

'Tom—really?'

He shook his head sadly. 'So much for my ego. And so much for the good money I've wasted on these tickets. Alas—she loves another.' He laughed. 'Don't look so stricken, girl—I'll survive. You're a very good dancer and very good to look at. Fair enough. I'm quite satisfied.'

There was no point in pretence. I said, 'I feel an awful fraud.'

He stood up. 'You shouldn't take life so seriously, my dear. It's a lot of fun if you take it as it comes.' He held out his hands. 'Come along,' he pulled me to my feet, 'let's join the howling mob on the floor.' But when I was standing he held on to my hands. 'At the risk of having my head bitten off I'm going to give you a stern warning.'

I said, 'Never to leave my keys around again. I promise, Doctor.'

'To hell with your keys.' He gripped my hands more tightly and shook them as if we were playing oranges and lemons. 'But there's something else which you'd be wise not to take too seriously.'

'What's that?'

He was silent momentarily, as if making up his mind; then he said, 'The prospect of a joint future with Peter Kier. He's—er—well, he's not exactly the home-loving type.' He was so obviously sincere over what he was saying that there was no question of my feeling annoyed with his gratuitous advice.

'He isn't?'

'No. Oh—hell.' He broke off. 'I don't know why I've let myself in for this—I like Peter and I like you—you're a nice——' he smiled. 'Any minute now and I'll ask you to be a sister to me. That's the point.' He said he had three sisters. 'That's why I know that this is a difficult fact for a young woman to grasp. What my sisters haven't told me on the subject isn't worth knowing. Fact. Yes, indeed. So you don't want to lose too much sleep over Peter—because if you do, all you'll end up with is insomnia.'

I said bleakly, 'Thanks, Tom.'

He let go of my hands. 'Don't look like that, Gill. You make me feel as if I've been pinching sweets from the nippers in Christian. Hell!' He frowned. 'I don't know what to do.' Then he said quickly, 'Yes, I do,' and put his arms round me and kissed me.

The room was suddenly full of light. Then the switch by the door was turned off and John said, 'Sorry,' and stepped backward into the passage. Before he had time to close the door we heard a woman's voice.

'Really! That girl is quite unsuitable! She wouldn't have lasted five minutes in St Martha's——' and the door closed.

Tom said ruefully, 'Well, I thought it was such a good idea,' and let me go. He asked what I wanted to do next?

'Dance? Isn't that why we're here?'

'It's a point.' He moved to the door. 'Are you frightfully narked with me, Gill?'

I smiled weakly. 'I'm not narked with you at all. I still think you've been very civil.'

'You do?' He shut the door. 'Then let's sit down again. I'll give you some more advice, shall I? Then I can kiss you again?

I liked that part—I liked it a lot.'

'No,' I said, 'no more advice—thanks. We'll dance.'

He offered me his arm. 'Let's go and find some apples.'

'Apples?' I wondered if I had missed something; it was more than possible.

' "Comfort me with apples," ' said Tom, ' "and stay me with flagons; for I am sick of love." Solomon. Unquote.'

7

NURSES DO NOT ASK WHY

LATER that night as I redid my face in the cloakroom Carol touched my shoulder.

'How's it going?'

We were alone in the room. I said, much as I had expected.

She took out her powder compact. 'Tom dances quite well, doesn't he?'

'Pretty well. No, that's not fair. Very well.'

She smiled. 'My dear, you're still full of the milk of human kindness. How long's it going to last?'

It was a relief to talk to her. I sat down and took off a shoe.

'I suppose this evening will have to end some time. It seems interminable.'

She said she wasn't having much fun either. 'I wish we could have made this a party. It wouldn't be so bad if we'd been a foursome.'

I did not have to beat about the bush with her, so I asked what was stopping us. 'I know Tom would be quite happy to mix.'

She peered at herself in the glass. 'I sort of gathered that Peter's allergic to parties.'

This did not upset me, although I saw she was afraid that it would. I knew Peter better than she, and the fact that he was against joining us meant that he was annoyed, as Tom had told me. If he had not been angry he would have been delighted with the prospect. As Tom had also said, Peter was a great man for a party. Carol would not know this because she seldom came to our parties. I did not remember her going to more than one other besides tonight's in all her years in Joe's.

I suddenly appreciated that I had let her in for an evening with Peter in a mood; and when he was in one of them, you had to be in love with him to find him bearable.

'Honey,' I said, 'I am sorry. It's too bad of him to behave like this and spoil your evening. He's murder when he's sulking. Look'—I had a bright idea—'shall I tell Tom to ask you to dance and then Peter will have to ask me and we'll have a heart-to-heart?' It was not the most tactful thing I had ever said, but I was shaken by her reaction. A small flame of anger leapt in her eyes. I had never known her really angry before, and I was so interested that I even forgot to feel guilty about my lack of tact.

'For goodness sake,' she said sharply, 'leave me a smattering of pride! I appreciate that you've managed to persuade one man to bring me here tonight; you really don't have to bulldoze another into dancing with me!'

'Oh Lor',' I said, 'I'm sorry—I'm bats—I just didn't think. And honestly I didn't persuade Peter to ask you. He thought it up for himself. You know that.'

The flame died, and her eyes were as calm as ever. 'I know you weren't thinking, ducks—you never do,' she said quizzically, 'do you? But it mightn't be a bad idea if you did.' She shut her compact with a snap. 'And you needn't worry about your young man's behaviour. He won't harm—me!' She walked away quickly before I had a chance to ask her what she meant. I wished I had called her back. Her words niggled in my brain for the rest of the night, and when I woke up next morning they were still there.

Out-Patients was very busy that morning, although it was Saturday. Sister was off for the weekend, and despite the rush there was an air of high holiday in the department.

I did not see Peter during the morning. I did not know whether he was avoiding me, or in the theatre. Probably the latter. Peter's bouts of bad temper seldom lasted long. I was glad not to see him. I had had enough on my mind without his disturbing presence, and I was tired of the well-intentioned, disinterested advice of my friends, old and new, on the subject of my future.

Tom was assisting in an eye clinic. Half-way through the morning he came over to the empty Children's Room.

'Have you a spare ophthalmoscope, Nurse? My battery's just packed up for me.'

I gave him our instrument, and he murmured, 'No hard feelings, Gill?'

'None at all. All that's bothering me this morning are my poor feet.'

He said, 'That's a bit of a dirty crack to your dancing partner, Nurse Snow.'

John came out of the office, where he had been writing notes. 'You wanting me, Thanet?'

'No thanks, sir,' called Tom cheerfully. 'I'm just scrounging an ophthalmoscope from Nurse Snow and fast returning to my eyes.'

John walked down the room and stood in the doorway. 'No more children coming along, Nurse Snow?'

'No, Mr Dexter. All the appointments have run through.'

I thought he would go, but for once he seemed in no hurry. He stayed where he was and watched the steady trickle of patients pass on their way to the main entrance.

'Place is clearing quickly this morning,' he remarked.

I agreed, I would have liked to have added that the place always ran smoothly when Nurse Blakelock was in charge, but although it was true, it would have been too obvious a crack. It would also have been very bad manners, since I knew of his relationship with Sister; and since he was invariably polite to us it was impossible, as well as inexcusable, to be deliberately rude to him. I went on tidying the comic-cupboard.

He looked round to see what I was doing. 'Enjoy yourself last night, Nurse?'

'Yes, thank you.' I wondered what he had thought when he saw Tom kissing me.

'That's good.'

I asked him the same question. He said, 'Thank you, I did.' He looked at his watch. 'I'm due in the theatre in twenty minutes. I'm going by the way of the canteen. Would you mind telling Nurse Blakelock that I'll be out of action in the theatre for the rest of the morning, and if she wants anything in my line will she contact Mr Henderson?'

I shut the cupboard. 'Yes, Mr Dexter.'

'No hurry,' he said; 'when you next see her. She's not likely to want me. The clinics are done.' So I opened the cupboard again, and he walked away down the corridor.

I finished the cupboard in a few minutes and went in search of Blakelock. I found her in Sister's office.

'Hallo, Snow. Your kids finished?'

'All gone, Nurse.' I gave her John's message.

'What fun for the theatre. I'll bet they feel just like a long list this morning.' She asked if I had enjoyed the dance. 'I hear it went well.'

'Very well. You should have been there, Nurse.'

Blakelock grinned. 'Not I, my child. I like my bed at night.' She said she had never been a one for dancing. 'I'm too heavy,' she said simply, 'and I start puffing.'

'Nonsense, Nurse. You nip round O.P.s fast enough without puffing.'

She said that was her armour plating. 'But you can't wear whalebone under an evening dress—so dreadful for your partner!' She asked how Sister had looked.

'Out of this world. She really did.'

Blakelock looked at the form she had been filling in. 'I

wonder if she's going to step out of this world——'

'Nurse, wouldn't it be bliss? And you could be Sister O.P.s.'

'Hush,' she said severely, 'what is all this, mutiny?' She relaxed. 'Be rather fun, Snow. Fun all round.'

I said it would be splendid, and we all thought she, Blakelock, would make a magnificent Sister O.P.s. I asked her what she wanted me to do.

She said, 'Thanks for the kind word. I hope Matron agrees. I'll admit I'd like it myself.' She looked up at the clock. 'Twelve. Perhaps it's safe to start the extra cleaning,' she said thoughtfully. 'I think it should be—but I always suspect a morning that starts as badly as this one did and then trails off by midday. We're too quiet.' She looked past me and through the open door. 'Or have I spoken too soon?'

I turned. Tims, the porter, was streaking down the corridor from switchboard. 'Message from Sister Casualty, Nurse Blakelock. Can you take a motor-cycle crash in the emergency bed? A young lad. Sister says as Casualty is full and hasn't a bed.'

Blakelock stood up. 'Yes, we can. The fracture-room bed is ready. But why is he coming in here? Surely if he's a bad crash he ought to go straight to the wards and by-pass us?'

Tims said he couldn't say, Nurse, he was sure—but he'd ask the Sister, and raced back to telephone.

Blakelock shrugged. 'I thought we were too quiet. Let's go and investigate.'

I followed her to the main entrance. Tims joined us immediately.

'Sister Casualty says as she's much obliged Nurse and the ambulance is coming alongside directly.' Tims had been in the Navy at some time, and in moments of stress always slipped back into nautical phraseology. 'Sister said to tell you as she's sent for Mr Henderson to come here, and she's asked the theatre to tell Mr Dexter.'

Blakelock and I looked at each other. Sister Casualty never panicked; if she had sent out a general alarm to the surgeons she must take a very serious view of the man's condition.

'Where's the injury, Tims?' asked Blakelock. 'And how bad?'

'Head,' he said briefly. 'Sister says she doubts as if he'll reach a ward, which is why she wants him in a bed here real quick.'

Blakelock and I looked at each other again and waited for the ambulance. There was nothing we could do until the men unloaded the stretcher. The accident bed in the fracture-room was always ready for something like this; the thermostatic blanket was on; the hot water bottles refilled two-hourly; a radiant-heat cradle; spare blankets; a dressing trolley; oxygen; a transfusion stand and setting; and a sheaf of blank notes were all there, waiting. Keeping that bed in readiness was part of the normal

96

16

routine of the senior probationer in Out-Patients.

There was nothing to be done but wait until the man arrived; and when he arrived, and the careful ambulance men wheeled in the stretcher-trolley with the help of Tims and an anxious young policeman, and we all lifted the boy on to the bed, it was unhappily obvious that there was little anyone could do.

Mr Henderson arrived as Blakelock covered the boy's head with fresh sterile towels. I looked up from the oxygen mask I was holding in position. 'Do you want me to move this, Mr Henderson?'

'Just let me have a look at his face'—I lifted the mask—'right. Give him some more, Nurse.' He touched what had once been a forehead with his forefinger, gently removed a corner of one of the towels. 'My God,' he said softly.

The room was very quiet, the only sound the hiss of the oxygen.

'How fast was he going, do you know, Officer?' asked Mr Henderson.

The policeman shook his head and stared at the floor. 'Not less than sixty I'd say, sir.'

Someone touched my arm. I glanced round and saw Blakelock was beside me. Her face was pale green, and there were beads of sweat on her forehead.

'Sorry, Snow,' she whispered, 'but I'll have to leave you to——' Her words faded and she went down. I caught hold of her with my free arm but she was too heavy for me. The policeman moved quickly, 'You leave her to me, Nurse.'

Tims was by the door. 'I'll fetch along Nurse Smith.'

'Thanks, Tims.' The policeman was dealing competently with the unconscious Blakelock. I looked back at the mask I was holding.

Bill Henderson said, 'I'll hang on to that, Nurse Snow. Can you clean his head up as Nurse Blakelock was doing?'

'Yes, Mr Henderson.' We changed places and I switched my mind off everything but my hands.

I swabbed, cleaned, swabbed, cleaned mechanically, and shut all the pigeon holes in my brain that might, if open, remind me that I was dealing with a human being. This isn't a boy's head, this is just something that has to be cleaned; that isn't a skull, it's just bone; and don't think, don't think, don't think. I had used this formula before; it was the only way I was able to achieve the necessary detachment to do some of the things we had to do. I could tell by the carefully controlled breathing of the man working with me that he was thinking what I was thinking, and feeling what I was feeling.

The ambulance men were still there, watching, waiting, although there was nothing they could do. Their kind, experienced faces were pale, their eyes heavy with fear. I had finished cleaning.

'What about his family?' I inquired.

Mr Henderson had fixed the mask and was preparing an injection.

'Did you contact them?' he asked the policeman.

The policeman said they had got a message to the boy's father. 'He and his wife are coming directly, Doctor, but they've got to cross London. It'll take 'em a tidy time to get here.'

Mr Henderson looked at me. 'I hope to God they make it.'

'Yes.' I went on with the new dressing I was applying.

He gave the injection. 'Mr Dexter know about this chap?'

'Sister Casualty sent a message to the theatre. He may have started.'

He nodded. 'Probably.' He took off his stethoscope. 'I'm going to give him some more of that. I'll use a long needle and get it into the muscle.' He looked at the trolley. 'Have we got enough coramine here?'

'There's a full box on that lower shelf.'

We gave him morphia; we gave him coramine; intravenous saline; continuous oxygen. We gave him everything else that could be given; everything that modern medicine and a modern well-equipped hospital could provide; but he had hit the road with an uncovered head at fifty or sixty miles an hour and there was nothing that was any use.

John came in about twenty minutes later. He had come straight from the table and had not even stopped to remove his white over-boots or pull down his mask. His boots squeaked on the rubbered floor as he came into the room. He stood in silence looking at the boy, and then as I lifted the dressing, at that broken head.

He said 'The poor young devil,' and nodded to me to replace the dressing. He turned to Henderson. 'What have you done?'

Bill Henderson told him. 'I didn't bother about taking any pictures.'

John shook his head. 'No need for that. We can see all we want.' He glanced at me. 'What do you make his pulse now, Nurse?'

For the last few minutes I had been taking his radial pulse continuously. 'I can't get it accurately now. It's barely perceptible.'

He nodded again without speaking, then remembered his mask, and pulled it down.

Bill Henderson turned up the oxygen, and the bubbles of air danced in the flow-water; John walked to the foot of the bed, which was raised on the highest blocks we possessed. He took the foot off the blocks and held it up higher. The policeman came forward and they held it at an angle that was nearly vertical.

'This doing anything, Nurse?' asked John.

'I'm afraid not.'

Bill gave him some more coramine; he used the long needle again and as the drug touched the heart I felt the beat under my fingers quicken very slightly and then fade again. One of the ambulance men was speaking to John. 'Shall I hold that for you, Doctor?' They changed over and John took Bill Henderson's stethoscope from the trolley.

'What did you get last time you listened, Bill?'

Bill told him, and again they looked at me. 'What is it?'

I said, 'Fading.'

They stood together watching the injured boy. John said very quietly, 'What a damned waste.' Later I remembered that it was the first time I had ever heard him swear. Now I shifted my fingers to get a better feel of his pulse. I moved my fingers three times, then twice more, then I said, 'I can't get it at all now.'

John fixed the stethoscope in his ears. 'I'll try this way.' He bent down and listened for the apex, then the aortic beat, he moved the end piece to the lungs, and then back to that eighteen-year-old heart. He took off the stethoscope and turned to the two men holding the bed. He said, 'Thank you very much. You can put that down now.'

Lisa came into the room and closed the door quietly.

'Mr and Mrs Downs are here to see their son.'

John took off his cap and pushed his hand through his hair. 'Keep them in the office, Nurse Smith. Say we'll be out immediately.' He looked at me. 'You had better come, Nurse Snow. Mrs Downs will want to see you.'

I said, 'Yes, Mr Dexter,' and followed him from the room, and the ambulance men moved their feet and avoided looking at us as we went by.

Lisa was outside the office door. 'I'll take over in there,' she said. She caught my eye, and I shook my head. She winced visibly, then walked away to the fracture-room.

His parents were young, very young to have a boy of eighteen. Mrs Downs jerked out of her chair and caught my shoulders with both hands. 'Nurse—can I see him now? He's all right, isn't he?' she gasped fearfully. 'He is all right? It's not too bad? Say—please say'—her voice cracked—'that he's not too bad?'

She was shorter than I, and over her shoulder I saw her husband stand up slowly, his eyes fixed on John's face. 'How is he, Doctor? How is the lad?'

John said gently, 'Won't you both sit down, please?'

Mrs Downs, still clinging to me with one hand, spun round. 'Oh, Doctor, can't I see him first?'

He said, 'Please sit down—I want to talk to you—please.'

She dropped back into her chair, her hand in mine. Her husband sat down stiffly, as if he was a very old man.

John pulled forward a chair and sat close to her, facing them both. 'I am very, very sorry,' he said 'to have to tell you this——' His voice was deep with compassion as he told them.

They sat very still. Mrs Downs stared at him uncomprehending, and then raised her eyes to my face, 'It isn't true, Nurse?' she asked softly, 'Tell me, please tell me—it's not true?'

I said, 'I'm sorry——' then broke off. What else was there to say? She did not cry; she gave a small gasp and then buried her face in my apron lap as if she was a child. She was not wearing a hat, and her hair was curly and very fair. I stroked her hair as if she had been a child, and felt my body shaken by her tearless sobs.

Mr Downs was twisting his hat in his hands, turning it over and over. He did not look at his wife. He looked at John.

'I gave him that machine for his birthday,' he said, 'I—gave it to him.'

Blakelock came in with tea and brandy. They refused both at first, but slowly we were able to persuade them to change their minds. John did not go back to the theatre; I did not know what was happening to his list, but was thankful to have him there. He took them in to see their boy, and then waited until the hospital car that Blakelock had requested arrived to take them home. Before they left, they shook hands all round, and then Mrs Downs kissed me. 'Thank you for what you did for my boy, dear,' she said as she let me go.

John took them out to the car and waited at the hospital gates as the car drove away. Blakelock came down the corridor. 'Leave that clearing up in the fracture-room to us, Snow,' she said. 'Just straighten the office, will you?'

John was back in the department. He said, 'I'll sign that certificate and the forms for you now, Nurse Blakelock.'

She said, 'Will you see to them, Nurse Snow?' and went back to the fracture-room. John followed me into the office. 'Let's have them and get them over.' He sat down wearily at the desk and tugged at the strings of his mask which was hanging round his neck. The bow on the upper strings had become knotted. He untied it slowly.

I found the necessary forms and put them, with my pen, in front of him. He picked up the first form. 'Do you know his Christian names?'

'Richard Samuel.'

'How did you have time to find that out?'

'The policeman got them off his driving licence. I heard him telling Tims for the admission book.'

'Right. Eighteen?'

I said, 'Yes.'

He stopped writing and laid one hand flat on the desk. 'What the devil can you expect if you give a boy that age a powerful machine? Of course he'll flog it—and of course he'll crash. Do you know what kind it was?'

'No.'

He told me. 'In case you're not up in these things that's just about the fastest machine on the road. A lovely job—if you use them sensibly. But who has any sense at eighteen?' He stared at his hands. 'We're all supposed to be so damned clever—all of us—and what happens? A boy plays the fool with a bit of machinery, and we can't do a thing. We just have to stand around and watch him die.'

I said, 'That's what's so awful. Nothing was any good. And she—that poor mother—she was so grateful. But——'

He looked up, 'Yes?'

'When they went off just now, I was thinking of them getting home—without him. His room, his things'—I shook my head helplessly—'it's Saturday afternoon—and he won't be there.'

His jaw set. 'No, he won't be there. And this time next week some other boy won't be there, and the week after, and the week after that.' He stood up. 'What could they expect—those pathetic parents? They didn't even see that he was wearing a helmet. They didn't think it mattered. They couldn't see that all this was inevitable.'

'Inevitable?'

'As night follows day.' He was silent for a few seconds. Then he said, 'Nurse Snow, I don't think a weekend passes in the whole year without my having to tell some parent what I've had to tell those two this morning. And it's always the same story; "He wanted one so badly, Doctor—we promised him one if he passed his exam—finished his National Service—anything." And the follow-up is identical. They crash.' He raised his hands from his sides, then dropped them helplessly. 'They don't wear helmets—they don't bother about brakes—they ride on white lines for fun—they try to beat the sound barrier'—there was no humour in his voice, only anger and frustration—'and they kill themselves,' he added more softly, 'and they kill themselves. And break their parents' hearts.'

I had never seen him so moved. I said without thinking, 'And we don't know how to fit the pieces together.'

'No.' He smiled faintly. 'I've often wondered how any man who's done more than ten minutes' medicine manages to have the God Almighty complex that some of them do have. They've all worked in a Casualty department at some period of their medical lives, and how you can work in Casualty and still consider yourself omnipotent beats me.'

I was thinking of Richard Downs. I said, 'Why did he have to die?'

He looked at me. 'You must have wondered that previously.'

'I have.'

He said heavily, 'Then you'd better stop. That's one question that you can't ask in a place like this. Not that I blame you for wondering—you can't walk into any ward without wondering.'

I said, 'How do I stop?'

He sat down on a corner of the desk, and our faces were level. He looked at me reflectively, as if he was considering whether to go on or turn back. We were very close to each other, and our proximity was not only physical; this was the first time I had felt this particular sensation with him, but I had known it previously with other men with whom I had had to stand by a bed and watch a person die.

He made up his mind. 'Personally,' he said, 'I find the only answer is acceptance. I have to remind myself that I can only see a fragment of the general picture; if I saw the whole I might have the answer.' He hitched his gown over his knee, 'There's another word for that—a better one, although it's the fashion to use a lot of high-powered scientific jargon to disprove it.' He was silent again, and then he said, 'Faith.'

'But in what? Life? God?'

'Same thing. And don't say you have to understand a thing to believe in it. Do you know how a wireless works?' he added quickly.

'No.' I grasped his meaning

'And I expect you're a shade hazy about a telephone.'

'More than that.'

He stood up. 'Well—if you can accept things like that—why stop there? You don't know those answers, but you're quite happy to believe in their existence and their efficiency.'

I said, 'I see.'

'That's right,' he nodded. 'You do. It's odd,' he went on, 'and people do not as a rule think of things this way—but you need just as much faith when you're trying to patch up somebody as does the person who needs the patching.' He asked when I was off duty.

'This evening.'

'Then you'd better have some brandy,' he said laconically, 'You look as if you could do with it, if you aren't free to go off.'

I said I felt all right, thanks. 'Would you like something, Mr Dexter?'

'Not I, thanks.' He pushed back his hair and I recollected what Tom had said last night. 'Not I.' He said he had better get back to the theatre. 'Fortunately Jamison was on to take over for me'—Jamison was one of the surgical registrars—'but I had better get back there if only to change. I'm sorry you're not off this afternoon; you look shot up.' He stopped with one hand on the door. 'Nurse Snow,' he said gravely, 'don't let yourself be too upset over this—over what you couldn't do. You did all you were supposed to do. So don't feel guilty because Mrs Downs was so grateful to you. You held her son's hand while he died, and you were kind to him and distressed for him. Most mothers would feel as she does.' He went out and shut the door behind him. I heard him tell Blakelock I was still in the office. I could not catch her reply, but I knew she would leave me alone. I sat down at the desk where he had sat. I did nothing. I sat and stared at the blank wall in front of me, too sad for thought or tears.

8

SUNDAY IN THE THEATRE

LISA came into the Children's Room at five minutes to six that evening. I was tidying the crêpe-bandage drawer.

'Dear Peter is searching the department, Gill. I don't doubt you are the missing object. Shall I tell him you're here, or are you incog.?'

I shut the drawer wearily. 'I'll tell him myself, thanks. He probably won't want me at all, but has come to borrow something.' I had no interest in what Peter might want—I had lost interest in everything since this morning—but I did not want to talk even to Lisa about it, so the simplest line was to do as she intended I should, and find Peter.

He was in the fracture-room. The room was spotless and impersonal as ever; the trolley setting replaced; a new mattress and bed clothes were on the bed; only the electric blanket and the hot-water bottles were the same, but even they had different covers.

'Looking for something, Peter?'

'Hi——' he smiled; 'you darling. When are you off?'

I looked at my watch. 'A couple of minutes.'

'Doing anything special on this gay Saturday night?'

Was it still Saturday? The day seemed to have gone on for ever. 'I'm going to bed. I'm whacked.'

He said surely I could postpone my collapse for an hour or so and have dinner with him. 'I can get off for two hours after seven.'

I looked at the empty bed. 'Don't let's talk in here—let's go outside.'

'Darling—what ails you? This is a perfect place for an assignation. Nobody uses this room on Saturdays.'

'It was used this morning.' I walked out to the corridor.

'Anything to humour the girl,' he murmured, 'but I wish I knew what was so wrong with the fractures. Old Rufford taken to haunting it?'

I said, 'We had a smash in there this morning.'

'That chap Bill Henderson was talking about at lunch?'

'I expect so. Motor-cycle crash.'

He said, 'Darling, you mustn't let these things give you the heebee-jeebies. You haven't a hope once you start doing that!'

I did not answer, so he said it just showed how badly I needed a little relaxation among the bright lights. 'It can only be a snack, I'm afraid, as I have to be back by nine. Come on, love, wakey, wakey! Or are you playing hard to get?'

'I suppose I must eat somewhere. Look,' I apologised, 'I'm sorry to be so up the pole—I just feel out.'

He smiled. 'I wish you'd stop shilly-shallying and come. I want to talk to you, Gillian. I do really.'

After that there was no question of my refusing. His smile had its usual effect on me; I said I would be ready when he was.

'I'll pick you up at seven, love.'

I was fairly sure that he meant it this time, but as I had been sure previously and spent the evening alone, I filled a hot-water bottle and put it in my bed. I could always go to bed early as I had originally intended.

He came for me punctually. The food was good; he was in one of his best moods, and when he kissed me on the way home I felt that life should be perfect. It was not, because somehow I was unable to join in the fun and games. I tried to, I tried very hard, but it was no good. I spent the evening mentally sitting on my shoulder and watching Peter and me. I was too emotionally exhausted to know whether I liked what I saw.

Peter said, 'I'm really very cross with you, Gillian. I can't tell you how put out I was when I saw you disappearing into the darkened room with Tom Thanet last night.'

I smiled weakly, 'Didn't anyone not see me disappearing into that room with Tom?' I told him about John and Sister O.P.s. 'She needn't have been so disparaging. Tom and I really only went in there to rest our two feet.'

He laughed. 'Poor old Tom. What a come-down for a natural born rake.'

'Tom's no rake! He wouldn't know where to start.'

He said I could be right at that. 'I should have known better than to panic. I might have guessed you'd give him the no-touch technique.'

I said, 'Did you panic?'

'Darling,' he rubbed his face against mine. 'I have a fine new crop of white hairs. I'm thinking of running for S.S.O. What's old Garth got that I can't emulate—saving the affections of a certain blonde?'

I rested my head against his shoulder, but for once his shoulder did not seem comfortable, so I sat up.

'Do you think he's serious about her?'

He pulled me back against him. 'Sit still, love. Yes, taking that affair purely at its face value, I do. Old Garth isn't the type to take a girl out just because he needs womanly companionship.'

'For heaven's sake! What other reason is there for taking a girl out?' He shouted with laughter. 'Don't be a goon, Peter. Tell me about them.'

He said, 'I see it this way. I've known him for six years and this is the first time I've seen him so much as look up from his scalpel. He's not sub-human, he's a-human. So the mere fact that he's asked the girl out seems to me fraught with significance.' He stopped suddenly. 'Hey. Whence this concern about the chap? Should I be worrying about him and not Tom?'

'You don't have to grow a single grey hair. I'm just fascinated—we all are. He's never looked at a Joe's girl and now he's lost his head over a product of the rival firm. We're furious.'

'Never mind,' said Peter; 'he doesn't know what he's missing. Joe's girls are all right.' He kissed me again. 'But to get back to the idle gossip, I wouldn't say old Garth had exactly lost his head—much though I'd give to see it. I saw quite a bit of them last night and I didn't get the impression that he was more than mildly interested—and yet I may be wrong at that; Frances Mack is an extraordinarily attractive young woman.'

I agreed that she was, and wondered why his saying that should make me feel so gloomy. I knew she was lovely; we all knew she was lovely; just as we had all reached the novel conclusion that Beauty Was Not Enough. To prove to myself that, whatever else might be wrong, I was not jealous, I asked how he had enjoyed the dance.

'It was all right,' he said noncommittally, 'but it could have been so much better if you had allowed me a couple of dances.'

'Allowed, my foot! You never asked me!'

'Did you expect me to?'

'Of course. I thought we would join up.'

He said, 'I rather thought the same.'

'Then why didn't we?'

He hesitated, 'We-ell, I sort of got the impression that the idea wouldn't be greeted by cries of joy from one and all.'

We were sitting on a bench in the park. It might even have

been the same bench on which I sat with John. The nearest park bench is the only place in which you can find respectable privacy if you live and work in an institution. Few of us had homes in London, or the money with which to buy privacy. That particular park was regarded as Joe's back garden; there were other parks in London and other hospitals, and on most evenings a census of the occupants of the various park benches would probably show that ninety per cent. were members of the nearest medical and nursing training school.

I bent forward and pretended to fiddle with my shoe while I thought over Peter's words. I did not believe him. I knew I could believe Carol.

'Who gave you that impression?'

He locked his hands behind his head and flapped his elbows. 'My love, when I was a boy my old man took me on one side and said, "Son, never lend money to strangers; always drink black coffee after dinner even if it poisons you; and never discuss with one lady what the lady you took out last night said to you." So let's talk of something else shall us? When are we going to have another war? Where do the patients go on Sundays?'

I did not ask any more questions. I knew he would not answer them if I did, as I also knew and had always pretended I did not, that he would swear black was white if it suited him. Now I was too tired to care much if he was lying; it did not seem to matter. Since this morning all our trivial affairs had faded into insignificance. I kept remembering that house in North London, and the childish yellow head that had pressed against me. I wondered how they could face going to bed tonight, and the silence of tomorrow morning. I was sure he had spent Sunday morning playing with the engine of that damned machine.

Peter said, 'Why the disapproving silence?'

'Not disapproving—plain coma.'

He stood up. 'Time I took you back. I shouldn't have dragged you out.'

That reminded me of something. 'Why did you?'

'What's that?'

'I mean—what did you want to talk to me about?'

'That what I said?'

'Yes.'

He laughed. 'I had to say something, Gillian. I was feeling sociable, and I couldn't face the prospect of spending two unnecessary hours in Joe's. Pretty smooth line, I thought.'

I said very smooth.

'That's my girl!' We walked back hand in hand. When we reached our Home he said, 'You go straight to bed, love. You're getting all introspective and gloomy. Big mistake. Not your line at all. You want to snap out of it.'

I promised I would, thanked him for the supper, and went inside. It was still early, but I did not feel like chatting to the girls in the sitting-room or watching television; I checked in at Home Sister's office and went up to my room. I would have liked to have talked to Carol and I wished she was not on nights. She had said nothing last night about being free tonight, and had obviously only had that one night free for the dance. Night Sister was very good about these things, and if Carol had been free she would certainly have told me, as we always did things together on our days or nights off. Apart from the occasion when she revisited her old school, we had combined for all our free times since her parents died.

I wondered if it was worth looking for Lisa; but Lisa was always surrounded by a tea-drinking assortment of our year at this hour of the night, and I was sick of my fellow-nurses. I discovered I was sick of doctors, too. I wondered if Tom was right, and there was any comfort in apples. I had some in my room and I ate one. I did not feel any better; I felt very lonely.

Next morning Lisa ran down the steps of the Nurses' Home at twenty-five minutes past seven and clapped my back, 'Think we'll make it, dear girl?'

We had five minutes in which to reach the dining-room, have breakfast, and be on duty. I waved a hand to save breath, and we galloped across the park in companionable silence and reached the dining-room just as Night Sister was reading the roll-call.

'Made it,' I said, swallowing my scalding tea. Lisa nodded, she was eating too fast for speech. Night Sister stood up to say Grace, and still chewing we stood with bent heads.

'Pleasant evening with Peter?' murmured Lisa out of the corner of her mouth.

'Very pleasant.' I beamed to show that life was a song again. I wanted to reassure Lisa about Tom; if she felt I was happy with Peter she would stop worrying about me in that other con- nexion. There was really no need for her to be upset, as there was no need for me to be upset over Carol and Peter at that dance; but young women in love do not need concrete reasons for having the vapours.

Out-Patients was officially closed on Sundays, and the O.P. nurses were sent jobbing. 'Jobbing' meant working in any ward for a brief period; for example, the morning in one ward, the afternoon in another.

Night Sister told Lisa to go to Ellen. She said she did not know what to do with me. 'Matron did not mention you, Nurse

107

Snow. I'm afraid I don't like to send you to one of the wards without her permission, so you had better go back to your department and make stock until Matron comes on duty at nine. I will tell her you are there.'

I liked being alone in the department; it was strangely peaceful, and not sad as an empty ward is sad. I went round all the rooms, opening windows, dusting benches, checking settings, and refilling the hot-water bottles in the accident bed. I hurried, not because there was any hurry, but from force of habit. After four years in a hospital, to move slowly is a physical impossibility. It is a good habit, if hard on the legs, because you never, in any hospital, know from one moment of the day to another exactly how much work you will have to do before the day ends, and you can never be certain of what is going to happen next. The only certain thing is that something will happen. Boredom is not an occupational hazard in a nursing career.

When I had finished the routine tidying I collected cotton wool, gauze, large scissors, a clean towel, and an empty dressing tin, and settled down at the corridor table to make stock (dressings). I had filled three tins when the telephone rang.

It was the Assistant Matron. 'Nurse Snow, have you had scarlet fever?'

Now—what? I said, 'Yes, Sister.'

'Splendid,' she said warmly, 'how convenient.' She asked if I had a cold or sore throat.

Curiouser and curiouser. 'No, Sister.'

'Then will you put away what you are doing and go straight to the general surgical theatre? Sister Theatre is short of a trained nurse this morning, and you were last there in the summer, so you should be able to be of some use to her.'

I said, 'Yes, Sister, thank you very much, Sister,' delighted at the prospect of being in action again, and she rang off.

Sister Theatre was a tall, plump woman with short heavy fair curls and deep-set blue eyes. She was around the same age as Sister O.P.s and had also trained at Martha's, but there the resemblance ended. Sister Theatre was never irritable and unfailingly considerate; she was also apparently tireless. She came out of her duty-room as I arrived in the theatre corridor. She was carrying a white enamel tray.

'There you are, Nurse Snow! Good morning!' She said she was delighted to hear I had had scarlet fever.

'Who's got it, Sister?'

'Nurse Brent [the staff nurse]. She was on this weekend, and went down with it last night. Fortunately, although I was off, I hadn't gone away, and equally fortunately you are spare this morning. Matron is afraid we may be in for an epidemic—these things never come singly—and she said she could not send me

anyone who had not had it in case they might be cooking it.'
She said would I go and change, and she would tell me what
she wanted done. 'We have a fairly long list this morning.'

'On Sunday, Sister?'

'On Sunday, Nurse,' she echoed dryly. 'So off with that cap
and on with a turban. This is going to be a Monday Sunday.'

The general surgical theatre was the largest in the hospital. It
consisted of the theatre itself, with its large glass-walled gallery
for the students; a sterilising room in which stood an auto-
clave; anaesthetic room; glove-room; duty-room; and surgeons'
changing-room. The whole place was cut off from the hospital
by large double doors and inside those doors, whatever the date
on the calendar, it was always midsummer. There were no
windows, and the air-conditioner and purifier in the roof
hummed like an overworked bee. While I was doing my theatre
training I had always felt as if I was at sea. There was the same
sensation as you get when you go below decks on a liner; and
you smell the tar in the air that rushes down the corridors
between the cabins, and the throb of the ship's engines makes
your ears ring. There was no tar in the theatre, but the ether
and chloroform hung in the air constantly, and the air plant
overhead made the same noise as a ship's screw.

I went into the duty-room and removed my cap and apron. I
tied on the long gown, a sexless garment worn by the surgeons,
dressers, and nurses alike. The one I had chosen would have
fitted John. It reached my ankles and I had to wind the gown
tapes twice round my waist. Sister came in when I was strug-
gling with the T-shaped turban.

'Like this, Nurse. Forgotten already?'

'I've lost the knack.' I stood still while she wound it round
my head, then pushed the whole thing slightly backward so that
it stood away from my ears. She removed her own cap and told
me about the day's cases.

'Mr Dexter wants to catch up on some of the cold [less
acute] cases, so he's doing a string of them this morning. Three
appendices, two repairs. And this afternoon we have a nephrectomy [the removal of a kidney].'

'Is Mr Dexter doing that, Sister? Why not Mr Smith [the
urological surgeon]?'

Sister's eyes smiled over her mask. 'I don't think this is a very
nice nephrectomy, Nurse. So Mr Smith thought Mr Dexter
might like it.'

I said, 'I see.' I gathered by that that this patient's prognosis
was considered poor, and consequently Mr Smith did not want
to spoil his statistics. Resident surgical officers do not have
statistics, they just have a job to do and they do it to the best of
their ability. As they are always highly qualified and experienced

young men, their best is very good. John was a Master of Surgery. Like most nurses in Joe's if I had to lose an appendix, a thyroid, a lung, or anything else, I would as soon have it removed by him as by any of the more exalted consultants. Sooner, in fact. The S.S.O. was the surgical dogsbody, but the variety of his surgery only made him, in our opinion, the better surgeon.

The three theatre pros had finished cleaning and they came to report for their morning's work. They were also wrapped up like white paper parcels. I did not recognise their eyes. The tallest parcel said. 'Good morning, Nurse Snow,' and I recognised her voice as belonging to a girl with whom I had worked in Christian. She was in her third year and was the Senior Pro.

Sister assigned us to our various jobs. She told me to stay in the anaesthetic room. 'And come in for the last case and watch. You may have to take a case this evening.'

The morning passed quickly. The anaesthetist and his attendant students grumbled quietly about working on Sunday morning, but the anaesthetist was efficient and neat, and there was little for me to do but stand by the patient's trolley and smile encouragingly. 'Just turn your arm over, my dear, and the Doctor will give you an injection. Now, start counting up to fifteen.' Only one man reached eight. The others dropped into the first stages of unconsciousness between five and six.

I went in with the last patient as Sister had said, and stood by her instrument trolley watching her. John was operating and Tom assisting. Two dressers stood by the table, but the gallery was empty because it was Sunday.

When the list was over the men disappeared to the surgeons' room to change, write notes, and drink tea. Sister went to lunch, leaving the Senior Pro and myself to clear up. 'The other probationers can carry on when they get back from lunch.'

Anstey, the head theatre porter, took off his cap and wiped his forehead. 'Cor stone the crows, Nurse Snow'—he came over to the sink where I was scrubbing kidney dishes—'what a carry on an' all.'

'Sunday isn't what Sunday used to be when I was last here,' I agreed.

'Ah,' he said darkly, 'be worse afore we're better. You mark my words, Nurse.'

'Do you think that nephrectomy is going to be heavy going?'

'Not 'im. Not with Mr Dexter. Now if it was Mr Smith it'd be different. 'E'd 'ave a real show—but you know what that Mr Dexter is'—he gesticulated as if John removed kidneys in his sleep—'all in the day's work it is to 'im, as you might say. Nah.' He shook his head gloomily and said there was a young chap as

110

was in Henry and he'd be down, mark his words, afore the day was out.

'What's wrong with him, Anstey?' I did not doubt him for an instant. Theatre porters are excellent diagnosticians; they also possess second sight about forthcoming operations.

'Cooking a perforation. G.U. On the bad side. They want to keep 'im quiet—on a diet and a drip, like. But it won't work.'

'It won't?'

'Nah,' he said again. 'He'll burst. You see, Nurse.'

When Sister returned I told her what Anstey had said, and she said Sister Henry had been discussing the man at lunch.

'Anstey's seldom wrong. Is Mr Dexter still here?'

'I'm afraid I don't know. I've not been out of the theatre since you left.' The Senior Pro looked up from the mackintoshes she was scrubbing. 'Mr Dexter left with Mr Thanet a few minutes ago, Sister. He said he was going to lunch.'

Sister hesitated. 'We don't want to tread on anyone's toes, and physicians can be touchy. I think I'll ring Sister Henry on the quiet. Id like to have that man's blood group just in case we need it.' She smiled at us. 'Then we can say "dear, dear, how convenient—we have some of that blood waiting in our 'fridge." '

Matron rang the theatre before I left for lunch and said I was to stay there for the remainder of the day.

'That's a mercy,' said Sister frankly, when I repeated this, 'because although I don't mind working straight through the weekend, I would like to be off for a couple of hours. My mother has come up to see me, and it's hard on her having to spend the time sitting in a hotel room.' She said she would not go out of the hospital. 'I'll be in my room in uniform if you need me.'

She sent me off duty, telling me to return at five. 'The nephrectomy should be over by then, and as we've nothing else scheduled—if Anstey is wrong—you should have a quiet evening.'

Anstey was not wrong. The man from Henry was operated on as an emergency during the afternoon, and when I got back to the theatre the sinks were piled high with mackintoshes waiting to be scrubbed, and Sister was sitting on a high stool drying rows of instruments.

'We've had them both,' she announced; 'wasn't that nice of us, Nurse? It's all over, the hospital is quiet, Mr Dexter has gone out to a very late tea, and Mr Henderson is on call.'

We changed places; she collected the two pros who had been working with her and sent them off duty, leaving the Senior Pro and myself to finish the clearing and then clean and reset the theatre for the night.

The theatre was always left ready for work, and if any emergency occurred during the night Night Sister had only to tell the porter to turn on the steam, wake the specific pair of nurses who were on call, and the theatre could deal with any case in approximately fifteen minutes—the time it took to get the necessary temperature in the heating pipes and the sterilisers.

It took us over an hour to deal with the results of the afternoon's work; then we systematically cleaned everything in the place, whether it looked dirty or not. That is one of the laws of a theatre: you leave nothing to chance. You polish shining surfaces, scrub spotless bowls and dishes, and wash the glass shelves, legs, and feet of trolleys, whether they have been used or not. We finished by six-thirty and sat down to test the gloves. Every glove was tested after use; those intact were dried and repacked for sterilising, the punctured ones repaired and left in the special basket where they were taken for use in the plaster theatre. We never used any repaired gloves for general surgical operations.

The Senior Pro was called Davis. She was a pretty girl, and she told me she loved the theatre and dreaded the thought of returning to the wards.

'You do or you don't,' I said, swinging a glove and testing it against my cheek. 'I'm not all that keen. I like people.'

She inflated her own glove. 'Messy,' she said simply, and I laughed.

'How about those mackintoshes? Weren't they messy?'

She said it was clean mess. 'And it's so much more peaceful in here—nobody stops you in the middle of your work to ask you to get out their biscuits or boil them an egg.'

The telephone rang, and I went to answer it. It was Sister Theatre ringing to know if we were quiet.

'Just mending gloves, Sister, that's all.'

'Good.' She said she wanted to take her mother to Euston. 'Poor darling, I've hardly seen her. I've rung the office to ask Matron if it was all right, and she said it was, but I thought I would ring you to make sure. I don't like leaving you alone like this.'

I rapped the desk top. 'We've got nothing on here, Sister. We haven't set eyes on a surgeon, even Anstey has gone off, and Brown [his opposite number] is helping at the switchboard.' I said I was sorry she had seen so little of her mother.

'That's not your fault, Snow. I couldn't possibly leave the theatre today. Well, if you're sure you're all right?'

'Truly, Sister.' She rang off.

A quarter of an hour later the telephone rang again. 'Acute abdo?' said Nurse Davis hopefully, and I went to answer it.

It was the Assistant Matron. 'Nurse Snow, will you set the theatre for a Caesarian section? Sister Mary will come over from Mary [the Maternity Wing] to take the case, and one of her staff midwives will be with her to look after the baby. I think you had better "dirty," and Nurse Davis can see to the anaesthetist. You had a Caesarian,' she reminded me, 'in June. Do you remember the setting?'

I said, 'I think so, Sister.'

'Sister Mary will be with you directly. She will tell you all you need to know.' She rang off.

Davis was beside me. 'What's cooking, Nurse?'

I told her, and she whistled. 'Wow! I've never seen that. What fun!'

I looked at her curiously. She was genuinely enjoying the prospect. 'I'm glad you think so. I don't care for Caesars.'

She said, why not? Surely they were just madly exciting?

'Madly,' I said drily, 'and madly dangerous, too, so I've heard tell.'

She asked who was doing it.

'Oh Lor', I forgot to ask.' I reached for the phone. 'I'd better ring Mary. I don't know what size hands the obstetricians have.'

I did not have to ring Mary because at that moment one of the two obstetrical house-physicians walked into the theatre, and he gave me all the details.

Sister Mary, a short, red-faced, well-corseted lady, arrived almost immediately.

'Well, Nurse—you Nurse Snow?' I said I was. 'Bustle to. Where is the instrument cupboard?'

I showed her the way, although she apparently knew it better than I did. She explained that the case was being done here as it was Sunday evening, and they had chosen this particular Sunday to repair some fault in the Mary Theatre heating system.

'This girl isn't one of our own bookings, she's an emergency. She hasn't been in long, although she's been in labour too long,' she added grimly.

I asked about a cot. 'Shall we borrow one from Christian, Sister?'

She said her staff midwife was bringing one from Mary.

'Look sharp, Nurse. I want to get this girl down as soon as possible. She's had a bad time. Time it was over. Are you going to "dirty" for me?'

'Yes, Sister.'

The 'dirty' nurse is the one unsterile person in the theatre; she wears a clean but not sterilised gown, mask, and cap, works as a liaison between the sterile gowned and gloved theatre staff and the outside world of bowl, forceps, nail-brushes, telephones, sterilisers, and anything else that they may require but may not touch themselves.

Sister suddenly bellowed, 'You know Mr Dexter is taking this, Nurse?'

I said the obstetrical house-physician had told me. 'I didn't know he did obstetrics here, Sister. I thought he was a general surgeon.'

Sister was busy with her trolley, and I was laying out sterile gowns and gloves on one of the tables draped with sterile towels. Nurse Davis was lifting the steaming nail-brushes from the steriliser and placing them in their bowls by the sinks.

Sister Mary said, 'Don't be ridiculous, Nurse. Of course the S.S.O. does obstetrics. And did you not know that Mr Dexter was an obstetrical registrar here before he became S.S.O.?'

I went out to the anaesthetic room to see if the patient had arrived. It was empty. Nurse Davis came out of the surgeon's room.

'The O.H.P. has got small feet. I've left him a large pair of our boots. I hope they'll fit.'

'What does he take?'

'Sevens.'

I smiled into my mask. 'He's going to enjoy wearing sixes.'

She said she wondered how the S.S.O. liked missing his tea-party.

I looked at the corridor clock. Ten to seven. 'Surely it was over long ago?'

'He was still here at five, Nurse——' she could not go on because the surgeons then arrived in a body. They said, 'Good evening,' and vanished into their room.

Davis said, 'This is going to be a party. Two O.H.P.s and two H.S.s. What's all the flap about?'

'It's useful to know how to do a Caesar. Nobody wants to do 'em—everyone has to once in a while. Those two'—Tom and Peter had come in with John and the obstetrical men—'are on this weekend, so they've come to see how it goes.'

None of the men had recognised me, which was not surprising since all that was visible of me were my eyes and my ankles. I had somehow found another outsize gown. The rule was that you took the first in a gown pile and did not bother about size. That camouflage was one of the things I liked about the theatre; I liked watching people work and talk, and not being visible myself. John and Tom had seen me all morning without knowing that I was there. It was a restful sensation.

I went back to Sister Mary and told her the men had arrived. Then, as we had nothing to do until the patient came from Mary, I asked why the operation was necessary.

She said, 'It would not have been necessary, probably, if this silly girl had had the sense to see us—or some doctor—in time. She's one of these intellectual young women who mistake common sense for an old wives' tale. Apparently neither she nor her husband hold with ante-natal care—which may be all right if you haven't her medical history.' She explained what this was. Then she sighed. 'A Caesarian section is now our only hope if we want a live mother and a live child. And whether we get that remains to be seen.'

We heard the soft rumble of the rubber-wheeled stretcher-trolley outside. The surgeons came in in their shirt sleeves, and in the gallery four students, probably midwifery clerks from Mary, settled down in the front row, and leant forward. The staff midwife came with her cot, and went over to one of the sinks to wash. The anaesthetist, the porter Brown, and Nurse Davis wheeled in the stretcher. John said, 'Right,' and turned to the instrument trolley.

9

MY MIND DECIDES FOR ITSELF

It was very hot in the theatre that evening; far more hot than was usual because the heat had been raised intentionally to counteract the shock of birth for the child who had yet to be born. Sister Mary's forehead was purple, as if her mask was too tight; and the men, standing directly under the great light that illuminated the table, breathed as if they had been running hard.

It was very quiet; so quiet that the faint sizzling that came from the anaesthetic machine seemed deafening, the muffled clink of instruments being replaced on Sister's covered trolley was a clatter, and the throbbing of the air-plant in the roof sounded ominous. Then even those sounds seemed to stop and the three young men round the table drew back slightly and stiffened like a well-trained chorus. The fourth, Tom, was holding the silver retractors in position. John lifted the baby and held him high over the table. The baby's skin looked very white against the brown of his gloves. The baby had black hair.

'Come on, chum,' said John, 'try breathing.'

The baby hung lifeless. John slipped his hands up and held both the feet in one hand, then slapped the fat, perfect little back.

'Come on, chum,' he said again, 'say something.' He squeezed the minute chest wall, 'Sister, I may need——' but he did not need anything. The baby suddenly disapproved of his manhandling and let out a pathetic little wail. A faint sigh echoed round the theatre, as if we too had all been holding our breath.

John wrapped the baby in a clean towel and handed him to the staff midwife. 'He's all yours, Nurse.'

She took the baby and laid him in his cot. She tilted the foot of the cot, so that the baby was nearly standing on his head; he went on crying for a few minutes, and then there was silence. I had a free moment, so I crossed over to look at him. The staff midwife jerked her thumb upward. The baby was lying with one hand pressed like a starfish over his mouth. He looked very bored, and very normal.

When it was all over, and the mother had been wheeled away, John peeled off his gloves. 'Is that girl's husband around, Sister?'

She said he was waiting in Mary.

He said he was glad. 'I'd like a word with him. I think it's time someone told him the facts of life. I wonder what he would have done with his wife today if he had been somewhere where there was no general hospital on tap?'

Sister sorted her instruments. 'I understand they consider child birth a natural occurrence, and did not bother about the possibility of complications.'

John stretched his fingers. The O.H.P. whose case this was said, 'I had a chat with him, sir, but I don't know that he took in any of what I was saying.'

'He didn't, eh?' John took off his cap and gown and dropped them on the table. The other men did the same, with the exception of Peter, who dropped his on the floor and then stepped on the gown as he walked out of the theatre.

Sister said, 'I think that husband thought I was just a fussy old woman.'

'One of those?' John nodded to himself, then smiled briefly. 'Right.' He nodded again, at her this time. 'Thank you, Sister— I'll see you in Mary later,' and followed the other men to the surgeons' room.

Sister Mary—who, like all midwives, could at times be terrifying, but was always more human than any general ward sister could ever be—said with satisfaction, 'Well, Nurse Shaw —there is one husband who is going to have the fear of God put into him! And he deserves it. The selfish boy.' She pushed her trolley towards me. 'I dislike doing this, Nurse, but I'm afraid you must do my cleaning for me. I must get back to Mary.'

I said Nurse Davis and I would be happy to clear up. 'We've nothing else to do now.'

She surprised me by thanking me for what we had done. 'You must come along to Mary and see that baby. He's a lovely child.'

When she had gone I called Davis. 'You had better go to first

116

supper. I'll start on this mess and go when you get back. We ought to eat now as we're free, in case anything else comes up.'

She agreed. 'This is obviously one of those days. What do you think we'll get next?'

'I dunno. What have we had, general—urological—and now midder? Oh, we haven't had any fractures, and it's not yet eight! Lots of time before we finish.'

She looked at the mackintosh sink. 'And lots of scrubbing. Do you know, Nurse, until I worked here I always thought everything stopped when the case ended?'

I said I had thought the same. 'I'm not all that keen on scrubbing brushes. Maybe that's why I'm no theatre girl. I'd rather be asked to boil an egg.'

She laughed and went out to change.

I washed the dishes and bowls, stacked the sterilisers, switched on the electricity, and placed the large silver egg-timers on each steriliser as I closed the lid. The sand dropped slowly through the glass waists. I washed the trolleys with carbolic solution, then remembered the nailbrushes, and had to dirty one of the sterilisers. I took a bowl, scrubbing brush, soap, and clean cloth, and started on the table.

My hands were busy, but my mind was now tolerably free. I wondered what John was saying to that husband. I wondered when I would have the opportunity to tell Peter what I thought of surgeons who dropped their gowns on the floor for nurses to pick up. I thought about that baby and what would have happened if he had not started breathing. And then I thought about midwifery generally, and whether I would train for that when I finished here in a few months. I had never bothered about my future previously, not only because of Peter, but because I knew my record here was reasonably good, and even if I was not in the gold-medal class I had a fair chance of getting that staff nurse's job in Christian. That would fill the next year, and beyond that I had never looked. Well, that job would not be mine now; Matron would not, and probably could not, overlook that business in Robert, so I would have to think of something else.

Peter? Not him. Not any longer. Tom and Carol had only told me what my subconscious had always known, and his recent behaviour merely underlined. He never had the faintest intention of marrying me, or to give him his due, had pretended that he had. I could hardly blame him for not fulfilling my wishful thinking.

Midder, I decided glumly, seemed the only answer. But did I really want to do midder? I did not.

I straightened my back; the water in my bowl was too cold,

and I needed a refill. I carried the bowl half-way across the theatre and then stopped. What did I want to do? I had to do something.

And then a most peculiar thought arrived in my brain. Two words, unasked and unexplained, that shook me physically as well as mentally. I dropped the bowl I was holding, then gaped idiotically at the mess on the floor. A steriliser spluttered and boiled over. I leapt at it, switched it off, and stupidly pulled back the lid. Quite naturally, a cloud of boiling steam hit my forehead. I yelped and jumped back.

A voice behind me said calmly, 'Nurse, have you gone quite mad? Don't you know that steam burns?'

I turned round, cursing inwardly. What on earth had he to come back for? I said, 'Thank you very much; it was nothing, Mr Dexter.'

He ignored my words and wandered round the theatre. 'Where's the soda bic.?' He took down the large glass jar marked 'Soda Bic.' from its place on the glass shelf by one of the sinks.

'Come here, Nurse. Take off that mask, and let me see what you've done to your face.'

I did as he said. He looked up from the solution of the stuff he was mixing in a small bowl. 'Oh. I hadn't realised you were behind that yashmak, Nurse Snow. I should have guessed. Come and put this on that forehead of yours.'

I felt an utter fool. 'It really is quite all right, thank you.'

He reached for the unsterile swab jar. 'Don't be absurd, Nurse. You don't want a blistered forehead, and you'll get one if you don't do something about it. Now, stand still and look up.'

I had expected him to leave me to apply the wretched stuff, but he did it himself, and since I could scarcely wrench the swab from his fingers I again did as he said. He did not take long, and then he threw the swab into one of the dirty-dressing buckets and looked at my forehead critically.

'Shift around, the light's behind you—I can't see if the line of demarcation has gone.'

'It isn't stinging any more.' I half turned. 'Has it?'

He looked down at me. 'Going. Did it hurt much?'

'Not really. Just gave me a bit of a shock. Good thing I had a mask on.'

He said dryly, 'Very good. How long have you been behind that mask? I didn't know you were in the theatre. You've done your time here, surely?'

'Oh, yes. Last summer.'

He washed out the bowl, left it to dry, and washed his hands.

'I remember. You were in on that last Caesar they did here. The one Mr Craddock did.'

I was quite surprised that he should remember so well. He had never given any sign of knowing that I existed at that time. I agreed that I had seen the previous Caesar in this theatre.

'Are you back for good?'

'Only one day, as far as I know.'

He smiled slightly. 'You're having quite a postgraduate tour of the departments, Nurse. Good experience.'

I said, 'Perhaps I need it—if I do daft things like leaning over a boiling steriliser.'

He said, 'Perhaps you do.' Then he asked me why I had dropped that bowl.

'Oh—that bowl?'

He nodded. 'Did you just feel you had to throw something?'

'No.' I hesitated. 'I just dropped it.'

He said mildly, 'That's what it looked like. Most extraordinary sight—a respectable Joe's nurse suddenly heaving bowls around an empty theatre.'

'Well—I didn't know anyone was watching.'

He seemed much amused. 'I was aware of that. I only came back for my watch—I'd left it somewhere and thought it might be by our sink.'

'I'm afraid you haven't. I've cleared over there and there was no watch about.'

He stepped across the pool on the floor and saw that I was right.

'Perhaps it's in Henry.'

'Yes. I hope so,' I said vaguely. I had noticed that all the egg-timers had run through.

He saw the direction in which I was looking. 'Instruments boiling to a jelly?' he inquired pleasantly. 'Hadn't you better get them out? Only watch out for the steam.'

'I think I had better.' I turned off the heat, stood back, and opened the lids gingerly.

He said, 'Nurse, before you start, hand me that squeegee beside you, please.'

I did as he asked automatically, then realised what he proposed doing. 'I'm going to do that later, Mr Dexter.'

He took the squeegee from me. 'You haven't got any sharps cooking in there, I hope?'

I said the needles, knives, and scissors were soaking in carbolic. 'Please don't bother about the floor.'

He was obviously in a very good humour tonight, and he had reason to be. He had had a successful day; eight adult patients were the better for his surgery, and in Mary there was a black-haired baby, who, but for him, might have been dead tonight, and there was his tea-party. Sister O.P.s was free, and I wondered if he had been out with her. By the way he was smiling, I thought it must have been a successful tea.

'You get on with your instruments, Nurse,' he said calmly, as he pushed the rubber squeegee and the water across the floor to the curved drain. The floor was almost dry when he finished; he left the squeegee to drip in the drain and washed his hands again.

'I have to go up to Henry now; I'll see if they found any spare watches there.' He walked over to the trolley on which I was unloading the steaming instruments. 'I hope we don't have to bother this theatre again tonight.' He picked up an artery forceps, swung it by the thumb grip to cool it, tested the spring, then snapped it shut. He replaced it in one corner of the trolley, as if it was the marker on a parade ground.

I said I hoped he would find his watch and I hoped there would be no more operations necessary that night. I thanked him for doing my floor. He nodded absently as if he was not listening.

'Turn to the light again, Nurse; let's see that forehead.'

I raised my chin and twisted my head round, reluctantly. I was very conscious of the fact that the steam and the soda bic. must have removed the last traces of powder from my forehead as successfully as my mask invariably removed it from the rest of my face. The only consolation was that he was unlikely to notice that I resembled a boiled egg; that my turban had risen and was now high on the back of my head, giving me a slightly Mongolian appearance because it took my hair with it, and the hair pulled on the skin of my brow. The light was directly on my face as he had requested, so I could not look up; I looked instead at his neat white shirt and sober tie (S.S.O.s always wear sober ties), and thought of my irrational dislike of men who wear coloured shirts. Peter once had a pink one; it took me months to get over the shock.

He said, 'Right. You can be quite happy about that. No marks.'

Oddly, he did not sound at all happy, and when I looked at him his expression had altered. He looked as if he was regretting having wasted the last ten minutes in here, and murmured, 'Good night, Nurse,' so formally that I was very sure he was. I said, 'Thank you, Mr Dexter, good night,' in a similar tone. I knew my place; I was quite happy to stay in it; I had not sought his ministrations or assistance. I made quite a point of telling myself all this as I heard him walk out of the theatre corridor. But when the outer door had closed and I was alone, I discovered I had picked up the artery forceps with which he had been fiddling. I held it in my hand for a long time and looked at it although it was not the first artery forcep I had ever seen. Then I put it back on the trolley and went on drying the others. The light behind me caught the metal instruments, and they glittered as if they were really silver and not merely plated.

Lisa limped into my room when I was undressing.

'Dear girl, my feet are killing me. This ward work is too much for a decadent O.P.s girl. I'm going to make some tea. Want some?'

'Love it.' I told her about my day in the theatre. 'It was such a relief to work with a pleasant Sister again.'

She said she was delighted to hear it; she personally wouldn't know. 'Dear Sister Ellen and dear Sister Out-Patients are blood-brothers—I won't say Sisters; I loathe puns.'

I giggled feebly and said Carol got along all right with Sister Ellen, and maybe Sister Ellen was just allergic to jobbers.

'She's always been allergic to me,' said Lisa sadly. 'She gave me hell while I was a pro—and she gave me hell today, the dear one. But I'm happy you were rescued from the stock scissors in O.P.s. Making stock all day is the bottom.'

'Oh, no!' I threw off my dressing-gown and pulled on my dress and blue belt. 'Lisa!' I struggled with my collar. 'I opened the department this morning and I haven't shut it. I'll have to go back.'

She groaned sympathetically. 'You will, dear girl. Sister will tear you to teeny weeny little pieces in the morning if you don't. Nip off, and I'll have the tea all set when you get back.'

I rushed downstairs, across the park, and through the hospital to Out-Patients. Fortunately I met no one, and I was able to close all the windows and doors I had opened, check on whether or not I had turned on the radiators (I had not), and leave it all as it had been when I arrived there alone this morning. I had switched off the last light, and was about to leave, when I heard someone coming down the stairs. I stepped back into the first dark doorway and waited. Two people came down the stairs and then walked along the corridor in the opposite direction to my doorway. They switched on the corridor light, but did not look round. I stepped gingerly round and up the stairs. I was moving slowly in order to be quiet. I had seen who it was, and as I went up the stairs I could not help overhearing a fragment of their conversation.

John said, 'I'm sorry to have been so late this afternoon.'

Sister O.P.s said that really didn't matter at all, she had so much to do over in the Home. 'But I wanted to see you tonight to ask you about your letter——' I heard a door close and nothing more. They must have gone into her duty-room.

Why not? I suddenly felt very tired. It was her duty-room. I went quickly up the rest of the stairs to the first floor, then along the corridor, and down by the next staircase. As I reached the main corridor that joined all the ground floors of the hospital I saw Peter loitering by the statue of one of our famous deceased physicians. Without stopping to consider why I did it, I shot into one of the telephone booths that lined that particular stretch of the corridor and, turning my back on him, pretended to make a call. After a little while I glanced round and saw he had gone, so I left the booth. Outside in the darkness of the park I smiled at my cloak and dagger act, but I was not really amused—I was only very puzzled.

When I was in that booth I had looked at my reflection in the small glass. There was no sign of any scalding on my forehead. If I had been alone like most nurses I should have done nothing but curse the perversity of sterilisers, and probably have had a blistered face as a result. I did not feel that it made any odds if a face like mine was blistered or not. It was too thin and too pale, and the only colour anywhere was in my eyebrows and eyes, if near black is a colour. That mirror had only confirmed the suspicions I had had since childhood, that I resembled a horse that had gone into a decline. If only, I thought, as I reached the steps of our Home, I had golden hair and violet eyes, I would not have to skulk in phone boxes because I looked too plain to meet my young man. I was quite savage about all this until I realised that my skulking in that phone box had had nothing whatever to do with Peter.

Lisa said the tea was stewing nicely and any moment now should be drinkable. 'O.P.s all serene?'

'Quite serene. I nipped in and out like a ghost.'

She glanced at me casually, then looked back a second time. 'You look rather like a ghost—has that miserable man been upsetting you again?'

'No. Actually he's been rather nice this evening. And he did a good job of work on that Caesar. He got a lovely baby.'

'Dear Gillian,' she said patiently, 'since when have the dear house-surgeons been doing Caesars?'

'Oh—you mean Peter?' I shook my head. 'No—he hasn't been upsetting me. I've been too busy today to remember his existence—apart from the time when he dropped his gown on the floor.' I told her how this had infuriated me.

'The devil.' But she was still looking at me in that peculiar manner. 'Gill, you sure you're all right? You look sort of pale green.'

I murmured, 'A pale green horse,' and then said more clearly that it must be the light.

She smiled. 'Not to mention the late hours you've been keeping?'

'Only on Friday. Have a heart, Lisa—I was in bed by ten last night.'

'Ten!' She poured out the tea. 'Dear girl, you aren't talking to Home Sister. Tom was standing in for Peter, and Tom told me this morning that he didn't stop standing until after one. Was it a good party?'

'I wouldn't know.' She stared at me. 'That's true, Lisa. I was back here shortly after nine. I don't know what happened to Peter after that—I thought he was on, but I could be wrong. It was Saturday night, and there's always some party somewhere on Saturday night, so presumably he went on to it. But not with me.'

Lisa clasped her hands. 'Dear girl, I'm terribly sorry. I was so certain he was with you. I knew he'd come to the department to ask for you, and then you weren't at supper and I worked it out.' She frowned. 'And Tom said so too, after supper when Blakelock and I were making stock, and he drifted by and was feeling chatty. And then our John also drifted by and asked Tom how long he was going to hold the fort for Kier, and dear Tom said, "Long as the party lasts, sir, I take it." '

I asked what John had said.

She grinned. 'John got all matey and asked where was the party, and Tom decided to be a devil and said that the lads were celebrating somewhere in the Medical school, but he thought this specific party was Nurse Snow.' She clearly expected some reaction, so I grinned back and asked how John had taken that?

'How would you expect dear Mr Dexter to take that? He raised his eyebrows and pulled some of his hair out, and said wasn't that nice, and please, Nurse Blakelock, could he have Mrs Smith's, Brown's, or Jones' follow-up notes, as he wanted to look up something.' She became serious. 'Gill, I wish I hadn't told you that.' She handed me a cup. 'Drink up. It's getting cold.'

'That's all right.' I asked if she had had a pleasant chat with Tom.

'Quite pleasant,' she said, and changed the subject, as she always did before long when Tom's name cropped up in the conversation. 'Have you to go back to the theatre tomorrow?'

I had not previously been able to understand her reticence to discuss Tom. She was reticent about no one and nothing else. Now I could understand, dimly. And I wanted to reassure her, not only because of what she had just said. I did not know how to do it, so I plunged straight in.

'Lisa, you do realise you don't have to worry about Tom and me?'

'Eh? How's that?' she asked lightly. 'Why should I panic about dear Tom and you or anyone?'

'Why should you?' I agreed. 'But you do.'

She looked at me, then grimaced. 'Wow! That hurt. Tell

me—was that a good guess, or am I that obvious?'

'You aren't obvious at all, and it wasn't a guess. I've known for the last few days—but I didn't know what I could do about it.'

She said dryly, 'Which makes two of us.' Then she smiled, not very happily. 'I wasn't worried about your side of it, but I wondered about Tom. I know he likes you a lot.'

'He wants me to be a sister to him,' I said simply, 'which shows.'

'Dear girl—you are telling me. What do you think I am? That man,' she said vehemently, 'collects sisters! It's agin nature. We've been pals for years—little schoolmates. That's what's so damned awful. He's so used to me that I'm as about as exciting as an old stethoscope.'

I said, 'How long, Lisa?'

She sighed. 'Years—I've always been this way about him.' Her sigh ended in a laugh. 'Under my flippant exterior, dear girl, beats an astonishingly faithful heart. It astonishes me. I never knew I was gold, pure gold, within—but I am. Poor Tom would have a stroke if he so much as suspected how I felt. He'd think it highly improper.'

I thought it over. 'I don't think he would.'

She spilled her tea, and her apron was ruined. She stared at it mournfully. 'Clean this evening.' Then she looked back at me. 'Say that again.'

I said it again.

She mopped her apron absently. 'And you find that technique works?'

'No, quite the reverse. That was where I've gone wrong. But perhaps, if you're crafty, you can profit by my mistakes.'

Lisa said I was speaking in the best tradition of a true St Joseph's nurse.

'That's me,' I agreed, 'Sister Tutor's blue-eyed girl. Even if they are black and I make the odd drug mistake. What does a little missing poppy matter? But don't deflect me, girl, I'm giving birth. To get back to Peter.' I was not wearing an apron, so that I could hug my knees with impunity. 'I think I've gone wrong through letting him see how much I liked him.'

'But, according to the books, dear girl, nothing builds up a lad's ego as much as an adoring young woman.'

'The books aren't always right,' I said sententiously. 'As Tom would say, fact. It didn't work with Peter—it'—I shrugged—'bored him. Yes, I know you think he has a thing for me,' I added quickly, as I saw she was about to interrupt, 'so he has—in a very minor way. I amuse him, and he's a possessive type, so he's hung on to me. It's been something to do in the long winter evenings.'

124

She said, 'Forgive me—but didn't you say everything was fine and dandy last night?'

'Oh yes, it was. He whispered sweet nothings into my ear and held my hand in the park, but he always does. It's his only line with a young woman. If he's not necking he doesn't know what to do.' I caught her eye and nodded. 'Yes, duckie. I have at last discovered that for myself. Taken a long time, I admit, but I'm no bright girl.'

She smiled, not unkindly, 'Very rude awakening?'

'Oddly, no. It just came; and there I was awake. And come to think of it'—I was getting fascinated by my theme—'I believe he only took me out last night because Tom asked me to that dance. He probably felt he had missed something Tom saw in me. Then he discovered something—that he hadn't. So he brought me home and went on to another party.'

She said she hated to rub this in, but if my approach was such a miserable failure with Peter, why did I consider it would work with Tom?

'Tom isn't Peter,' I said obviously; 'he's a very different breed. He's good-natured and rather sweet. I know you know him very well, and he's a tolerably new buddy to me, but that probably makes me see him more clearly than you. I liked him very much in Robert; he was nice to the men and used to get really worked up when they were ill. He's got a kind heart —and, having all those sisters, he's not conceited.'

She laughed. 'He comes in the middle. His mama tried to spoil him, but the Thanet girls weren't having any. No he's not conceited.'

'Which reminds me——' I told her about his kissing me. 'There was nothing to it, but I'm telling you in case that wretched woman makes a song and dance about it when she comes back tomorrow. She never lets an opportunity to crack go by.'

Lisa said Sister not only might make the crack; she already had.

'She had coffee with Blakelock in the canteen after lunch yesterday—I suppose she drifted over from the home to see her beloved John. You knew she hadn't gone away for the week-end?' I nodded. I knew. 'Blakelock told me all as an item of gossip over the cotton wool on Saturday evening. She had no conception that it affected me and said she had been very glad to hear it, which annoyed Sister more than somewhat. Blakelock also said she hoped it showed that you were getting dear Peter out of your system. She—she doesn't go for Peter, much.'

'I gathered that. But, Lisa, you didn't hold that against me? That was nice of you.'

She coloured slightly, 'I didn't love it, but I didn't lose any

125

sleep. Why shouldn't he kiss you? It's a free country.'

I said I still thought it was very nice of her. 'You must do something about Tom. You and he make a good pair.'

'Do I throw my arms round him in O.P.s tomorrow?'

I smiled. 'That mightn't be such a bad idea at that. But you've got the general effect. Try less of the old-pal-of-me-youth angle and a little more of the little woman.'

She snorted. 'Can you see me as a little woman?'

'You'll have to do it,' I said sternly. 'Practise simpering.' She experimented in front of the glass. 'He'll run screaming if I do this!'

'Rubbish. Flap your eyelashes. Watch Sister; she's got it taped.'

I went on to say that, although very bad at my own affairs, I thought I was splendid at running other people's. Then I recollected how I had upset Carol. 'I take that back. Only some other people's.'

'How's that?'

I was worried about Carol. I hated to have hurt her, no matter how inadvertently. I told Lisa what had happened.

She said sensibly, 'I don't suppose she took serious exception. You and she are buddies. You don't take exception if you're fond of a person.'

I thought, that's true.

'Do you think she was warning me about Peter? Do you think he used his line on her at the dance?'

'Looks like it,' she said reluctantly. 'Do you mind very much about all this?'

'I haven't had time to work out whether I minded or not. This has been quite a weekend.'

'Think of it now. No time like the present for facing unpalatable facts—and I'll stand by with hot tea.'

'Right.' I looked at her. 'So Peter is having a splendid time gallivanting with one and all? And last night I was the first instalment of his evening's entertainment?'

She said, 'Right.'

I looked at her, and she looked at me anxiously. Then, quite suddenly, I wanted to do something I had never before been able to do about Peter.

I relaxed, lay back on her bed, and rocked with laughter.

I laughed and laughed, and when she saw that this was no act and I really was shouting the place down, she laughed too.

'Dear girl,' she spluttered when she had breath for speech, 'I can't tell you how glad I am you've seen the light. I never fancied that supercilious young man for you. If he had lost his head and married you he would have made you utterly miserable.' She grew serious. 'You know, losing that morph. was the

126

best thing that ever happened to you. It made things come to a head. Good thing.'

I agreed that it had done that. I was not yet sure if it was such a good thing. A lot of peculiar things had been happening to me in the last few weeks, and my new outlook on Peter was not the least peculiar.

She dropped on to the bed beside me. 'Gill—who took that stuff?'

I said, 'No! No! No! Not again! We've been into it too many times. Please!'

She was not to be put off. 'But it went.'

'Dispenser's mistake.' I was firm. 'Can't be anything else. Who wants a grain?'

She ignored me. 'Not Tom'—she ticked him off on her fingers—'wouldn't be John—not the pro, she'd be scared—Carol's your pal——' She gazed at me triumphantly and tapped her thumb. 'Do you suppose Peter took it? I've never dared ask you before.'

'Just for sheer devilment?'

She shrugged. 'It did bring things to a head. Maybe he was worried—thought you had him hooked.'

'No,' I said thoughtfully, 'he wouldn't have done that. Peter's no fool. Only a fool or a lunatic would have touched that stuff.' I told her now what John had said in the park. 'It didn't add up. It just doesn't.'

She yawned. 'So we blame the dispenser?'

'No one else does—but I do.'

I went back to my room shortly after that. There was a note from Home Sister on my pillow. 'If you get this before ten-thirty, will you please come to my office.'

It was ten-fifteen. I tidied my hair, put on a cap and cuffs, and rushed along to the lift with my heart in my mouth. What had I lost in the theatre tonight? What had I forgotten to do?

Sister called me in calmly. 'I'm glad you were back in time, Nurse Snow. Theatre working late?'

I said I had been drinking tea with Nurse Smith.

She inclined her head graciously. 'I merely wanted to see you as I knew you would want to hear about Nurse Ash.

'Nurse Ash, Sister?'

She said Carol was very poorly and had been admitted to Susan, the sick nurses' ward, with acute bronchitis.

'I'm very sorry, Sister. How did she get it? She was fine on Friday night.'

'Nurse Ash apparently had a temperature this morning. The foolish child did not report sick, but hoped that she would be fit for duty tonight after a day in bed. Fortunately Sister Ellen noticed how ill she looked immediately Nurse reported for duty. Sister took her temperature. It was over one hundred and three, so she sent for Dr Cutler, and he sent Nurse to Susan.'

'Was she all right last night, Sister?'

Sister's brows drew together. 'Nurse Ash was off duty last night, Nurse. You must have seen her at the party in the Medical School? You both asked for late leave.'

I reminded her politely that I had not asked for late leave and had come in early. She turned the pages of her Late In book absently.

'You're quite right, Nurse. I checked you in myself. That is why I like to have it all written down—I do get so muddled at times.' She beamed at me. 'I know why I thought you must be together—because of Mr Kier.'

'Mr Kier, Sister?'

'Yes, Nurse.' She told me that she had seen Peter call for me at seven, and then met him later coming out of the Night Nurses' Home with Carol. 'And knowing that you and Nurse Ash are great friends, I assumed that you must have been at the same party.'

I said, 'Yes, Sister.'

She said she would let me know when Carol was allowed visitors. 'That was all I had to tell you, Nurse. Good night.'

Lisa was coming out of the bathroom when I got up to our floor. 'Where are you off to in your cap and cuffs? Theatre call?'

'Home Sister.' I told her Carol was ill. 'The poor girl! How on earth did she pick it up?'

'Nights,' I said shortly. 'You can pick up anything on nights. And she's not a girl for the fresh air. She hasn't had my farm-yard upbringing, and now that I'm off nights, and not handy to drag her round the park in the morning, she probably never sets foot out of the building.'

'Fresh air,' she lectured, 'is the thing for a night nurse, if you want to stay a night nurse. Otherwise you never see the light of day for three months.'

'You do have nights off.'

She said she was on a soap-box and was not going to be pulled off it with frivolous talk of nights off. 'Show me one nurse, dear girl, who doesn't spend her entire nights off asleep.'

'I've got you there,' I said slowly, 'Carol. Sister told me she was off last night as well, although I didn't know it.'

Lisa was a bright girl. She said, 'She wouldn't perchance have been dear Peter's second instalment?'

'Apparently.'

Another girl came into the corridor. 'Don't you O.P.s girls ever go to bed?'

128

'Never,' said Lisa, 'the ever-open eyes, that's us. But we won't disturb your beauty sleep, dear Nurse—we're going to Gill's room to put up our feet for the odd hour before dawn.' She swept me along the corridor with her and in to my own room. When she had closed the door she said, 'Maybe we ought to have another good laugh?'

'I dunno.' I unbuttoned my collar. 'Maybe we should.'

She said kindly, 'He may have just rung her when he got back—or something. He probably felt at a loose end—had the night free and didn't know you were determined to get back early.'

'He didn't have to know. My invite was quite specific—two hours. I thought he was on at nine.'

She had another idea. 'Perhaps Sister mistook him for someone else. The place is stiff with fair-haired housemen. And Sister's an old waffler at times.'

'Could be that.'

She redraped her dressing-gown around herself. 'Supposing it was him—so what? Don't forget he now rates nothing so much as a hearty laugh.'

I said, 'I wasn't bothering about him.'

She said gently, 'I didn't think you were,' and we looked at each other in a gloomy silence.

I broke it. 'Lisa—where have I gone wrong?'

She did not answer me directly. 'You are pretty fond of Carol, aren't you?'

I nodded. 'We've always got along so well—and although we aren't really alike, we've roughly complemented each other. We liked the same things—we worked together a lot as pros—and she was wonderful to me during my first year.'

Lisa said, 'You had a black first year, dear girl.' Her expression was very sweet. 'I remember you went off to stay with the Ashes that first Christmas. You liked them, didn't you?'

'Immensely.'

'Gill.' She was suddenly brisk. 'Aren't we making far too much of all this? Even supposing it was Peter—well, now you don't mind, what of it?'

I said, 'I don't give a damn about Peter, but I give several for Carol.' I smiled with humour. 'No doubt Freud would have a word for our relationship. I just know I like her as much as I like anyone in this world, and I hate to think that for some reason she's avoiding me and didn't tell me she was off or going out.'

'She was feeling ill. This bug was cooking yesterday.'

'All the more reason—she had only to crawl to the corridor phone to have an S.R.N. on unofficial tap. She knew I'd be off duty some time. I could have got her some aspirin or tea or something.'

Lisa said she simply had to have a cigarette, and when I produced one she gazed at the lighted end as if it was a strange and beautiful object.

'I wonder if dear Peter asked her not to tell you.'

'But she wouldn't take any notice——' I broke off as I grasped her meaning. 'You think—she and Peter——?'

She spread her hands expressively but said nothing.

'I never thought of that, Lisa.'

She said she had a Gallic mind. 'I always think of these things, dear girl. Sleep on it—it might account for a lot. And now I must go to bed.' She collected her washing things which were now strewn around my room, rewrapped her dressing-gown, and left me.

For once I did not drop asleep immediately I was in bed. I thought about Carol. Peter and Carol. And then I thought how strange that sounded, but how it was no more strange than the odd thought I had in the theatre, and which had caused me to drop that bowl. I fingered my forehead in the dark; it was not even a little sore. I hoped I would be able to see Carol soon; I wanted to tell her that as far as I was concerned she was welcome to Peter. I decided to be tactful about this; no wonder she had been so annoyed with me at that dance. I smiled to myself. At last something added up. I turned over and went to sleep.

10

OUT-PATIENTS IS A TENSE DEPARTMENT

TEN days passed before I was allowed to see Carol. Her bronchitis turned to bronchial pneumonia, and she took longer than usual to respond to the anti-biotics with which she was being treated. I inquired daily in Susan; Sister Susan took the flowers, magazines, or notes I brought with an adamant 'Not today, Nurse Snow. Perhaps, tomorrow!'

Matron, unfortunately for me, produced a spare staff nurse to take the place of the scarlet-fevered Nurse Brent, so I was sent back to O.P.s and my children. I enjoyed the children, but found the department over-heated, over-full, and, what with the constant presence of a disapproving Sister, over-powering. I was not alone in this; one of the probationers handed in her notice, a second demanded to be transferred from O.P.s, and even Nurse Blakelock looked haggard and as if she had dropped from her normal twelve stone to a wornout ten.

John was around the department as usual, and when he was

about Sister was more often than not with him. But she seemed to take no comfort from his presence, and in his absence became quite unbearable. A Sister makes or mars a ward or department. The work was the same as it had always been, Blakelock was sweet and soothing, but not even the patients and a pleasant staff nurse can compensate for an unhappy Sister, and she must have been miserable to have spread her gloom around as she did. O.P.s became an unhappy department, and we nurses lived for our own—and Sister's—off-duty.

I watched John to see if he noticed the increased tension among the staff. If he did he gave no sign, but the housemen were well aware of the situation.

'So help me, Gill,' said Tom, 'you girls are sterling characters, but now I loathe this place. Fact. Even old Rufford's caught on. Heard him creating in the canteen the other day. Wanted to know what had got into the department—apparently his clinic had been messed up.'

'It certainly was messed up.' I told him how Sister had played havoc with the appointments list, to the fury of the mothers and the dismay of the almoner. And then she thought it would be quicker if we did things according to St Martha's methods. 'We did it,' I said grimly, 'but we won't do it again! Rufford nearly went through the roof. She wanted kids only in here—Mums outside.'

He grinned, then, as Sister appeared at the far end of the corridor, rushed on. She had seen him, of course. She sailed up to me.

'Nurse Snow, if I find you neglecting your duties again and flirting with the house-surgeons I shall send you straight to Matron.'

I said, 'Yes, Sister.' She knew quite well I had an empty room and was waiting for the first patients to arrive. I would have liked to have advised her not to say 'flirting.' It dated her. I put her age at least ten years above my own on that showing.

That evening she was off. Before she went she left instructions that Nurses Smith and Snow were to scrub out the splint cupboard before going to supper. The splint cupboard was the pros' province, but we were so delighted at the prospect of having her out of the department that we would gladly have scrubbed each of the ten waiting-rooms.

'This is sheer bliss,' said Lisa, as she arrived with the bowl of water. 'Peace, perfect peace—and dear old Blakelock in the office, smiling! Imagine that, Gill—smiling! Some one loves us after all!'

I rolled up my sleeves. 'Poor old Blakelock—she has the worst of it. Fancy having to staff to someone like that—for a two-year stretch! No wonder she's lost weight.'

131

'Before she goes, dear girl, our chubby Blakelock'll have a waist like yours.' She shuddered. 'Thank heaven my days are numbered. I've done over four months. I must be off any moment—or I'll go to Matron like that kid Martin. You watch out. And I'll tell Matron why. I'll tell her'—she climbed on a stool—'that if I haven't wept by eleven each morning I consider it's a bumper day—and how poor little pros are all reduced to acute melancholia. Heck.'

'What's up?'

She said she was not tall enough.

'Come down, and I'll do the top.' We changed over. 'But, Lisa, what's got into her lately? Why is she so much worse? I'd have thought everything was what the doctor ordered. She's got John in her pocket—what more does she want? If she doesn't like the job why on earth did she take it?'

Lisa removed a pile of aeroplane splints from the next shelf.

'What makes you so certain he's in her pocket?'

I soaped the brush. 'Obvious.'

'No more obvious than before. I know he took her to the dance, but he has to take someone, and it has to be a Sister. That's positively traditional.'

I said unthinkingly, 'Is it also traditional for S.S.O.s to have tête-à-têtes with Sisters in darkened departments?'

'How's that? Having a which with who?'

Having said so much, I told her the rest.

'Wow! You devil, to keep that quiet all this time! But'—she tugged at my apron—'hey! when was this?'

'Weekend before last. Pass me your soap. I've dropped mine.'

She held her bar absently. 'Something mighty queer about that.'

'Why?'

'Because she's been so foul-minded since then. Haemade-mentia, plus. And she shouldn't have been. If she had had a merry weekend chez John——'

'Don't forget he was on—she can't have seen much of him——'

'Phooey. She knows the score there—she's a nurse. That wouldn't be a snag. No. They must'—she beamed up at me triumphantly—'have had harsh words that weekend. Otherwise she'd have been full of the joys of spring—like she was when she first set eyes on the dear man. And, come to think of it'—she scrubbed feverishly in her concentration on the love-life of our betters—'our John has been glowering round the hospital lately like one vast thunder cloud. Maybe that love has withered like the leaves in autumn.'

I said my heart bled for them. I was glad I was standing on that chair and well above her head. Lisa would want to know why my emotion should make me grin idiotically at the wet shelf.

'The course of true love,' she said sadly, 'runs no more smoothly for the upper classes than for a lowly fourth-year. Life is set with pitfalls. I've finished this shelf.'

'So've I.' I lifted an aged Thomas's splint off a nail by the ceiling. 'I'll do the wall. Hang on to this, honey.' She straightened and held out her arms. 'No progress with Tom?' I asked, as she clasped the long unwieldy object against her chest. 'Haven't you taken Aunty Gill's advice and let him see the lovelight?'

She shook her head mournfully. 'No dice. Look at Sister—even you. It doesn't work, Gill. Thanks, all the same. Tom doesn't see me at all these days, like I said.'

She was standing with her back to the open door. The department was officially closed, the clinics had ended, the patients gone, but our corridor was a short cut to several wards, and was used as such by the men. A trickle of white coats had drifted by in the last twenty minutes, glanced incuriously at us as we scrubbed, and passed on. Now a white coat lingered in the doorway. Tom Thanet, who could not have failed to overhear what Lisa had said, was staring at her back. I was about to welcome him, when he shook his head slightly. He did not move.

Lisa grappled with her splint. 'It's funny,' she said, 'how corny you can get. All I can think of now is how I let him slip through my hands when I was a bright young pro, and how I didn't know what I was losing until I found I'd lost him.'

Tom came in slowly. He said very quietly, 'Looking for something, Lisa?'

I got off my chair. 'I must get another brush—this one has no hairs left.' I gave them no chance to answer, but I doubted if they even heard me. Lisa was clinging to the splint and looking at Tom; Tom was gaping at her as if he had never seen her before. I thanked Heaven and Matron's Office that Sister was off and went to find Blakelock. 'Something else I can clean, Nurse? Nurse Smith is just finishing the splint cupboard.'

Blakelock nodded impassively. 'No doubt Mr Thanet can reach the top shelf.'

'Yes, Nurse.' I did not ask how she knew Tom was in there; Blakelock always knew what was happening in the department, and the knowledge never worried her, which was why she was such a good staff nurse.

She told me I could go off duty. 'I expect you want to visit Susan. How is Ash?'

'Getting on. I haven't seen her yet. Sister Susan gives me a nightly report.'

She sighed. 'Sister Susan is a Joe's girl. Makes a difference.' Which was the only criticism of Sister she ever allowed.

Sister Susan promised that I might visit Carol next evening. She asked me to fetch some of Carol's belongings.

'Now Nurse is better she will prefer her own nightgowns. And as you are her friend she will not object to your going to her drawers. I have her keys here.' She gave them to me. 'And will you bring her face powder and hair-curlers, Nurse Snow? Nurse is particularly anxious to doll herself up again.'

After supper I asked Home Sister if I might go to the Night Nurses' Home, and explained my reason.

'Of course, Nurse. You will save me a job.'

Carol was a neat person, and I found what I wanted immediately. I shut her make-up box; collected a brush and comb; pyjamas; bed-jackets; then, remembering her love of bed-socks, I opened the drawer again. I could not find them at first, so I unlocked a lower drawer. They did not appear to be there either; I shifted the clothes carefully, I did not want to untidy anything. I found a pile of bed-socks and pulled out two pairs. The toe of one of them was bulky. I smoothed it, then felt something small but hard under my hand. I shook the sock over the bed casually, wondering if some hair-curlers were caught up there. But at the same time my hands, trained to think for themselves, had recognised the familiar contours of what they had touched, even when disguised by the woollen sock. Consequently I was not very surprised when I picked off the white bed quilt four small glass ampoules of morphine sulphate. I was not very surprised, but I was very shocked. And I did not know what to do with them. I held them in the palm of my hand and jiggled them thoughtfully. Then I put back the empty socks, took an alternative pair, closed and relocked the drawers, took the things I had come to fetch over to the hospital, left them with Sister Susan, and went back to my own room.

Later, when I was in bed, someone knocked quietly on my door.

I called, 'I'm not asleep,' and reached for my bed-side lamp.

Lisa bounced in, her face illumined with happiness. 'Gill, you devil. Why didn't you tell me he was standing behind me when I was letting down my back hair?'

I blinked at the light. 'Discretion and I go hand in hand. Now tell me, how's it going?'

She flopped on to the foot of my bed and took off her shoes. She said everything was going as well as could be expected. 'But, dear girl'—her eyes danced—'I never knew anyone could be so happy.'

I lay back and smiled at her. Tonight she looked beautiful.

'So the course of true love can run smooth?'

'Wonderfully smooth. Do you know what he said?'

I said, 'That until tonight he never realised that you took anything or anyone seriously?'

Her jaw dropped, 'But that's uncanny. That's just what he did say!'

'Not uncanny. I've always thought that myself until these last weeks, and I've known you nearly four years. How did you think he could guess?'

She said she was long past thought. 'But Gill—how did you know he was even interested in me?'

'I didn't,' I said honestly, 'but I didn't see why he shouldn't be. Every other man in the hospital is, ducks, so I thought on the law of averages——'

'That's been the snag!' She clapped her hands together. 'All those stupid men—getting in the way—no, don't laugh'—she waved me down—'it's true—they're a bind and a bore. Do you know why he didn't ask me to the rugger dance?'

I shook my head.

'He was sure I was booked,' she said mournfully. 'See what being a one for the boys does for a girl! He'd got the idea I was the Toast of the Medical School and the Belle of the House-Physicians—and thought I was just bound to be booked! Everyone thought so—and I didn't go.' Her voice died away in laughter. 'Now I'll have to take the veil.' She sighed with pleasure. 'Won't it be restful?'

I asked how much progress she and Tom had made in the last three hours. 'When I left you in the splint cupboard you were barely on speaking terms.'

She said they had made quite a bit of progress. 'We've dealt with everything from engagement rings to country practices. You know how I talk, dear girl—and what with one thing and another my tongue sort of ran away with me.' She stopped short. 'I clean forgot. How was Carol?'

'I didn't see her. Sister said tomorrow.'

'That'll be nice,' she said, 'you'll be able to get everything straight then.'

I said it would be very nice, and as I knew that her delight in life would not be able to blunt her intelligence if we started discussing my affairs, I pretended to yawn. 'Sorry, ducks,' I apologised.

She jumped off my bed. 'I shouldn't have woken you! I am sorry. You look all heavy-eyed and blurry. But I had to tell you what you'd done.'

I smiled at her. 'I'm glad you did. And I can't tell you how glad I am about all this. I always said you and Tom would make a good pair.'

'Liar—you only said it a couple of weeks ago.'

I said I refused to be put off. 'Time is immaterial. Only not now it ain't—so if you don't mind, honey, I must go to sleep. Otherwise I shall be out on my two feet in O.P.s tomorrow.'

She laughed and said she would love to see Sister's face if I laid my little head on one of the benches and slept among the nippers. She said she was even looking forward to O.P.s tomorrow; that she loved everything and everyone in the department, including dear Sister, but best of all she loved the dear splint cupboard.

I woke early next morning as you always do wake early when you are worried. I lay and watched the cold grey October dawn turn into a colder and still more grey morning. The heavy clouds moved sluggishly across the sky; they were no heavier, no more threatening, than my thoughts. I wondered if I had done the right thing in getting rid of that morphia.

I was past minding its original disappearance; I was not happy about the mess it had made of my life, but I had accepted it. What I could not now accept was that Carol was responsible. And I wondered how many more of my little problems were due to her.

Peter. The change in his attitude since that night. I had automatically assumed he had cooled towards me because I was under a cloud. But I now remembered that only on that night had he grasped that she was Ashton Ash's daughter. He was a practical young man, and not one to confuse business with pleasure. If Carol had shown herself even mildly willing he would have had no compunction in transferring his attentions to her. And in fairness, why should I blame him? We were not and never had been engaged and, as Lisa had said, a rich wife is as useful to an ambitious young doctor as to any other man.

I smiled wryly; that last date I had with him—why had he asked me? Relaxation before the serious business of the evening? Or had he told her he just had to ask poor old Gillian—she was so blue—and had they enjoyed a splendid laugh over it?

I did not mind them laughing; I had no feelings at all about that angle, no gloom to spare from the shock that Carol had taken that wretched stuff—that, and the general depression I felt these days. But why she should have done anything so infantile and pointless I could not understand. What had she to gain? It was so stupid.

I longed to be able to unburden to someone. I could not talk to Lisa about all this. It would not be fair to hand her this baby; she might feel that something should be done about it, or she might tell Tom, and somehow it would get around. Everything got around Joe's. It was a chatty hospital.

I stopped pretending to myself and thought how much I would like to talk to John. I let my mind relax into a glorious bout of wishful thinking in which there were no Sister O.P.s, Matrons, inquisitive colleagues, or traditional barriers between myself and him. I thought how restful he was, how kind, and above all how sensible. I could do with some of his sense, and his strength. That quality, where he was concerned, was not only physical.

It was not yet seven, but I got up quickly. There was no future in this kind of wishful thinking. I dressed and went over to breakfast, where for the only occasion in my training I found I was the first nurse in the dining-room.

My room was busy that day. Mr Rufford had an orthopaedic clinic all morning, and from one-thirty to four John took a mammoth general surgical clinic. The benches were full of old appendices, repairs, removed glands, and an occasional once-fractured skull that should really have been seen by Mr Ravel the cranial surgeon, if Mr Ravel had not been occupied in the theatre with a freshly broken head.

Clifford Brown was one of these old injuries. He was a small ten-year-old who had fallen from a ruined building on a bomb site two years ago. He had fallen on his head and had been dangerously ill in Christian for several months when he was first admitted. He had been home two or three times and then returned to Christian for varying periods; the last of these coincided with my time there as a relief night senior this previous spring.

Technically he was too old for a children's ward. Eight was the usual age limit, but since he was a special case he had been nursed in the small room which lay off the main ward. He slept badly and was much disturbed by headaches; consequently he was a law unto himself, and when he did get to sleep was never woken for anything. Meals, teaching rounds, washing, and so on were arranged to suit him, and not the other way around. For some reason he slept best in the day-time, and generally ate his meals with us at night.

He loved being read to and above all he loved poems. Whenever we were quiet we read to him in turns during the night, and when we were not quiet—which was more often than not— I used to lift him out of bed, wrap him in a blanket, and carry him back to the centre table in the ward, from where I could keep an eye on the other children, write the night reports, and read or recite to him in the intervals. He and I passed a good many hours this way, while I whispered the King's Breakfast or the saga of King John who was not a good man. I often wondered how none of these ever penetrated to my night reports. Clifford had a passion for those two above all others, with the Hunting of the Snark as a runner-up.

His mother pushed forward his wheel-chair that afternoon

137

and smiled with relief when she recognised me. 'Ever so grateful it's you, Nurse Snow. I was just wondering how I was going to manage. My man's on nights and I had to leave the baby with me neighbour. My man said as he'd get his own tea and for me not to worry if Cliff and me was kept, but I know he won't wake until the last second—gets that tired, he does—and it worries me, him going off without a proper meal.' She asked if she could leave Cliff with me and come back for him later. 'You'll be all right with Nurse Snow, won't you, duck?'

Cliff lowered one near-transparent, blue-veined eyelid knowingly.

'Hi-ya, Nurse—know any more of them stories?' Then with an adult look he nodded to his mother. 'I'll be O.K., Mum. Don't you worry.'

I did not care for the expression on his face. It was too wise. Not precocious, but unnaturally wise. No small boy should have that much wisdom.

'Of course I'll look after him, Mrs Brown. How's he been?'

He had only been sent home because there was nothing more the hospital could do for him. He would have to come in again soon. His mother brought him out to Out-Patients weekly, and every week she drew me aside and whispered as she did now, 'He does look a mite better, don't you think, duck? His dad was saying this morning as he's got quite a nice little colour these days. You see it too, don't you, Nurse?'

Every week I had lied. I lied again today. He seemed to me to be fading weekly. His parents adored him and would have given their right hands for him, but it needed more than that to stop the tumour that was growing in his brain as a result of that accident.

Clifford looked at me reassuringly. 'I'm O.K., Nurse.'

'Just a fraud, Cliff?'

'That's right, Snowwhite.' And again that strange adult expression flickered over his face. I think he knew what was happening; he never mentioned being well, going back to school, flying a jet, letting off an H-bomb, or any of the other topics our small boys discussed. Even his semi-tough 'Hi-ya' was an act assumed for his mother's benefit.

'Before you go, Mrs Brown,' I said, 'I'll ask Mr Dexter if he wants to see you today. If he doesn't, any time you come back for Cliff will suit me, and if he does, we can work out roughly when that'll be, and that will be easier for you.'

'Ta, duck,' she said gratefully, 'I'd be ever so obliged. But I don't want to interrupt the doctor.'

'He won't mind.' I left her and walked quickly to the office as John opened the door, and ushered out his patient and attendant Mama.

'Next please, Nurse.'

A strong-jawed lady rose like a jack-in-the-box from the front bench and hauled her little daughter up after her. 'In you go, Marigold—just where the doctor is. And don't be frightened of him, dear. Mother's here!'

I nipped between her and John. 'Just a moment, please. I would like a word with the doctor.'

John said, 'Yes, Nurse?'

The lady interposed her large self between us. 'Now see here, young woman: it's my daughter's turn next, and don't you forget it.'

'I won't be a minute,' I apologised; 'do you mind waiting just a few seconds more?'

She tapped her foot impatiently and said she didn't know she was sure, and I was afraid we were in for a scene. The other mothers watched with interest, and the children squirmed with pleasure. Behind them I saw the tired, embarrassed face of Mrs Brown.

'My turn,' said Marigold's mama.

Marigold wailed suddenly, 'Ain't I going to see the Doctor, Mum?'

John tweaked one of her hair-ribbons. 'I thought you were supposed to be scared of me, chum?' he said gently, then he smiled at her irate mother. 'It's so good of you to be so understanding,' he said; 'it helps us so much. Thank you.'

To my surprise and relief she subsided on to the bench and settled her skirt. 'That's all right, Doctor,' she said mildly, then turned on poor Marigold. 'Sit down, love! Can't you see the Doctor's busy?'

He held open the door. 'After you, Nurse.'

He shut the door and leant his broad back against it, shutting out the patients. He was still smiling. He rubbed his jaw. 'That was a close thing,' he murmured. 'Now—what's up?'

'Mrs Brown. Clifford's Mum.' I explained the domestic complications. 'Will you want to see her today?'

'How's he looking?'

'Not good.'

'I see.' He looked at his watch. 'I'd better see her. Say an hour from now? She doesn't live far, does she?'

'Two roads away.'

He nodded. 'Right. We'll make it then definitely, and if I haven't reached him you'll have to slide her in under the counter. I won't have that poor woman kept hanging round, so when she gets back come and haul me out, no matter what I'm doing. Right?'

'Yes, Mr Dexter.'

He smiled faintly. 'If anyone is after your blood because of it, let me know.'

I was not clear if he was referring to mutinous patients or Sister. I said, 'Yes, Mr Dexter, thank you.'

I wanted to get back to Mrs Brown but he was still against the door. 'I suppose Cliff hasn't got one of his headaches again, has he?'

'Not by the look of him.'

'Well,' he said, 'that's something.' He moved and opened the door. 'Now let's have the tough lady on the front bench.'

He came out with me and waved at Mrs Brown. 'See you later, Mrs Brown. Nurse will explain. But don't kill yourself getting back. We'll be here and we'll keep an eye on Cliff.' He held out a hand to Marigold. 'Come on, young Marigold. How's that middle of yours behaving?' Marigold said her scar was ever such a lovely line, Doctor, and went with him, followed by her graciously smiling mother.

The clinic settled down; the children moved along the benches; Cliff told me confidentially that his Dad was working nights to get the extra money to buy a television set.

'Dad reckons as how a telly is what I need to give me something to do of an evening when I'm not sleeping.'

'That's kind of him, Cliff. You'll enjoy a telly.'

He looked at his thin hands. 'It'll be ever so nice, I'm sure, Nurse,' he said politely.

I knew him well from that spell of nights; I knew that something was wrong now and was fairly sure what it was. I took one of his hands absently. He was as undemonstrative as any other normal boy of his age, but there are times when it is normal to want to hold on to somebody. I said, 'Do you miss your dad a lot now he's working nights?'

His hand stirred in mine, but he made no attempt to move it away.

'Bit,' he admitted.

'Would you rather he went back to days and got you that telly later?'

He tilted his face to look at me. His face was very white apart from the two patches of unnatural colour on his cheekbones, the colour which made his parents so pathetically pleased.

'It's not as I wouldn't like to have one, Snowy—it'd be nice for me mum now she can't never get out of an evening with Dad like what she used to—but I don't see as how I'd look at it much. I keep getting me headaches, and I don't think I'll have much time for watching the telly, see.'

I said quietly, 'Why won't you have much time, Cliff?'

He was thoughtful. 'It's this way,' he said at last, 'I'm always in an' out of this place. Fat lot of good it'll do me when I'm up in that Christian ward again, and Dad's gone to all this trouble to get a telly back home.'

'Your mother said your headaches were getting better, Cliff. Are they?'

He gripped my hand and grinned sheepishly. 'I has to say that, Snowy. You know what Mums are! Talk about panic!'

I smiled at him. 'I do indeed. My mum used to create all winter because I always got my feet wet. According to her I was bound to be ill for life—but I never ever caught cold. And look at me now—a fine figure of a nurse who's not missed more than three days in all my training—and that was due to a septic finger.'

He wanted to know all about my finger; whether I had had the nail or all five nails pulled off; what sort of a drain had been used?

'Through and through, Snowy?'

He was quite disappointed when I explained it was only a simple whitlow. Like all old patients of any age he was very knowledgeable about hospital life and his conversation was strewn with pseudo-medical jargon.

Every few minutes or so I left him to see to the queue, but the clinic was running itself well that afternoon, and my ministrations were unnecessary. However, Sister liked to see her Nurses nipping smartly round their waiting patients with lists, pencils, and harassed expressions, so every so often I nipped. As luck would have it, this was never when she was passing the room. Each time she went by I was back by Cliff's chair, apparently gossiping aimlessly.

A short while before his mother was due to return I asked if he would like me to say anything to her about his dad going back to day-work.

'I'm sure he'll like to hear that you miss him in the evenings.'

He looked concerned. 'I wouldn't want to upset him, Snowy. He's that set on getting that telly for me.'

'Shall I just mention it to your mum? She'll know what to do and she'll like to know how you feel. It's not,' I added, 'that I want to turn into a grown-up and tell on you—but I think she should know.'

'Garn,' he grinned scornfully, 'you couldn't turn into a blooming grown-up, Snowy. You ain't old enough!'

'Of course I am, you disrespectful brat! I'd have you know I'm a State Registered Nurse AND twenty-two years old. Any minute now and I'll have white hair.'

'Nurse Snow!'

Sister was standing beside me. She said would I please come into the corridor? I followed her meekly, then waited while her eyes swept over me from the tip of my cap to my shoes.

141

'Nurse, you will kindly behave in a more dignified fashion when on duty in my department. What did you imagine you were doing? Telling a patient your age!'

'But, Sister—I was only joking with Cliff——'

She said she did not mind to whom I was talking, and I certainly had no business to be joking on duty in her department.

'You are running a clinic, Nurse. Not a children's party.'

I said yes, Sister, sorry, Sister, and she repeated what she had said, and asked if I would be good enough to bear that in mind while I was on duty. For once she forgot to echo 'in my department.'

There was nothing in the room that needed my attention, but I walked round, and the children shifted under my gaze. I even brooded by the glass wall of the office. My burst of superfluous efficiency must have annoyed John as much as it did me. He came to the door.

'Wanting something, Nurse Snow?'

'No, thank you. I was just checking my list.'

'What's wrong with it? Are you running late?'

'No, Mr Dexter.'

He looked as if he thought I had gone quietly mad, and went back to his patient.

Cliff moved restlessly in his chair and touched his neck. I went back to him. 'In a draught, duckie? Or your head playing up?'

'It gets a bit tired like,' he admitted; 'sort of aches most of the time, only sometimes it seems more. Wish I could take it off and put it down somewhere.'

'I wish you could,' I said soberly. 'Shall I'—I glanced at the door; Sister was out of sight—'shall I tell you a story?'

'What'll she say?' He jerked his head downward and winced.

'Sister won't mind,' I lied cheerfully; 'what's it to be?'

'Give us the Snark.'

We had the Snark. Then the Walrus and the Carpenter; Old Father William; then back to the Snark.

His head drooped. 'I got a boojam in my head, I reckon.'

I altered his cushions, his position, but he could not get comfortable. He moved his head as if it was literally too heavy for him. At last, with the room nearly empty, I said, 'Like to sit on my lap like you used to? You could generally get comfortable that way.'

He said simply, 'Can I?' and I lifted him out of his chair.

I sat down on the back bench. Nurses do not sit down in hospital, but there were extraneous circumstances that caused this rule to be broken in the wards, and I did not see that that should not also apply to O.P.s. He settled on my lap and, as I had hoped, was shortly asleep. He was not heavy. He had probably always been slight, now he was the size of a frail child of six.

The few remaining mothers smiled sympathetically and tiptoed up with their cards and stray questions. They kept their children quiet. 'There now,' they whispered, 'don't you go waking up that poor little boy. You sit still, duck, and I'll buy you an ice for your tea.'

There were three children still to be seen before the queue reached Cliff, when Sister shot back into the room.

'Nurse Snow—what do you think you are doing? Put that child back in his chair at once!' She made no attempt to lower her voice, and that was her mistake. The mothers bristled with indignation, and the office door opened.

John said evenly, 'Did you want me, Sister?' He walked across to us. 'I'm glad,' he murmured, 'that chap's got off. Hang on to him until I'm ready, Nurse Snow.'

I was quite amused at the sight of Sister hastily recomposing her features. She achieved a smile. 'I was just inquiring how your clinic was progressing, Mr Dexter?' She was obviously not aware, since she had never been a nurse in O.P.s, that the glass wall of the office was not sound-proof. John said the clinic was going along all right, thank you, Sister, and went back to his office.

Sister left us alone. The mother nearest to me smiled encouragingly, although her face was still red with indignation. When her infant had been seen she came over. 'Don't you take no notice of the likes of her, dear. Red tape—that's all as matters to some! Call themselves nurses! I dunno.' She looked down at Cliff, who was still happily sleeping, and shook her head. 'The poor little mite, I seen him up afore. Is he going to——' I shook my head in warning, and she swallowed her last word. 'What's his name, dear? I'd like to know. I'd like to say a little prayer for him. My own done so well—I like to help another.'

'Clifford,' I said softly.

She nodded, 'Ta, dear.' Her eyes narrowed with compassion, 'Seems a shame—to see a kid like that.'

Mrs Brown returned and sat silently beside me. A few seconds later she whispered, 'Shall I hold him, duck?'

'No, thanks. I'm fine, and the doctor will be ready for you—he is now.' John beckoned to her from the office door, and she tiptoed towards him, lifting her feet high in her anxiety to make no noise. Cliff did not wake. He was having a sedative mixture four-hourly, and when he managed to get to sleep the medicine kept him asleep for a couple of hours. He did not stir when they came out of the office and back to the bench on which I sat.

Mrs Brown said, 'I'll put him in the chair, Nurse.'

John said, 'I'll do that,' and lifted the sleeping child from my lap. He stood, holding Cliff, waiting for me to straighten the chair cushions. I stood up and stretched my stiff arms.

Mrs Brown pushed forward the chair. 'It's ever so good of you, Nurse, to have held him all that time.'

John said, not disparagingly, 'I expect Nurse was very glad of an opportunity to sit down.'

'I was indeed.' I had had no opportunity yet to talk to Mrs Brown about that television set. I said, 'Before you go, Mrs Brown, there's something I'd like to talk to you about.' I had plumped the cushions. 'Ready, Mr Dexter.'

He sat down on the bench with Cliff still in his arms. The boy's head flopped weakly against his chest.

'Why don't you two go into the office, Nurse? I'll hang on to this chap.' He smiled at Mrs Brown. 'I'm one person who is not in a hurry.'

It was just after four; he was due in the theatre at half-past. There was no hurry, if he missed tea. I thanked him and took Mrs Brown back to the office.

I asked her to sit down, pulled a chair close to her, and when we were both seated I said I hoped she would not mind my interfering, but I thought there was something she and her husband might like to know.

'Cliff knows I'm going to tell you, and we thought we'd leave it to you.' I told her about the night-work.

She sat with her work-worn hands clasped in her lap. She listened without comment until I had finished, then she said simply:

'Ta, duck. I'll fetch his dad off nights.' She was silent again. Then, 'I know from what the doctor's been telling me that our Cliff won't never see that telly. But you know what men are, duck—they get helpless when they see illness. And I got a good man. He wants to help out all he can, and this is his way. But I'll fetch him off. Mind, I'll be tactful, like, but he'll come off.' She looked at me steadily. 'If we aren't going to have our Cliff with us much longer his dad'll want to see all he can of him—an' if he works the day-shift he'll get the evenings and nights when the boy's mostly awake. So I'll tell him, duck. And ta. Ta ever so.'

I said, 'Mrs Brown, I am so very sorry. You know how we all feel about your Cliff. We love him.'

'That's right,' she said with a brisk little nod, 'I know, duck.' She leant stiffly against the back of her chair as if she needed the support. 'I never,' she went on, 'thought this could happen

144

to me. I never thought as I could stand it. I don't know as I can. I just knows I will. I will.' She looked beyond me to where John was sitting. 'That's another good man, duck. An' he talked to me real lovely, just now. Know that he called me, Nurse?'

I said quietly, 'Tell me?'

She looked back at me. She was a young woman, possibly thirty, but her face was middle aged. 'He said I was the bravest woman as he'd ever seen. He said that of me, duck. Alice Brown.' Her eyes were puzzled as a child's and there was no trace of pride anywhere in her face or her voice. 'He told me as I was to go on pretending to our Cliff—and if I didn't think his dad could take it I was to go on pretending to him too. For his sake, as well as the boy's. And he said—I could do it.'

I said, 'I think you can too. And I think he was right about you. I never realised that you knew.'

She smiled; a sweet, shy smile that transformed her tired, homely, unpowdered face. 'Well, it doesn't do to make a fuss, does it, duck? But ta. Ta ever so.'

11

THE QUIET WARDS

I SAW Carol that night for the first time since her admission to Susan Ward. She was in one of the small single cubicles at the far end of the ward. She took off her reading glasses when I appeared round her curtains, and smiled.

'Gillian, how nice! How are you after all this time?'

I said I was fine, and how was she? I had no notion of what I was going to say to her or why I had come. My feet had wandered automatically to Susan when I had left the dining-room after supper, and so I was here. I wished I was not.

She said she was fine too, but dead sick of injections. 'I'm a human pin-cushion. But give me the news. How's O.P.?'

'Quite pleasant—apart from Sister.'

'Foul as ever?'

'As ever.' I talked 'shop.' It was the safest thing to discuss. All nurses, whether ill or well, are content to talk shop indefinitely at any hour.

I watched her as we talked. She looked better than I had expected to find her; she was thinner, but her colour was good and not feverish, and since she had been in bed for nearly two weeks she was no longer tired. There was something else about her appearance that I could not place immediately. She looked very much alive, and not as if she had been seriously ill.

I asked if she liked being warded. 'Sister Susan nice?'

'Sheer joy.' She almost purred. 'They all run round you in small circles. I don't think I'll bother to get up. I like being the centre of attention, for a change.'

I let that pass. I said I was very glad.

She asked after Lisa. 'Blakelock was up here visiting one of her set who's warded next door. Miggins. She came and had tea with me. She told me that Lisa Smith—according to Blakelock —had purloined your latest scalp?'

I was genuinely amused. 'Not poor old Tom?' I was academically interested to see how annoyed my obvious amusement made her. 'Carol, that's an old affair. He and Lisa have been buddies for years.'

'You never mentioned it.'

'Didn't think you'd be interested.'

'Why did he take you to the dance?'

'Wheels within wheels,' I said darkly. 'A splendid scheme that came off.'

'It did?'

'Yes, indeed. Oh—by the way——' I asked how Peter had known Tom was going to ask me before Tom knew himself.

She picked up her glasses and tried them on. 'I probably got that muddled. You know how it is on nights.'

I agreed, as once before, that I did, and waited for her to go on. She took her time.

'Been very gay lately, Gillian?'

'Not at all. I've had one brief dinner date—the night after the dance——' I added casually, 'and since then my work has been my all. Very tedious.'

She said it must be, and I stood up to go. 'Sister Susan will chase me off if I stay too long.'

'But you've only just come. Sit down, girl, and wait until she starts chasing. I've been so cut off I've dropped the threads. Tell me all. Who's doing what with whom?'

She sounded so normal that for a brief instant I wondered if I had imagined finding those drugs. I sat down on her locker.

'What do you want to know specifically?'

'Everything. How's Peter? If our John and that blond piece are engaged; where I'm going when I leave here; what's happening to you; are you staying in O.P.s? Has Matron said any more about Robert?'

'Hey—let's start again.' I smiled. 'Peter I've not seen. He must be well, or I'd have heard, but beyond that I can't say. I haven't seen him since you did.'

'Since the dance?'

'The next night. He took me out to supper. The night you got ill.'

'Oh, yes.' She sounded relieved. 'How about our John?'

146

'Your guess is as good as mine. And that goes for the other things too. I haven't seen Matron, and nobody's said anything about any future plans for either of us.'

She was still playing with her glasses. 'We'll hear in time,' she said absently. She looked round at me. 'I've been wanting to talk to you about Peter.'

'You have?'

She nodded. 'Remember,' she said slowly, 'that night in the cloakroom?'

'When you said he wouldn't harm you?'

She half smiled. 'I didn't think that got through.'

'It did. I meant to ask you what you meant, but you got ill.'

'That's why I wanted to see you.' She said she hated to say what she was going to say, but she thought it was something I ought to know.

'It's odd,' I said, 'how people always think you ought to know the unpleasant things, never pleasant ones. What's on your mind, Carol?'

'Well'—she smiled in the same way—'you remember that night you lost those drugs——'

I said softly, 'The night my drugs were taken? Yes. I'm not likely to forget it.'

Her expression never altered. 'You've swung round. I thought you considered it was a mistake.'

'No. No mistake.'

She did not ask how I knew. If she had I would have told her then. Later I was sorry that I had not.

Her eyes watched me keenly. 'So at last we're getting somewhere. Now—do you understand who took them?'

I said flatly, 'No. I don't understand at all.'

She sat up suddenly. 'You must understand if you know it was him. It's too obvious why he did it.'

'Why? Carol, who are you talking about?'

'But, darling—who else but Peter? Of course it was him. I've always been sure. And look how he's behaved since—dropping you, rushing round after me. Remember that was the night he found out who I was and he must have felt desperate. He had to get rid of you somehow——'

I said, 'Stop that.' I used the tone I used when the children in O.P.s were out of hand, and it worked as well with her as with them.

She gaped at me. I knew I was white with rage. I do not often get angry, but when I do I make up for lost time. I was flaming. It was not that I still loved Peter—I did not—but I had and would always have a soft spot for him. We had had a lot of fun together, been to a lot of parties, drunk gallons of

147

coffee, and I was not going to allow her to talk of him this way.

She said hesitantly, 'Gillian, you look grey.'

'The light,' I said shortly.

'Why did you stop me? I hadn't finished.'

I stood up and walked to the end of her bed. I hung on to her bed rail to remind myself that she was a patient in bed.

I took a deep breath. 'Look'—my voice shook with anger, but I had it under control—'there's no point in chatter. I know Peter did not swipe that stuff; nor did Night Sister or Tom or John or that pro—whatever her name was. I never thought they had taken it. I never thought you had either, until it dropped out of your bed-socks last night.'

She did not attempt to deny it or seem surprised. She asked, 'What have you done with it?'

'Smashed the ampoules, burnt the labels, and poured the broken glass and the drug down the bath in our Home. What did you expect me to do with them? Leave 'em there? Take 'em myself?'

She lay back on her pillows, and then she laughed. 'Gill Snow,' she said breathlessly, 'you—the bright girl of the set! You haven't the *nous* of a two-year-old. Now—how on earth can you prove that I took 'em?'

I said, 'Why should I want to prove that?'

She stopped laughing. 'Well, you must be going to do something about it?'

I shook my head. 'Why?'

I saw she neither believed nor understood; that made us quits. I did not understand her. But I wanted to. I asked why she took them.

She sat up again. 'I'll tell you why.' Her words were stifled by a spasm of coughing. I remembered that she had been very ill. I was still very angry, but I was also a nurse. You do not shed four years' training so easily; certainly not a training received in St Joseph's Hospital, London.

'Don't bother now. Tell me another time. It can wait.'

'No, it can't!' she panted. 'Don't you dare go until I've finished! I'm not having you brooding over my bed-side as a perfect little ministering angel again!'

I said, 'Don't get so worked up or you'll cough again.'

She was furious. 'Stop being such a ruddy little nurse!' She spat the words. 'And just listen to me for the first time in all these years. You've always done the talking—now you do the listening for a change! Yes, you! Sweet Nurse Snow! Kind Nurse Snow! Popular Nurse Snow! The Sister's pet—it's made me sick.' She looked as if she could easily be very sick. 'The whole of our training, that's all I've ever heard. And what

148

was I? Your wretched little shadow tagging along behind, because no one thought I had the personality or the brains to do anything else.' She coughed again. 'Don't go!' she hissed.

I waited at the foot of the bed, my hands on the iron rail. The rail was no colder than my hands.

'It was the same with the boys. Tom this and Peter that—you went to the parties and I read the damned good books! And of all the men in Joe's you had to grab Peter Kier.'

I got in a word at last. 'I never even realised you even liked Peter——'

'You never realised anything! You never will realise anything! You just drift around being sweet and forgiving—well, don't start forgiving me, because I'll never forgive you!'

I stared at her. 'For—what?'

'For being you. For what you've done. You had everything all taped. You were so sweetly clever'—her lips twisted—'you—the daughter of some insignificant farmer. I'm Ashton Ash's daughter. My father did something worth doing. I never pushed that around because I thought everyone knew it. I didn't understand how clever you had been until I discovered how carefully you had kept it dark.'

I made no attempt to defend anything. 'Peter?'

She smiled. 'Peter. See what's happened since he found out? He was a changed man. And the hospital has changed, hasn't it? Since you've been found to be fallible? Do you know'—her smile was fixed to her lips and did not touch her eyes—'I never guessed quite what I was starting when I took that grain out of the box on my way back to you and the Admiral. I thought there would be a bit of a fuss—and I thought it would do you good to find life can be complicated at times—but I never thought that Matron would make such a shining example of you.'

Now I recognised what it was I had not been able to place in her appearance when I first came in. Triumph.

I did not say anything, and she must have finished, because when Sister Susan put her head round the curtains a few minutes later we were still staring at each other.

Sister said brightly, 'That's enough for one day, Nurse Snow.'

'Thank you, Sister,' I said. 'Yes, I think it's enough.'

Sister beamed down at Carol. 'Nurse Ash, you are looking much improved for your friend's visit. Quite cheerful again.'

Carol agreed that she felt quite cheerful, thank you, Sister.

Sister Susan held back the curtains. 'Come along, Nurse Snow.'

Carol said, 'Good night, Gil—thanks for coming.'

I said, 'Not at all. Glad you're better, good night,' and followed Sister into the corridor.

Sister Susan was feeling chatty. 'It does one good to have a cosy little chat with someone of one's own age when one is ill, Nurse. You must come again tomorrow.'

I said I would love to come back tomorrow, if my off-duty coincided with the Susan visiting hours.

Sister said, 'If not, I am sure Sister Out-Patients will allow you to pop up for a few minutes.'

I was not sure that Sister Out-Patients would allow anything of the sort, but Sister Susan was a kind old lady, a contemporary of Home Sister's, so I murmured, 'Yes, Sister, thank you, Sister, good night, Sister.'

Susan Ward was on the top floor of the oldest block in the hospital. The block next to Susan had been badly damaged in the war and stood, an ugly, gaping ruin, in the centre of the busy hospital. The block was due to be pulled down and rebuilt any day, and with this object some temporary scaffolding had been erected to strengthen the ruins. But there were so many new wards being opened in the undamaged parts of the building, so many new extensions being added to the departments, to cope with the fantastic increase in the number of our patients that had come with the last few years, that the ruins were left untouched, apart from their ghostly skeletons of steel and wood.

I walked out of Susan, then stopped at the top of the stairs. My head was hot and my hands freezing. My legs shook. I badly wanted to sit down, and quickly. I could not sit down on the stairs, and if I went back to Susan Sister would start taking my temperature. I remembered the ruins, and the piles of new bricks on the grass between the blocks. I would go and sit there. I did not want to think or talk or do anything but sit.

I went down by the iron staircase that ran up every block. There was no chance of my meeting anyone there. It was dark outside and very cold; the clouds were low, but it was not raining. There was no moon. Through the moving clouds I saw an occasional star. I was glad the stars were there even if I could not see them. Having been raised in the country, I needed to see stars; I could dispense with the moon, but I felt lonely when the sky was low. My father's farm had been miles from the nearest village, and street lighting was something that annoyed us when we drove through that village—'Can't see an inch with all these damned lights, Gill'—but out on the marsh there were only the stars and the very occasional slender gleam of the flickering marsh light.

I drew my cloak more tightly around me, not solely to keep out the cold, but to hide my white apron. An apron or white coat was visible against the black grass from a hundred yards away. Not that what I was doing was against any rule; the grounds were open and the iron staircase was often used in the day time. It was merely that I wanted to avoid being seen.

I was on the top step of the bottom of the five rungs of stairs when I saw a white coat coming along the grass below me. I stopped, and leant against the wall. My rubber-soled shoes had made no sound on the ironwork, and if whoever it was had not noticed my cap already there was little likelihood that he would do so now I was standing above him.

The footsteps stopped. John's voice said, 'What are you doing up there, Nurse? You shouldn't use that staircase at night without a torch.'

Oh, no, I thought—does he have to be everywhere?

I walked down the rest of the steps, cursing all itinerant doctors in all hospitals and specifically Joe's. I should have known that this was bound to happen. He was always handy when I was making a fool of myself, which must, I thought savagely, give him a lot of quiet amusement. He was waiting for me, so I went up to him.

'Good evening, Mr Dexter. I came down that way because I wanted fresh air.'

It was too dark to see his face. That staircase wound round the old block and ended at the path that led through the ruins to the rest of the hospital. There was no light. The ground floor of the block was part of the physiotherapy school and locked at five each evening. The staircase was only floodlit on the weekly fire-practice nights.

He recognised my voice. 'Tell me, Nurse Snow,' he said mildly, 'are you sure you're a human being?'

I said I was quite sure. 'Why?'

'You keep appearing in such an astounding variety of places. Highly disconcerting. One minute you are hiding behind a child in O.P.s, then behind a mask in the theatre, and now I discover you hiding against the wall on the fire escape.'

I could not think of anything else to say, so I said I was sorry.

'Why were you hiding?'

I said obviously, 'Because I didn't want to be seen.'

He said, 'Why not? You weren't committing any crime—merely being rather absurd.'

I was so used to being lectured by everyone with whom I came into contact these days—and also so used to his calling me absurd, with reason—that I stood docile and waited for the lecture to proceed, ready to murmur a mechanical, 'Yes, Mr Dexter, no, Mr Dexter, anything you say, Mr Dexter,' at appropriate intervals. He did not say anything. He seemed to be still waiting for my explanation. I had no energy for invention,

151

so I repeated that I had wanted fresh air.

He said, 'And you find the air up there peculiarly beneficial? I must try it some time.' His voice sounded as if he was smiling.

'Yes.'

Roughly thirty yards from where we stood, and almost hidden by the block on our right, was the concrete-covered ramp that connected all the blocks of the hospital. Now we heard more footsteps, and then men's voices. This was to be expected, and was one of the reasons why I had chosen to come down by the irregular route. The resident staff walked miles up and down that ramp every night as they went on their rounds.

Peter and one of the obstetrical house-physicians were walking in our direction. The O.H.P. said, 'I'll hop on to Mary, Peter. Give her my regards!'

Peter called back, 'I'll do that. See you later, Roger. This little sociability won't keep me long. I'll be back for that beer before I start my round.'

The O.H.P. walked across the grass in the opposite direction, and Peter disappeared round the block.

John said, 'I won't keep you, Nurse,' and was gone before I realised he was moving. For once my reflexes worked quickly. I shot after him without bothering to work out why I wanted him back.

'Just a moment, please, Mr Dexter.'

He was near the ramp. When he turned, his face was in the darkness again. 'Want something, Nurse?' he asked coolly.

I said, 'Yes,' and ran out of courage.

I knew there was no point in what I had done; what did he care if I hung around corners waiting for young men? He did not care to help me explain either. He said, 'Oh?' and I dried up completely. Possibly this was apparent from my expression. The ramp light was now on my face. He said at last, 'Why not say it and have done, Nurse Snow? You do want to tell me something, don't you?'

'Yes.' I hesitated. 'I wanted to tell you that I was doing what I said, taking the air. I wasn't hanging around waiting for Mr Kier.'

'Would it have mattered if you were?'

I said, 'Not to you, naturally. But it would have to me. I don't like—dark corners.'

He said he was sure I did not.

'I suppose you've been visiting Nurse Ash?'

'Yes.'

'How is she?'

'Better.'

'Good.'

I wished I had never started this asinine conversation. I

wished all the routine wishes you have when you are acutely embarrassed: that I would fall through the ground, be struck by lightning, or simply dead. Anything was preferable to this.

I mumbled, 'I'm sorry I've delayed you. I just wanted to explain.'

He said evenly, 'That wasn't necessary, but thank you.'

I shivered and clutched at my cloak. 'I think I've had enough fresh air. I'd better get back to the Home.'

He nodded. 'Far better. But if you are cold why not go back through the hospital and out of Casualty? It's the shortest way.' He noticed my hesitation. 'Or are you anxious for exercise as well as air?'

'No. I've had enough exercise. I've been on all day.' He walked down the ramp, and he told me he was going to Peter and Paul. 'I did four chaps from there this evening. I thought I'd look at them before I started my round.' He asked again how I had found Carol. 'Cutler told me she had a nasty chest when she came in. I'm glad she's picked up again.'

He was being extremely civil, and I was grateful to his flow of hospital small talk. I was dumbfounded by my own folly, and above all by the new folly that I could no longer ignore. I was so busy with my thoughts that he had to ask the same question twice before I answered it. He wanted to know if I had any idea how Carol had become so ill.

I shrugged. 'I suppose it just came on. She probably got very run down through being on nights.'

'Hardly, in her fourth year. You get acclimatised to it by then. We wouldn't have any night nurses around if you didn't.'

We were in the hospital now. I glanced up at him. 'If it isn't the effect of nights, I've no idea.'

He grinned quickly. 'Off the record, Nurse, what did go on at that last party in the Medical School? I can't help feeling it must have been some party, judging by the aftermath.'

'What aftermath, Mr Dexter?'

'Nurse Ash has had bronchial pneumonia,' he announced calmly, 'two of the dressers, who were the hosts, I gather, are down with feverish chills, and one of the clerks has a broken nose. And they all went down the day after the party. I remember one or two affairs in my past, and I merely wondered what particular line of student hilarity caused this. That's all.' He looked down at me. 'I hoped you could assuage my curiosity.'

I was just going to say that I was unable to tell him anything, since I had not been present, when he went on.

'Once—just before I qualified and we were all pretty lit up, as everyone is at the prospect of finals—we had a terrific affair. We asked some Martha's men across; they came over the river

153

in hordes and brought roughly a hundredweight of flour and a gallon or so of gentian violet to make the party go. It certainly went.' He grinned again. 'I can't describe what we looked like.'

I looked at his spotless coat, equally pure shirt collar, and neat tie. 'You got in a mess?'

His eyes were disappearing with amusement. 'Mess is an understatement. We were soaked in deep purple.'

'What did you do?' I forgot my embarrassment in my fascination at the idea of a purple giant.

'Only one thing to do. We frog-marched them to the lake in the park and threw them in. Then we jumped in after them, and the party degenerated into free for all water-polo. We used an air-cushion as a ball,' he said reminiscently, 'until the cops broke it up. And this was in November—and colder than it is now.'

'Did any of you get ill?'

He said he thought they all got colds. 'My main recollection of those next few days is hazy with the smell of eucalyptus, swallowing aspirins and whisky, and trying to rub that wretched gentian violet off myself.'

'Did you get it off in time?'

He shook his head. 'Only on the more visible areas of my person. I hoped the examiners would consider my pale mauve face and neck as an unusual symptom of examination shock. And that,' he added, 'is why when I heard about Nurse Ash and those boys, I wondered if perhaps the party might not have contributed to their being warded. After all, Nurse,' he said reasonably, 'you don't break your nose because you are on night-duty.'

'That's true,' I admitted. 'But I'm afraid I can't help you about the party. I wasn't there myself, but I haven't heard of anything unusual going on and I would have done. Three of my set besides Nurse Ash were there.'

We had reached the foot of the stairs that led to Peter and Paul.

He stopped smiling at the past and came back to the present. 'But Kier was at that do?'

'He was.'

'Why didn't you go?' he asked curiously.

I said, 'I wasn't asked.'

He put his hands behind him and stood with his feet apart like a guardsman at ease. He looked genuinely concerned that an unimportant young man should not have asked an equally unimportant young woman to a party. I was reminded of something a man in Robert once said: 'You feel that big chap minds what happens to you, Nurse. Not just that he wants to get you better and out, but that it makes him feel bad to see you're bad.'

I knew the other patients felt that too in different ways; they all liked John, and not because of his skill. Patients in reality care very little about the skill or qualifications of the doctor treating them; a doctor is a doctor, any doctor as skilled as another—to them. But they care a great deal whether a doctor is kind or not, and whether he is able to project that kindness.

I had never experienced his concern when applied to myself before. I understood what that man in Robert meant very well.

He said, 'How old are you, Nurse?'

'Twenty-two.'

He smiled slightly. 'Dust and ashes? That's how it seems, doesn't it?' His voice was very gentle.

I had avoided thinking of Carol since I left her; I could not avoid the thought any longer. I nodded.

He said, 'And this is where I'm supposed to tell you that you are very young and have your life ahead, and all you need is hard work and a good digestion to see you through.' He lowered his eyes. 'Only I'm not going to. You've endured enough strictures from me on a variety of subjects and occasions. You,' he said deliberately, 'are a very patient young woman, Nurse, and you'll pick yourself up very nicely without any assistance from me.'

I said, 'It gets exhausting.'

'Picking up the pieces?' I nodded again. 'It does. And the snag there is,' he went on slowly, 'that every time one gets floored, although one can get up again, one leaves a piece down there on the floor.'

I said, 'I didn't know other people felt that way, too.'

He did not answer for a few seconds, then he said,

'Oh yes. They do.' He shifted his shoulders. 'And now I had better get moving on to Peter and Paul. And I expect you are anxious to get moving back to your colleague Nurse Smith, and the cup of cocoa, or whatever it is you drink at this hour of the night.'

'Tea.'

'Tea, is it?' He smiled slightly, 'And I expect it never keeps you awake?'

'Never, Mr Dexter.'

'So much for its powers as a stimulant,' he said briskly. 'Right. Good night, Nurse Snow.' He turned and walked up the stairs two at a time. I did not move away immediately. I stood and stared at the empty space where he had been standing. Then I heard someone coming down the stairs; I walked away slowly, in case it was him coming back. It was one of the housemen. We exchanged good-evenings, and I went back to our Home.

Lisa was presiding over the tea-cups. 'How's Carol?'

'Much better.'

She said soberly, 'Carol's dead lucky to have got away with it. Blakelock told me tonight how bad she had been. She heard it from Miggins.' She filled the cups. 'Really, Carol Ash is a complete fool to play about with her chest in that way.'

'She couldn't help it,' I remonstrated. 'Anyone can get pneumonia. It's just one of those things.'

'Phooey! It's not one of those things if you rush round to parties and dances with a temp. of 102.'

'She had that temp. at the dance?' I recollected now how ill Carol had looked that evening. I had put it down to night-duty; a temperature half-controlled by aspirins would give the same appearance. 'How do you know all this, Lisa?'

'Straight from Carol—via a couple of Staff Nurses. She told Miggins how she'd worked it—staying in bed all day and causing no talk because she was a night girl, and then getting up and gallivanting by night. Miggins told Blakelock that Carol was very pleased with herself. Thought she'd been no end cute.' She frowned. 'I've no patience'—she spoke sharply for her—'with people who fool around with their health. Surely to goodness, we see enough of what can happen to the poor unfortunates who get these things through no fault of their own! Playing the fool for the fun of it makes me mad! It's plain stupid—and plain inconsiderate. There's Ellen without a Night Senior—and have you heard that Kirsty's got scarlet? Night Sister will be having kittens.'

'Night Sister never has kittens. She says, "Och aye," and copes.'

'Dear girl,' said Lisa, 'don't be dense. You know how Night Sister loathes not having a spare senior up her sleeve for emergencies. And you know how whenever we are short that's the time when the emergencies come flocking in.'

Which was true, as I agreed.

'I know she's a friend of yours,' she continued, 'but really she is a trying girl. Why couldn't she have been decently ill and left you to go to that dance with Peter? Then Tom might even have asked me, and we'd have had none of the soul-searching we've been through lately.'

'John,' I said thoughtlessly, 'wondered if she had been chucked into the lake among the ducks.' I had then to explain myself and she was so enchanted at the prospect of John heaving the Martha's men into the lake, that she forgot to ask why I was taking air on the fire escape.

'If only I'd been born twenty years sooner, Gill! I can't bear to have missed seeing our cool, calm, and collected S.S.O. dressed in flour and gentian violet and going berserk with an air-ring.'

'Cushion.'

'Ring, dear girl, makes a better story. Tom will die laughing.'

I said, 'No. This isn't for publication. He probably wouldn't mind—but I'm not spreading it abroad.'

She took no notice. 'It's the best thing I've heard in years. The old devil—keeping it quiet all this time.'

'Hey!' I said firmly. 'Listen. No.'

She stopped laughing. 'No?'

She looked at me for a long time. Then she groaned. 'Oh, no—dear girl—you don't tell me?'

'I don't tell you anything.'

Her eyes appraised me intelligently. 'So that's why we can have a jolly laugh at dear Peter?'

I said, 'A girl has to laugh at something.'

She said that was fair enough. 'And you can have another little bout of hysteria.'

'Sister O.P.s?'

'No. I was thinking of your pal, Carol. Her pneumonia was all in vain. You've got a laugh coming to you there, dear girl.'

I said carefully, 'How come?'

'You know very well how come. She was determined to risk anything—even, glorious melodrama though it sounds, her life. People,' she reminded me, 'do still hop it with pneumonia. She must be pretty attached to your ex-young man.'

I said I thought she probably was.

She said, 'Well, take my tip, and don't give her your blessing. It won't go down well.'

'Why not?' I had always known Lisa was quick on the uptake, but not that she was as quick as this.

She hesitated. 'To be candid—which isn't easy or wise as you are fond of her, but what the hell—because sometimes a kind thought gets read as patronage.'

She said she had to go and ring Tom. 'Help yourself to more tea, only don't wait if you want a bath. I may be chatting quite a while.' She put on her shoes. 'One thing,' she added slowly, 'they aren't officially engaged yet. That's a point.'

I agreed that it was, and poured myself another cup of tea.

12

CHRISTIAN IS A QUIET WARD

THAT seemed to be that. All the ends neatly tied, and only my own was flapping loose. I concentrated on work, and was very conscious how lucky I was to be able to do that. Blakelock went down with scarlet, which meant an extra pressure of work on all the O.P. staff; oddly, Sister's temper improved as the work increased. There was no time to worry over trifles and she even ignored Johnny Brandon's yell of 'Watcha, Snowwhite!'

Lisa and I each ran two clinics simultaneously, as Sister had to deal with the whole administration of the department single-handed. A staff nurse's job resembles that of a Commander on a ship in the Royal Navy. The Sister owns the ward or department, the staff nurse runs it. Matron sent us an extra first-year pro; all the other pros moved up a step, and the Senior Pro took over from myself in the Children's Room; I was substituted for Lisa, and she, to her horror, was officially acting staff nurse. Sister, with a complete staff again, retightened her lips and her discipline, and we were on the verge of going to Matron to demand a transfer *en masse* when two of our pros caught scarlet fever.

'The dear children,' said Lisa when I told her this, 'aren't they just too wonderful? I suppose Sister hasn't got it?' she added hopefully. She was having a morning off and was still in bed. We were too busy to have whole days off, and so our weekly day off had been split, and we had either an afternoon or a morning.

'She hadn't got it this morning.' I had rushed over to change my apron. 'I'll have to scoot now—she was livid with me for getting in her way when she spilled that carbolic, and only sent me to change because she said I was bound to get the ugly gangrene.'

She clicked her tongue against her teeth. 'You are so trying, Gill. Fancy letting yourself get burnt with raw carbolic?' She shook her head despairingly. 'Now if you'd been a senior nurse at St Martha's Hospital, London, it would have rolled off you like water. Seriously, did you burn yourself?'

'No. Only a few drops got through and I washed 'em off at once. But Sister was mighty marked. And it was she who didn't cork the jar. She used it last for her instruments.' I buckled my belt. 'See you on duty this afternoon. Enjoy your breakfast.'

I did not see her on duty that afternoon because Matron sent for me half-way through the morning.

'Christian ward is now in quarantine for scarlet fever, Nurse Snow. You have had it?'

'Yes, Matron.' I guessed what was coming and looked at her right ear to hide the relief I felt at the thought of leaving O.P.s.

She said the night staff was very depleted.

'Yes, Matron.'

She pursed her lips. 'I had not intended moving you from Out-Patients as soon as this, but circumstances have forced my hand. Night Sister and Sister Christian are both willing to have you back on night duty, so you may return to Christian as night senior tonight.'

I said, 'Thank you very much, Matron.'

She asked if I had had a day off this week. 'I had the morning on Sunday, Matron. I was due for a half-day tomorrow, but I am not doing anything special.'

She looked up at me. 'I dislike you nurses missing your off-duty—you should have sufficient free time. You have been very busy in Out-Patients recently,' she said reproachfully, as if I personally was responsible for Blakelock's scarlet, 'and, now those two probationers have contracted the disease, Sister will be even more rushed.' Suddenly she smiled. 'I do not know what Sister will say to me when I remove one of her two remaining senior nurses, but there is no alternative.'

I thought Sister would probably give three loud cheers. I said, 'No, Matron.'

She told me that four night seniors had been in the latest batch of victims, 'and the entire Christian night staff. That was one of the reasons that decided your case. I cannot have two new night nurses in that ward; one of you must know the ward, and you were there as a senior relief and a day senior.'

'Yes, Matron.'

She said she was glad I did not mind forgoing my half-day. 'And I am afraid you will have to manage without off-duty today, Nurse. Will you ask Sister to send you to lunch at half-past one, and then you must go straight to bed if you are to work tonight.' She picked up a list. 'I shall be sending Sister Out-Patients a spare Senior Probationer to take your place, and a junior probationer to stand in for Nurse Waller and Nurse Dulain, who were warded this morning. Would you tell Sister that for me, and say I am sure she will be able to manage?'

'Yes, Matron.'

She had not dismissed me, so I waited, holding my hands behind my back in the traditional stance of Joe's nurses.

'I sincerely trust,' she said, 'that this epidemic terminates shortly. If it does not we will have to close some of the departments, possibly even more wards. We have thirty-one nurses either at, or on their way to, the isolation hospital. And it has now spread to the resident staff. Two of the house-physicians woke with suspicious sore throats this morning, so Dr Cutler

159

tells me.' Her eyes were anxious and yet amused. 'I may find myself back in a ward yet, Nurse—if I do not find myself in the isolation hospital.'

'Have you not had it, Matron?'

She shook her head. 'I have not, Nurse.'

I said I hoped she did not get it.

'None of us are indispensable—but I hope not, too. My nursing staff are quite sufficiently pressed without their having to do my work as well.' Then she asked if I felt well. 'You have been looking very tired recently, Nurse.'

I said I felt quite well, thank you.

'I do not like having to send you back on night-duty,' she said. 'You have already done two months as a night senior, but, apart from any other concern, I need night senior nurses.' She pursed her lips. 'That morphia has never been traced, Nurse. It appears quite inexplicable.'

I said, 'Yes, Matron.'

She nodded. 'Home Sister tells me you were extremely upset about leaving Robert Ward.'

'Yes, Matron.'

She looked at me steadily, and then she smiled. 'You will enjoy going back to Christian. Not,' she added quickly, 'that that in any way enters into why you are going back there, but I am happy that you will be able to settle down again. That will be all, Nurse.'

Lisa was at lunch, and delighted for my sake. 'Dear girl, how splendid for you. But I'm going to miss you at the daily round, the common task! There won't be a soul to laugh with!'

'Try Sister. Learn to love her. Maybe that's all she needs.'

She leered. 'Is it, dear girl?'

'The love of a good woman.' I told her how nice Matron had been. 'Really matey.'

She said Matron was crafty. 'She's got us all taped. She knows just when to crack the whip and just when to relax. But she's not a bad old soul at heart. I like her—quite.'

'A Joe's girl, that's why. Can you imagine what she'd be like if she came from Martha's?'

She had lost interest in Matron. 'Seen John this morning, Gill?'

'No. The pundits have rallied, and O.P.s was stiff with titles taking clinics. Also the fishing season is over. I expect he was in the theatre. Not that it makes any difference. He and I are back to square one. "Morning, Mr Dexter," "Afternoon, Mr Dexter," "Good night, Mr Dexter." Our sole conversation.'

'Snappy dialogue,' she said, 'keeps a man interested.' She sighed. 'I dunno, Gill. Wish I did. I'm fond of that man, you know. I think he's a good type—and I hate to think of him spending a lifetime hanging round that woman—but what can you do when a girl looks like she does? Expect he just doesn't see what she's really like.'

'So she's so damned lovely that you can't expect any man to see through it.' I turned to her. 'Except your Tom. He doesn't like her.'

She said thoughtfully, 'I'd love to say Tom was perfect, but he's not the only one. I've told you that before. In the days when the young men and I were well acquainted I gathered that most of them loathed her guts.'

'Oh well, John's just different. That's what we like about him.'

She said, 'Trouble is, he's been too busy. Now he's fallen— *whang*. Always happens that way—and he's getting on—nearly forty—dangerous age.'

'He's not forty—he's thirty-seven.' I was indignant.

She laughed, not unkindly. 'He was thirty-seven last year, dear girl. But, if you like, time can stand still. Anything you say.' She stood up and pushed in her chair. 'Back to the inferno. How well I know how Dante felt. You're lucky to be out of it.'

'Very lucky.'

She said, 'And you'll be glad to get back to a ward. That'll be fun for you.'

I agreed, and thought how even she, who was the soul of optimism these days, could not pretend that she saw any future for me anywhere in anything but my job.

Christian was very quiet, and the twenty-two children were asleep. Two cots in the ward, and the small room in which Clifford Brown had been, were empty. Sister Christian told me the ward had closed that morning.

'We are keeping these children until they are clear, then we'll wait until we empty, fumigate, and spring-clean before re-admitting. One good thing about scarlet is the short incubation period. We won't have to wait long to see if those two this morning have handed it round.' She told me her staff nurse had gone off with a suspicious sore throat that afternoon. 'I expect she's on the way to the isolation hospital now.' She smiled ruefully. 'That place is going to bless the name of St Joseph's.'

When she had finished giving me her report I thanked her for telling Matron that she was willing to have me in her ward.

'I was quite satisfied with your work when you were last here, Nurse Snow. Why should I not be willing to have you back?' She unpinned her drug keys. 'I don't suppose I need remind you not to leave these out of your possession.'

'You don't, Sister.'

I felt a new woman with those keys jangling against my bib,

and normal for the first time in nine weeks. I was sorry the girls had scarlet, but was selfishly grateful that there was this staff crisis. Christian was a pleasant and peaceful ward, although not often as silent as it was tonight; Sister Christian was the closest thing to a friend I had among the Sisters, and there would be no strain. It was wonderful to be able to look forward to going on duty again; until this bout in O.P.s I had been able to do that since my first year. First years—irrespective of your private affairs—are terrible things. No nurse in her senses can enjoy that year—I have never met one who did—but once you have passed it, slowly, your attitude alters, until half-way through the second year you discover that it is not bad at all, and in the third, that yours is a very pleasant job. Fourth years are the best. You have not the responsibility of a staff nurse, but you are treated as a semi-staff nurse, you know what you have to do and why, you know where everything is, and who everyone is. These are important points. One of the worst points of most hospitals, when you are new to them, is the state of profound ignorance in which you find yourself. Sister says, 'Have you seen the pathologist?' 'Get this or that from the steriliser,' 'Set a trolley for a lumbar puncture—a dry dressing—a cut-down transfusion,' and you have no notion of what she means, or how to do it. Sister Tutor has taught you all this in the class-room; but no class-room resembles a ward with forty beds and forty pairs of eyes watching you all day long. Naturally you are not supposed or expected to manage alone; but you do not discover this until you are past caring. Pros are frightened of doing things wrong, never realising that they are never given anything of importance to do, and if they get a setting in the wrong order the staff nurse is there to correct it.

Pros are also taught never to make excuses, and that 'I haven't time,' or, 'I don't know,' are forbidden explanations; you have to make time, you have to learn how to do this, that, or the other, and the quicker you learn the easier your working life becomes. Consequently whenever a ward was slack at Joe's the pros flocked to the staff nurse for instructions, and passed quite half-hours laying unnecessary trolleys, and learning the positions of the bowls and instruments parrot-wise. It may seem a peculiar system, but it worked. And the day appeared when you stopped being a parrot and found yourself thinking: what's he going to need for his dressing? But when a ward is rushed a mechanical pro is a useful person.

My new junior, a girl called Stane, was an intelligent child. As soon as she had finished her routine she came up to me.

'Nurse, can I do some settings?'

'What don't you know?'

'Aspirations—tappings—I'm hopeless at that.'

'How about transfusions?'

She said she thought she was all right on them.

'Look,' I said, 'you must know them backwards. Set an emergency transfusion with the blood box, and a cut-down, on one trolley, and a chest aspiration on the other. Don't bother to cook the things—we don't want the steriliser on, so do them in the bathroom. I'll come and go through them with you when you've finished.'

She said, 'Child or adult?'

'We've masses of time. Why not do both?'

Tom was the first houseman to come round. 'Well now, isn't this a nice surprise, dear Nurse.' He grimaced. 'I know. I've caught it from "dear Lisa."' After we had dealt with his half-dozen surgical children, we sat down at the centre table that in Christian, unlike the adult wards, was not hidden behind screens at night. I handed him a sheaf of forms. 'Sister wants these filled in, Tom.'

He murmured, 'I wish to God they'd let us use carbon paper,' and obliged. 'That the lot?'

'Yes. Apart from one thing.' I turned to smile at him. 'I gather I have to congratulate you. I certainly do.'

'Aw-shucks!' He looked faintly embarrassed but very happy. 'I rather think I owe you a vote of thanks. You—and that splint cupboard.' He wagged his head. 'Splendid co-operation went on there, Gill.'

I said both he and Lisa were dead crafty. 'It wasn't until I saw the way you were looking at her back that I really tumbled to it. You are a couple of goons to have wasted so much time.'

He said he had no conception how he looked, he only knew he had his ears pinned back. 'You aren't the only person who didn't tumble. I can work myself into a state of acute neurosis when I consider how narrowly we missed going on wasting time. I had practically given up. There didn't seem any point in pushing myself in among the encircling horde.'

'You don't seriously mean you would just have done nothing at all?'

'If you hadn't let Lisa give me that lead——' He smiled self-deprecatingly, then shrugged. 'Possibly.' He sat quiet for a few seconds, then he said, 'Want some more fraternal advice?'

'Love some.' I was interested.

He shrugged again. 'You asked for it. It's this question of laughter. It's no good. It's all right for a jolly evening, but no man can take the thought of being laughed at—when he's serious. Lisa is a gay girl; she laughs at everything and every-body. Which put me off.'

I said, 'She never laughed at you.'

'So I've discovered,' he said quietly. 'It's been a pleasant discovery.'

My pro came out of the bathroom as Tom left the ward. She rushed up to me. 'I'm sorry I missed Mr Thanet, Nurse.' She looked quite upset.

'Why? Did you want to see him specially?'

She said, 'I mean—he didn't get any coffee. It's all ready in the kitchen—I'm sorry, I should have been on the look out.'

'Hey! What is all this?' I was intrigued. Sister Tutor never taught us this in my first year. 'Are you supposed to be running a ward or a coffee stall? The housemen don't have drinks as a routine. That's for bad nights—crises.'

Apparently I had not reassured her. 'I'm sorry. Nurse,' she repeated diffidently, and turned to go.

'Wait a minute.' I looked round the circle of cots. Not one had stirred. 'Sit down,' I pulled out the chair beside mine, 'and tell me how long you've been on nights and where you've worked.'

She said she had been seven months in the hospital and spent the last two as night junior in Ellen.

Her mouth turned down when she said 'Ellen.' I asked why she hadn't liked it. 'Don't you care for convalescent surgery?'

'The women were sweet.'

'Was Sister Ellen the snag? She can be—I know. I was a second-year in Ellen. But you don't want to let Sisters get under your skin. They always have a thing against night pros, it's nothing personal. The technique is to keep out of their way as much as possible, and when you can't, always have a spare clean apron with which to confront them, put your hands behind you and say "yes, Sister, sorry, Sister" to everything. And for goodness' sake,' I begged her, 'never make excuses—even if you have a good one. If you do you get a reputation for being argumentative, and God help,' I added piously, 'any pro that gets that.'

She nodded to herself, as if I was only underlining facts she already knew. 'Thanks, Nurse—that's useful to know.' She smiled. 'The Senior Pro in the Home told us that our first night. I had forgotten it.'

I did not think she had for one minute; I thought she was an intelligent and tactful young woman. 'Then what was wrong with Ellen?' I asked curiously.

She hesitated, 'Well—I suppose it was my fault. The S.P. told us juniors just had to get on with seniors, and that was all there was to it—but I couldn't hit it off with mine.'

'You couldn't?' My surprise was honest. 'That's odd. I suppose Nurse Ash was feeling tired and sickening for this illness. Most juniors get on with her.'

'Oh, but they don't,' she assured me; 'they dread working with——' She broke off, 'Nurse Snow, she isn't in your set?'

'Not only in my set, my child—she's'—well, I thought what could I say, when everyone considered Carol and I a female David and Jonathan—'she's a great friend of mine.' I smiled. 'You want to watch out, Nurse. You can never tell in a place this size who's a buddy of whose.'

'Oh, Nurse,' she said, 'that was a brick.'

'Don't let it bother you. But I know how you feel. Dropping bricks is one of my favourite pastimes.'

She said quickly, 'It was bad luck that morph. being taken. Jean Fraser told us all about it—she was your pro'—I nodded—'and she's in my set. She was terribly sorry when they took you off. She said she'd never had such an easy——'

'Hush'—I held up a hand—'don't drop any more or you'll wake the kids. You nip back to the bathroom—or have you finished the settings?'

She said, not yet. 'Wouldn't you like some coffee, Nurse Snow?'

'I'll help myself later when the men and Night Sister have been.' Since she seemed to have a fixation about coffee I thought we had better get it straight. 'Don't ever wait on the housemen. If they want any, they can help themselves and wash up their cups, or they don't get it again. I don't hold with pros waiting on housemen. The only people we have to run round are Night Sister, the S.M.O., and the S.S.O. And running round offering them drinks is my job.'

She said thoughtfully, 'Of course, Sister, Dr Cutler, and Mr Dexter are different. I mean, they're pretty old, aren't they, Nurse?'

She was only saying what I would have said myself at eighteen, but now I rushed in to defend them. 'They aren't old, Nurse.'

She gaped, 'But, Nurse—they must be forty. And Mr Dexter has got white hair.'

'So he has,' I said, as if I had just realised this, 'it is quite white in front.' I stood up. 'I'm going round. Call me when you want me.'

We had three children with rheumatic fever. Mabel, Margaret, and Joe. The little girls were comfortable, but Joe was damp and twisting in his sleep. I warmed a towel, blankets, and clean nightgown, then dried him, redressed him, and remade his cot. He did not wake properly, but kept his eyes firmly shut as I moved him. When I had finished I said quietly, 'Like some lemonade, Joe?' I hated having to disturb him to drink, but he needed the extra fluid to compensate for what he had just lost in perspiration.

He mumbled, 'I'm thirsty, but I don't want to wake up.'

'Then don't you. Just pretend you're asleep, and I'll pretend I'm filling a motor bus.'

'Petrol or oil?' he asked intelligently.

'Petrol.'

'What make?'

'Oh——' I thought of a well-known advertisement. 'That do you?'

'It's good,' he remarked. 'My dad uses it in his delivery van.'

I slipped my hand under his head and raised it slightly, then held the spout of the feeding-cup to his lips. 'Swallow, Joe.'

He squeezed his eyelids even tighter and drank half the cup. 'Do I have to have more?'

'Buses need a lot of petrol,' I suggested, and he drank the rest, sighed, murmured ' 'nk you,' and was asleep again.

I added the amount of drink I had given him to his fluid-chart and moved on to the next cot. We had five infants in a row, separated from Joe by one empty cot. Their ages ranged from eleven to nineteen months. They were all dry, but one of them had removed his napkin in the last fifteen minutes and had it tucked round his ears. I lifted him out, found the missing pin—happily closed—underneath him, and fixed him up back to front. 'You'll have to be Houdini if you are going to get that off now, honey,' I told him, but he took no notice and went on sleeping.

I heard someone come into the ward and saw Peter was standing at the door. I walked across the ward—Christian was circular and not oblong as were the other wards. 'Something I can do for you, Mr Kier?'

'Good Lord!' He stared at me. 'What are you doing here?'

'Working. Back to the old routine.'

He grinned swiftly, 'Don't tell me the drugs have turned up at last? Is all forgiven and forgotten? That why you're back?'

I said I was back because I had had scarlet fever. I beamed at him because I was glad to see him. We had not been alone together for over a month, and now he was here I was delighted to find that his presence meant as little to me as Tom's had done. Perhaps less. I had become very attached to Tom lately. Kindness is an endearing quality, and Tom Thanet was a kind young man.

He misunderstood my beam. His eyes narrowed as he said lightly.

'So we're back to square one?'

I said, 'Everyone seems to be saying that around Joe's lately.'

'You don't seem to approve?'

'Isn't it,' I said, 'always a mistake to go back?'

He raised his eyebrows. 'Darling—what is all this? If we

aren't at square one—where are we?'

I said evenly, 'In the middle of Christian and you are about to do a round. Right?' I turned on my beam again to show I meant no offence but was just stating a fact.

He bowed, 'As one keen type to another, I salute you. Let's look at the chaps.'

I led the way to the table. 'I'm still a bit vague about which are yours and which Tom's. He looked at all the surgical kids.'

'Tom's an eager beaver these days. I think he's brooding about stepping into old Garth's footsteps ten years from now.'

'But I thought he was going to G.P.?'

Peter looked up from the diagnosis list. 'You mean because of this business with Lisa Smith?'

'Yes. They won't want to hang around Joe's for years waiting to get married.'

He was considering the list again. 'William—he's mine; Anthony Blake—infant hernia in eight; Dorothy; Elaine; Trevor Green—chap with big ears by the cupboard; Mabel Dick.' He jerked his head. 'That bunch over there.'

I looked at my own notes. 'Tom saw them.'

Peter said he had better look at them again. 'Otherwise the boss will be raising the roof again.'

'Again?' I glanced sideways at him. 'Our John being difficult?'

'Being ruddy awful. And not only to my humble self. The whole resident surgical staff is creeping round on tip-toe and falling over backward in their efforts to keep on his good side. Real hard it is for us. We've always had to watch our step slightly—fair enough—but he was easy enough on the whole. Don't know why we're being treated to this sudden show of temperament from him,' he added glumly, 'but personally I wish he'd snap out of it. Snap is the operative word where he's concerned these days.'

This was the first complaint about John I had ever heard from any of the young men. It was also the first time I had discussed him with anyone but Lisa for some weeks. I had noticed no change in his general behaviour in O.P.s, but then Sister Mack was in O.P.s.

I said, 'Maybe you boys ought to send a deputation to Sister O.P.s. She might know the answer.'

He sat back in his chair and leant his elbow on mine. 'Darling, I always thought you were a sensible girl, but you do talk the damnedest rubbish at times. First Tom—now old John.'

I looked round the ward. Christian was not darkened in the same way as the adult wards, and I could see every child's face from where I sat. They were all right, so I asked him to explain himself.

'All this true love and romance,' he said, 'is very touching, in its place, but it's hardly the be-all and end-all of life.'

'But it does complicate matters.'

He threaded his stethoscope through his fingers. 'Only'—he watched the rubber tubing as if it fascinated him—'if you let it. And neither old John nor young Tom are exactly fools. They aren't the types to mess up the job by taking the lighter side of life too seriously.'

'But Tom and Lisa are engaged.'

He tugged at the rubber and smiled faintly. 'Frankly, I take all these red-hot affairs with a grain of salt.'

'Are you still of the opinion that Tom is a rake?'

'He's fairly serious these days, I'll admit. But even a serious type has to have an occasional evening off.'

'I see.' I did. I also saw exactly what I had been to Peter for the past couple of years. And once again I had to remind myself that he never for a moment had given me reason to think I was anything else.

He rethreaded the stethoscope. 'I suppose there are times when it's a good thing to marry early at this game, but those times are pretty few.'

This was a glorious opening for me, but I had no desire to take it. It was not solely my nice nature; I appreciated that he might be warning me that he was considering doing exactly that himself. It might have been unintentional, but I doubted if it was—Peter never spoke without thinking—which was why I could not now have the satisfaction of blaming him for leading me up the garden path. I almost suggested that he changed his profession; he was a born diplomat. It seemed a shame that he should not be let loose among the United Nations.

I stood up quickly, 'I think that's Harry waking.' It was not Harry, who was snoring loudly, but it broke up the party. Peter left the table, looked at his children, and, since Tom had written all the notes and filled in all the forms, once he had seen the children there was nothing to keep him in Christian.

Night Sister, two medical housemen, a medical registrar, and Dr Cutler the S.M.O. came and went in quick succession. Christian, being a mixed ward, was a very social spot at night. John came in after midnight, just as I had given up any hope of seeing him and decided that he must be away for a long week-end, as it was Friday night.

'Good evening, Nurse Snow. How's the family?'

I said they were all quiet, thank you, Mr Dexter, and we walked round the cots. He did not say that he was surprised or pleased to see me; he did not ask why, or if, I was happy to be back. He looked at the surgical children, then said formally, 'That all you have for me, Nurse?'

'That's all, Mr Dexter.'

'Good. I'll push off. Good night.'

I said, 'Good night. Thank you,' and he went.

I sat down at the table, pulled the report book towards me, filled in the date and time, and wrote 'Christian Ward, Night Report.' Then I put down my pen, and asked myself what else I had expected him to do? His behaviour had been his usual behaviour on his night rounds. I had seen him walk in and out of wards endlessly in the last few years; S.M.O.s and S.S.O.s are like Felix: they just keep on walking. He had been quite civil and quite impersonal, as he invariably was. And I thought that because I needed to have my head examined that was no reason to suspect that he was in similar need of an encephalogram. I picked up my pen and wrote my report.

None of the other children in Christian caught scarlet fever, although several more pros went down with it. Since most of the children were convalescents, and the ward continued to be very slack, Matron decided that Nurse Shane and I should not have any nights off duty until the ward closed, and then have them in a bunch at the end.

'Which is all very nice,' I told Lisa, 'but what am I going to do with five days? I don't want to go to a hotel.'

She said, 'Of course, Carol has gone down to Cornwall with that aunt of hers. Don't you want to join her on her sick leave?'

'Too expensive—and too much travelling. I'd spend it all in the train.'

She offered to ask her mother. 'I know she'd be delighted to have you, dear girl, and you could meet Tom's sisters.'

'Sweet of you,' I said gratefully, 'and I mean it, but I don't think I will.'

She said she knew so well how I felt. 'Night Nurses cannot mix in civilised society. You want to go somewhere and sleep. What about someone near your old home. Couldn't they put you up?'

This business of having nowhere to go for my holiday was a new problem. Since my father died I had spent all the succeeding holidays with Carol or at her parents' home. They had been very good to me, which did not make me feel any happier now.

Lisa had given me an idea, so when my holiday was only a few days off I rang up Ann Black. Ann was one of my oldest friends, and she had married the junior partner of our local G.P. the year I started training. When my father died she had written to me, 'Any time you want a breath of the old air, just ring, or wire, or turn up. If the back bedroom is full you can always share the loft with the apples.'

I had not seen Ann for years; I had not been back to that part of the country since my father's funeral. While I waited for the call to go through I wondered if she had moved, or would remember me.

'Gill who?' The wire crackled, our wire had always crackled. 'I'm sorry, I didn't catch——'

'Gill Snow,' I said hopelessly.

'Gill!' She bellowed so loudly that she could have dispensed with the telephone. 'Gill, how wonderful! How are you? And when are you coming to inspect my youngest?'

'Is that Tim? How is he?' I remembered my mother sending a Christening present in my name. 'He must be pretty grown-up.'

'Tim my foot! This one's called Clare! She's nearly one. When are you coming, Gill?'

I said, 'That's why I rang. I want to cadge a bed. Can I?'

Ann and I had been at the same kindergarten, and later at the same day school. Her father was my father's oldest friend and greatest rival. When I put down the telephone her voice was still in my ears. I had shed four years in that number of minutes. I remembered something my mother once said: 'You make a host of acquaintances once you grow up but few friends; but when you are a child, all your acquaintances are your friends, and they stay friends all your life.'

Lisa came over to the Night Nurses' Home next morning and I told her about Ann. 'Just what you need, dear girl—a real break. You haven't been away from the hospital for months.'

She was off until twelve-thirty, so we went for a walk in the park. She said she needed the air after O.P.s. 'For two pins, Gill, I'll play truant and come down to Kent with you.'

'Bad as ever?'

'Worse.' She added that she was a glutton for punishment. 'I'm just a merry little masochist. But, seriously, if it wasn't for dear Tom I'd slit my throat.'

'That affair can't still be standing still. It's unnatural.'

She said we all lead unnatural lives, and she wanted to feed the ducks.

'We haven't any bread.'

'I have.' She produced a breakfast roll from her pocket and began chucking it absently. 'I'm not a one,' she went on, 'for the false raising of hopes, but I'm beginning to wonder about that affair. I've been talking to Tom.'

'Lisa! Not about me.'

'Dear girl, don't be dumb! We girls must stick together! No. About John. And Tom says he thinks we're barmy?'

'Why?' I asked hopefully.

She grinned sympathetically. 'Straw-clutching? Well, listen. Tom says he doesn't think John ever had much of a yen for our

Frances Mack. He thinks John was probably attracted by her face, as they all were when she first arrived, and they were wondering what the Martha's men were doing letting her get away. Then they saw a bit more of her and understood only too well.'

'But how about those dances and tea dates?'

'Dance. Singular. And tea—well, as dear Tom says, the fact that a man takes a girl out to tea doesn't automatically mean that he's going to marry her. Fact.'

I was not reassured. 'He didn't have to ask her out,' I said gloomily. 'Does Tom explain that?'

She said, actually he did. 'He says that the only reason why she has had dear John in tow when every other young man in the hospital has been running like a stag in the opposite direction is because she got her hooks—forgive dear Tom's crude expressions—on to John before he saw them coming, and John, being that sadly old-fashioned thing, a little gentleman, has tried to let her down lightly. And that, Tom says, is why she's been so foul-tempered to one and all lately.'

I smiled half-heartedly. 'Lisa, you have got it badly. "Tom says" is your main theme.'

She laughed. 'I know. So much for my strong mind, dear girl!'

The ducks had finished the roll and were clamouring for more. We walked away, much to their disgust, and they complained to each other loudly. Lisa glanced back at them, 'They are so like the skin clinic,' she murmured.

I said, 'Has Tom found John trying, lately?'

'You've heard that too? Yes, slightly.'

'What's the oracle's opinion?'

'Not very helpful—he just says the chap is obviously overworked, and due to retire to the glory and leisure of a Consultant. He's been S.S.O. the heck of a time.'

'That's true.' I had not thought of anything as obvious as that. Maybe Peter was right about me. I did have the damnedest ideas. Perhaps Tom was right too. It was a comforting thought, in a way. I admitted this to Lisa. 'If he must marry someone, I'd rather it was anyone but her. She'd make him so wretched.'

She flushed. 'I'll tell you something, Gill. When I was all worried about Tom suddenly falling for you, at least I did know that if you were in love with him too, he'd be all right.' She gave me a small, unusual smile. 'Couple of mugs, you and I. Proper soft.'

SATURDAY NIGHT IN CHRISTIAN

ON my last night on duty before Christian emptied, the children were all so well that, beyond the routine treatment and the small amount of nursing necessary for the acute rheumatisms, there was nothing to do. By ten-thirty I was sitting at the table sewing name tapes on sheets, and the pro was writing up a lecture in the kitchen.

It was Saturday night and half the men were off; those that were on duty were too busy to do more than put their heads round the ward door, murmur, 'All right, Nurse,' and vanish again. I did not know what the flap was about until Peter shot in at ten to eleven. 'Want me, Gillian?'

'Only two signatures.' I passed the forms to him. 'Your kids are flourishing.'

'Thank the Lord for that. I'll nip off—I haven't started my round proper yet. I came here first because I knew I could get it over quickly.'

'What's the panic?' I walked to the door with him to save time.

'Saturday night in Cas.,' he said grimly. 'Just routine.'

'Road accidents?'

He nodded. 'Two cars. Both overtaking. They met in the middle'—he pushed one fist into the other palm—'like this. A concertina—according to the cops.'

'Many hurt?' I asked soberly.

He said, 'Three involved. Two drivers, one passenger.'

'How are they?'

'They aren't,' he said laconically. 'At least two of them aren't. The boss is working on the other one now, but she is booked if anyone is.' He looked at me, 'If those poor devils could come and spend the odd Saturday night in Cas. they wouldn't be so damned keen on that last drink and a spin down the by-pass. Know what I've just been doing?'

I had never known Peter so grim before. I shook my head.

'Digging large lumps of by-pass and steering wheel from a poor devil's face with my two hands,' he said savagely, 'so that we can get what's left of him presentable by the time his wife gets here.'

I winced. 'Just like that.'

'Just—like—that.'

I went back to my sewing; my hands worked mechanically; my body was in Christian, my mind in Cas. I had worked in Cas. on Saturday nights; I could visualise very well what was going on there now; I knew the mixture of frustration, compassion, and anger that affected everyone who had to deal with road accidents. It was in the faces of the policemen, the porters, the staff; and the scene was repeated so often, and was so futile, and so fatal.

Until then I had forgotten it was Saturday. You lose all account of time at night; and since your nights-off seldom fall at the weekend—as the weekends were the busiest nights of the week, because of the increase in the accident cases from Friday night to Monday morning—weekends disappeared from your life during your three months night duty.

I did a little mental calculation. That weekend I worked in the theatre, John had been on. That made him on last weekend and officially off tonight. I wondered why he had not gone away.

Bill Henderson, the Senior House Surgeon, looked in at midnight. 'All quiet, Nurse?' Dr Cutler—the S.M.O.—followed him in, and they left together. I expected no more round that night. All the firms had been represented.

At a quarter past one the outer door opened, and John came in. I had finished the sheets and was making a child's split nightgown. I put down my sewing and stood up.

'Sorry I'm late, Nurse Snow,' he said wearily, 'I got held up.'

I said I had heard about that accident. 'Mr Henderson has been round.'

'Has he? I didn't realise that. I knew the theatre was working again and I thought possibly he had not managed to get here.'

'Is this Mr Henderson's weekend on?' I asked, to be sure.

He nodded briefly. 'Yes. I'm off. I meant to go away, but got delayed and decided against it. Since I'm here—how are your children?'

'Very well.' I thought he would go, but he was leaning on the back of one of the chairs and made no attempt to move. I asked if he would like to see the day report on his cases. He had sometimes asked to see that in other wards.

'Thanks.' He pulled out his chair and sat down. I sat beside him, as etiquette demanded, and gave him the book. He turned the pages absently, found what he wanted. 'They seem all right.'

'They are.' I asked after the road accident.

'Which one, Nurse? We've had three more since then. Two motor-bikes and one cyclist.'

'Bad?'

'Not too bad. They had no pillion passengers and were both wearing helmets; they're rather knocked about and shocked, but they haven't done anything serious. The cyclist is in the theatre now. Compound tib. and fib.' He was silent. He closed the

173

report. Then, 'I lost that first girl—the car passenger.'

I said, 'I am so sorry. Was she young?'

He glanced at me. 'About your age. I think she was on her way to or from some dance. She was,' he said very slowly, 'wearing an evening dress. A blue one.' He was silent again. He sat staring at the pool of light on the table that came from the pulled-down centre light that barely cleared our heads as we sat there. Then he said, 'She was a nice-looking girl.'

I said nothing, because there was nothing I could say that would not sound superficial or hackneyed.

At last he roused himself. He looked round at the children. 'They are quiet tonight.'

'It's been like this for the past week. Makes me feel very guilty to be sitting here doing nothing when the place is so busy.'

He said, 'Someone's got to sit here. Another night you'll be up to your eyes in it, and the rest quiet. That's the way the swing goes. Are you on alone?'

'My pro is writing notes in the kitchen. Night Sister can't use her elsewhere as we're still in quarantine.'

He nodded. His face was drawn and heavy, and he looked as old as my pro considered him. He also looked deathly tired.

'The rush is over now,' he said laconically. 'It's all quiet. Until the next time.'

I asked if he was doing Mr Henderson's night round anywhere else.

He did not answer me directly, 'This is my last ward. I knew you were slack in here; I thought I'd finish on that note.'

Peter had said something like that to me once, but his meaning had been different. John meant only what he said. Christian was a peaceful ward.

'Would you like a hot drink before you go to bed?' I wanted him to have one; he looked in need of it, but I expected him to refuse. We all offered him coffee nightly, but I had never yet heard of him accepting it from any nurse. I was much surprised when he said, 'I'd like some coffee if you've got any handy.'

'Coffee? If you've finished?' I hesitated. 'Won't it keep you awake? Won't you have cocoa, Mr Dexter?'

The ghost of a smile lit his eyes. 'Nurse Snow, nothing will keep me awake tonight. And I detest cocoa—thank you very much.'

I got up. 'Black or white, Mr Dexter?'

'Black as you can make it, please. I have still to get from this ward to our house.'

My pro had finished her notes and was sitting on the bread bin in the kitchen knitting a highly complicated jumper. She jumped up and dropped a needle.

'Relax,' I said, 'I'm only getting coffee for Mr Dexter.'

174

She took two cups off the dresser and laid a small tray while I reheated the much stewed coffee. I saw what she was doing. 'Thanks. But only one cup, Nurse. I'll have some later in here with you. I'm not yet a member of the upper classes.' I smiled. 'Nurses in training do not drink coffee in the middle of the ward with the S.S.O. Quote, Sister Tutor.'

He was standing by Joe's cot when I went back to the ward. He jerked his thumb at Joe. 'That chap's looking better. Cutler was worried about him when he came in.' He walked back to the table and sat down again.

I put the tray in front of him. 'Do you take sugar, Mr Dexter?' As I asked that I thought how odd it was that I knew so little about him; and then I thought of the one-dimensional view we all had of each other. The hospital was too large for you to have more than a handful of close friends; you made a host of familiar acquaintances who were part of your life today, forgotten names tomorrow. It was like living with a set of playing cards, seeing just that one professional side and never knowing what went on behind the white starch. I did not know if he took sugar, had parents, read thrillers, liked the movies, was kind to dumb animals, had any serious political views, or views on anything beyond surgery. All I did know was that he was good at his job, infinitely calm, and that as far as I was concerned he did not have to do anything, he just had to be around, and that was all I wanted.

He glanced at the tray, 'What about you, Nurse? Don't you take coffee?'

'Not just now, thanks.' I offered him the cup and saucer.

'Thank you.' He frowned briefly at the coffee.

'Isn't it black enough, Mr Dexter? I can make stronger.'

He looked up at me. 'It's quite right, thanks,' he said absently. He asked about the closing of the ward. 'What's happening to you nurses?'

'The day staff are having two days off, then coming back to spring-clean when it's all fumigated; my pro and I are having five nights off.'

'Going away?'

'Yes.' I explained about Ann. 'It'll be pleasant to see her again.'

'I'm sure it will be. What's her husband's name? Is he a Joe's man?'

'Edinburgh. He's a David Black. But he's got an English M.R.C.P.'

He nodded. 'I met a couple of Blacks in the Army. One was a Scot. Might be the same chap?'

I said I would ask David. I knew he was not really interested in my friends or my affairs, but that he wanted me to keep on

175

talking to take his mind off his own thoughts, so I told him all I could remember of David Black, and then we went on to discuss G.P.s in general and country G.P.s in particular.

He finished his coffee but made no move to go. 'Holidays'— he glanced round the sleeping children—'are a problem when one hasn't a fixed home, aren't they?'

'Yes.' I wondered again about his background, and that house by the river in which he had grown up but which was now a block of flats.

'Of course there are advantages in that situation,' he went on thoughtfully, 'especially in this line. Take tonight.' He looked at me. 'This is supposed to be my weekend off. I've scrubbed it— doesn't make any odds to me. But it's the sort of thing that would make a deal of difference to one's wife. Which is fair enough. A wife has a right to expect to see her husband on his weekends off.'

'I suppose so.' I wondered about Sister O.P.s. Was this the snag? But surely, being a nurse, she knew what marrying a doctor entailed.

'You agree with that, Nurse?'

I hesitated. 'Yes and no. I'd say it depends on whether you marry someone who knows anything about hospitals or not. If she's used to hospitals she'll understand that kind of thing is inevitable—and, come to think of it, not only to resident men. G.P.s wives never know when they are going to see their husbands, and they certainly never have a meal on time.'

He twisted his empty cup. 'Perhaps you're right. But it's always seemed to me that to hand a woman that set of circumstances with a proposal of marriage is hardly a fair bargain.'

That was it, indeed. He did not feel it was fair to ask her to marry him.

I said, 'Resident doctors do marry, Mr Dexter.'

He looked at me. 'And lots of their marriages go astray, Nurse Snow. Cause and effect?' He was still watching me. 'I see you do not agree?'

'No,' I said slowly, 'I don't think I do.' He waited for me to go on, so I did. 'Obviously I look at this from a different angle to yourself; but most women probably feel as I do. When you marry a man in a specific profession like medicine—the Church —even farming—you marry the profession as well. I think you'd accept the peculiar snags as part of life and not want to change it.' I remember my mother's urban upbringing; her dislike of early meals and mud; her love of summer holidays. Yet she made a very successful farmer's wife; she accepted the holidays in late November, the mud, the twelve o'clock dinner hour, and the loneliness of our marsh, not merely with equanimity, but with whole-hearted enjoyment. She wanted to be where my father was and, when that was not possible, she wanted to be waiting for him. Her marriage was a happy and successful one. I explained a little of this. 'Precious few women would want to change their husband's jobs; because a job is so much more part of a man than it is of a woman. If you change the job you'll probably change the man. And if you love someone you wouldn't want to change anything about them.'

'Academically'—his expression was reflective—'supposing—for the sake of argument—you were my wife, and you'd been expecting me tonight and I hadn't turned up. Wouldn't you have been annoyed?'

I felt as if I was driving a nail into my own coffin; I also felt consciously grateful for Sister Tutor's training. 'A good nurse,' she lectured us, 'should always look pleasantly interested, or gently compassionate.' My facial muscles were stiff with the effort of assuming the former expression.

'I might have been annoyed because some food had been ruined, but not seriously so.'

'Why not? Go on, Nurse,' he prompted. 'This interests me.' He sounded as if he were discussing the weather.

'Partly because I'd know roughly why you were held up, and partly because'—I shrugged—'this may sound absurd—but I should think that if you were fond enough of a person to marry them it wouldn't make much odds where they were. In hospital —South America—anywhere. You wouldn't really be apart.' And as I spoke I thought how extraordinary and how easy it was to talk to him this way.

He said very quietly, 'You would just have to put your hand out in the darkness and not feel alone?'

That was exactly how I did feel. I nodded.

He had not taken his eyes off my face. He half smiled. 'I wonder which you are—very young or very old?'

I shrugged, wishing now I had not talked so much. He was silent. We sat there for some time, and there was no sound in the ward beyond the soft breathing of the children; and the occasional chewing noise babies make in sleep. Even Harry had stopped snoring. It was a peaceful silence, one in which there was no strain.

I glanced sideways; he had not moved anything but his eyes, and he was staring again at his empty cup. I recognised the way he sat. I myself had sat as he was sitting, on mornings that followed heavy nights, when I was too tired to get out of a chair. I knew he was a very strong man, not only because of his build, but because of the years he had spent walking the wards of Joe's. Tonight he had reached his limit. He was temporarily too exhausted to make the effort necessary to walk the approximate half-mile of corridor and park to the doctor's house.

177

'Would you like some more coffee, Mr Dexter?'

'No thanks.' He straightened his shoulders. 'I must push off.'

I looked at my watch. It was nearly two. I said, 'It's getting late.'

I took up my sewing without thinking, then saw he was watching my hands and dropped the nightgown on the table. 'I'm awfully sorry,' I apologised, 'I forgot what I was doing.'

Nurses do not sew when waiting on a senior member of the resident staff.

He said, 'Don't stop. It's soothing to watch. I'm hardly doing an official round. What is it? Operation gown?'

I held it up. 'Yes.'

He moved his hand and pushed it through his hair, and I discovered I had been waiting for that gesture. Since Tom drew my attention to his reason for making it I had watched out for it. At first because I was curious and then because I was always watching him. Tom was right. It was a reflex action when John was worried. I suddenly understood why he had made it now. I said, 'Did you have to see her family?'

His lips were a straight line. 'All their families. The police told them, but they came up. I saw them.'

I said, 'I know you told me you can get used to anything, but I don't see how you can. I don't see how you can stand it.'

He turned in his chair and was facing me. 'At times,' he said, 'I can't.'

He stood up slowly and pushed in his chair. He puts his hands in his pockets and his shoulders were back. He looked down at me impassively. 'I seldom admit that to myself. I've never admitted it to another person. That way I like to delude myself into believing that it does not happen. But like most delusions, it doesn't hold water. Thank you'—he inclined his head—'for your—coffee. Good night.'

He walked out of the ward and closed the door quietly behind him. I put down my sewing and went round the children. They were perfectly all right and needed nothing from me. I went back to my sewing.

Next morning Christian was closed and fumigated. The con-valescent children were bathed and had their hair washed and were sent home; the majority in tears, after what had been for them a gloriously protracted party. The few that remained were taken to the private ward to be nursed there until Christian reopened. They were extremely proud of their lingering ail-ments.

'Spect I'll be in for years! Not like you, just an appendix! Now me—I got glands! Will I see them students again in the private ward, Nurse?'

Joe, the one stretcher case, was the smuggest of all. 'Got to be carried, I have,' he announced to the admiring ward, 'not just be pushed in one of them wheel-chairs.'

But before he went there was a minor crisis caused by Harry, who said hopefully that he was sure his throat felt ever so sore and he felt very itchy. This was at six o'clock in the morning. I could not see anything down his throat, nor any sign of a rash; he had no temperature, but he swore that he could not swallow. 'It hurts, Nursie, it does.'

I rang Night Sister; she called a house-physician. The house-physician was a solemn and conscientious young man; he was also very recently qualified; he called the medical registrar.

The medical registrar arrived with his white coat over his pyjamas. 'Tell me the worst at once, Nurse Snow. How many have got scarlet?'

I said I did not personally think anyone had scarlet. 'I'm only a nurse, Doctor—I don't diagnose. I just report. Harry says he's got a cruel throat—and he feels itchy. I thought I had better ring Sister.'

He smiled coldly, 'At six in the morning, Nurse?'

'We close this morning,' I reminded him. 'Some of these children are supposed to be breakfasting in the private wing. I couldn't risk not reporting it.'

Mr May, the house-physician, said, 'That was why I called you.' He sounded as smug as Joe.

The registrar gave us both an ugly look and said he was damned if he hadn't forgotten. He looked at Harry's throat and apparently unblemished skin without comment, walked over to the table, and damned himself again.

'I'll swear that's not a scarlet throat, and that's not a scarlet rash. But I won't,' he said mournfully, 'swear it isn't measles. Anything can be measles.'

'I didn't see any Koplikses,' said the house-physician helpfully.

The registrar scowled. 'Nor did I. But I'm going to get Dr Cutler out of bed. We'll see what he sees.' He turned to me. 'No temperature?'

'No, Doctor. That's what's so odd.'

'Think it's polio?' said the cheerful ghoul of a house-physician.

The registrar did not deign to answer. 'I'll talk to Dr Cutler, Nurse.'

I thanked him. 'I'm sorry to get you up so early.'

He touched his unshaven chin. 'You have my sympathy too, Nurse,' and walked away.

Dr Cutler, a pleasant, round little man, bounced in like a ball.

'What's going on, Nurse? More scarlet?'

'Harry has a sore throat and feels itchy, Doctor.'

The house-physician, who was having the time of his life thinking up different diagnoses, said, 'He's very red in the face. Perhaps he has pinks disease, sir?'

Dr Cutler was a better early riser than his registrar. He said politely, 'Might be so. Of course, it could just be plain health.' He looked down Harry's throat, then went carefully over Harry's body. Harry was delighted, and the other children began unpacking.

'Reckon we'll have to stay, eh, Nursie?'

Dr Cutler looked round at their expectant faces. 'If you think, my little dears,' he said, 'that we are going to keep you all in here because Harry's got a pair of mildly inflamed tonsils, you've got to think again.' He turned round and looked at the registrar, house-physician, and myself, who were standing in a line behind him.

'Mild tonsilitis,' he said shortly, 'I'm going back to bed. I advise you to do the same. Good morning, Nurse Snow.'

'What about Harry, Doctor? Can he go to the private wing?'

'Harry,' said Dr Cutler, 'may take his tonsils—to the private wing. With my love.'

The house-physician said seriously, 'How could you tell it wasn't scarlet, sir?'

Dr Cutler looked up at the earnest young man. 'I've been looking down scarlet throats and at scarlet rashes for the past four weeks. I eat, sleep, think, and dream scarlet. I'm a walking encyclopaedia on fevers. And you ask me how I know? May I tell you? Because it don't look like a scarlet throat and it isn't a scarlet rash! Good morning.' He bounced off again.

The registrar was happy at last. 'I didn't think it was,' he murmured basely, 'but I always like to pass the buck. Morning, Nurse.'

'Oh, God,' said the house-physician when we were alone, 'have I done the wrong thing, Nurse?'

I was very sorry for the poor boy; he was really upset.

'If it had been scarlet and you hadn't called them they'd have murdered you. I don't think you did wrong, Mr May.'

He did not seem at all satisfied. 'How could Cutler tell?'

I recollected that he had only been qualified three weeks. 'He does get a bit of experience in these things.'

He wandered off, shaking his head on the follies of spot diagnosing. I could guess that he was longing to call a pathologist, fever specialist, and possibly the Consultant Paediatrician as well. I did not say anything else. He would find out for himself that Dr Cutler was seldom, if ever, mistaken in a diagnosis. He was not this time. Harry, I heard later, had a mild temperature that evening, and then his throat settled again with as little reason as it had flared. Children's throats do these things.

That afternoon I went down to Kent. Ann and her husband welcomed me warmly, her children were sweet, and I enjoyed my stay with them and the opportunity it gave me to meet again my old friends in the village. While I was there I had a note from Matron telling me I could have two more days added to my holiday, to compensate for the off-duty I had missed in Out-Patients. I was due back on duty on the following Monday night.

Although I was pleased in a way to return to my past, I was happiest when I was alone. I did a lot of walking over the wind-swept marsh and curled inland along that part of the coast and lay lonely and treeless, haunted by the ghost of the lost sea. It was odd being back on my home ground, odd and reassuring. I felt complete for the first time in months. I knew who I was and where I belonged. I did not have to explain my presence—every-one in a village knows about everyone else—and it was perfectly natural that I, Gill Snow, should be staying with Ann Black. My friends asked a few questions, 'Did I like nursing? Wasn't it terribly hard work?' But these were merely opening gambits to give them the excuse to tell me how the church roof had broken again, and something had to be done for the organ fund.

Something had always had to be done about the organ fund. And had I heard about the Parish Council meeting? There had been the most terrible scene about the bell-ringers.

My father had been on that Council, and I never knew him to return from a meeting in which there had not been a terrible scene. My mother's first question was 'What was it this time, Bill?' And I had to hear about the harvest. 'Imagine, Gill, a whole field of clover seed wasted in all that rain! The stuff wouldn't dry, and with so much turning the seeds fell out. Six hundred quid went up in a bonfire! Remember that happening to your father in '46?'

And the local hunt was having trouble. The Master was a good type, they said, 'But M.F.H.s these days are not what they were. No discipline in the field.'

I wondered when M.F.H.s had been what they were.

It was all very pleasant and soothing, and if only I could have stopped thinking of John I should have been very happy. I never thought at all about Carol, the drugs, Peter, or the mess that had resulted from her one night in Robert. If she had not done that I wondered if she might not have done something with perhaps even more serious consequences. I never cared for the word 'hate' and was slow to use it even now. I could not understand how she could bother to dislike me so much; I was not important to her. Perhaps it was work, and the shock of her parents' death, that had temporarily unbalanced her. What she had done was not normal, and abnormal people are ill people; that I had learnt in my training. I thought all this out when I was still in the hospital, and now I was home I did not bother with it again.

What did bother me was the prospect of a future without John. Try as I could, and I tried hard, I could not see anything else for myself. I avoided thinking of that Saturday night in Christian. His defences were down because he was tired. I was just the available pair of ears. I would probably see a lot of him when I went back. Night Seniors do see a lot of the men—that's one of the minor attractions of night duty; not merely from the obvious point of view, but because the men, being doctors, know a lot more than we do, and most of them are keen on their jobs, and like to talk shop, and their conversation makes interesting and instructive listening. But when I left Christian I would be near the end of my training and, having done so much surgery lately, would almost certainly finish in one of the medical wards. I would have to be content with Dr Cutler, a nice little man and a clever physician. I was not at all content.

14

A STRANGER ON THE MARSHES

SATURDAY night was dreadful. I went to bed early, hoping to sleep long before 1 A.M. I did not sleep; I lay and cursed myself for being so weak-minded, Matron for giving me these extra two nights, and the country outside my window for being so quiet. There was nothing to distract my mind, which was behaving in the usual way for the small dark hours. I married John to Frances Mack, Peter to Carol, Lisa to Tom; I had every girl in the place married and saw myself carrying my lonely lamp through the years until, arthritic and ailing, I ended up as a Home Sister in some provincial hospital that was too small and insignificant to afford a lift in the Nurses' Home. I got really excited at the thought of their expecting me to drag my old legs up the stairs, and was composing an irate letter to an unborn hospital committee when I finally fell asleep.

When I got back from church next morning I found Ann had packed me a picnic lunch. 'I remembered our passion for picnicking in mid-winter, Gill. I thought you might like to spend your last day shivering in the open air!'

'It's a lovely day.' I was delighted with the prospect. 'I think it's a splendid idea.'

She looked doubtfully at the window. 'At least it's not raining yet. Where'll you go?'

I hesitated. 'I'm not sure. I think I'll walk over our—I mean the Frand's—land towards the sea. I'll probably eat in a net-house. There'll still be a few birds to look at.'

I had avoided this specific part of the marsh since I returned, but now it looked so normal that at times I felt my father was walking with me. I saw his straight back, the old tweed hat he always wore, the leather patches on his jacket, and his mud-spattered boots, the insignia of a working farmer.

I did not feel morbid or sad; I knew that his shadow would walk that marsh until the sea came back. He had dug, pumped, and farmed those acres for forty-two years, from the time he left school and joined his father when he was seventeen. I was the fifth generation to be born in the stone house that crouched on its knees against the wind. The fifth and the last; and, as we were a family that went in for only children, when my father died the farm was sold. There had been little profit from the sale, but what there was was sitting in the local bank until I was twenty-five.

I stood and looked at the house, then turned towards the sea. There might be another family living there, but it was unchanged; the out-houses were painted in black and white as we had kept them, and the swinging fox over the oast-house was the one my grandfather had put there.

The land beneath my feet altered; it grew firmer, there was less soil, and then miles of pebbled green rock; the pools through which I splashed were pools of salt water. The wind was rising as I reached the sea, it tore open the tight faces of a solitary carpet of sea-pinks, and the big gulls screamed over my head.

I had no watch, but took my time from the pale sun. I ate my lunch in one of the ruined net-houses that were dotted at irregular intervals on the low rocks. After lunch I climbed on to the sea-wall.

The wind was worse up there; it tore into my lungs and stifled my breathing. The wall was being strengthened against the spring flooding. There were no men working there today, as it was Sunday, but they had left their bricks and sandbags in neat mounds. I took shelter against one of these and got my breath.

When I could breathe normally I looked round. I could see inland for miles, while behind me the urgent sea reached to the sea-wall, and demanded its lost entry. The noise was overpowering, and the sandbags against which I leaned vibrated. I relaxed and listened, and my body swayed slightly with the movement of the sandbags.

Something that was not a bird moved from one of the far net-houses. I looked again and saw a man walking across the rocks far off on my right. I watched him out of disinterested curiosity, wondering if he was one of the Frands, or a local bird-watcher spending a Sunday with a cine-camera. The marsh in all seasons was a bird-watcher's paradise.

He stopped at a second net-house, stooped, and went in. Then he came out, straightened after the low doorway, and took off his hat. I could not see his face from this distance, but at his next movement I jerked away from the sandbags. He was pushing one hand through his hair, and even from this distance I could see his hair was black. I ignored all possibilities that this might be a stranger—that the world is full of men who tug at their hair in moments of stress. I moved from my shelter and yelled; the wind was with me, and although he could not have heard what I said, he caught the sound of a voice. He turned my way, raised a hand in a slow wave, then came towards me.

I half jumped, half climbed, from the wall, then slipped and skidded across the wet rocks, not stopping to wonder why and if he had come to find me. All I wanted was to reach him, and until I did that I would fight nothing but the wind.

Suddenly he was in front of me, and he was looking at me as no man had ever looked at me. He said, 'Your friend, Mrs Black, told me that I would find you somewhere here.' His voice was slightly breathless, as if he too had been battling on that sea-wall. 'I hope you don't object to my asking her?'

I said I did not object.

He held his hat in one of his hands; his hands hung heavily at his sides. 'I found the house quite easily, and Mrs Black was kind enough to ask me to wait with them until you returned; but I explained that I hadn't very much time, so she suggested that I came over the marsh to look for you.'

I felt dazed. 'That was nice of her.'

He said, 'She seems a very charming person.' He did not take his eyes from my face. 'I hope'—it was then that I saw he was actually, and incredibly, nervous—'I hope you don't mind my coming down like this? I heard in town that you were having an extra couple of nights off, and I did so want to talk to you. Somehow I have never been able to manage that in town—so I came. Do you mind?'

I said, 'No.'

The wind from the sea hurled itself between us, and five plovers rose in a black and white cloud over our heads. He watched the birds, and then looked round the marsh and over towards the sea-wall. 'We seem to be standing on the edge of the world'—he smiled slightly—'but this is your world. It's not very easy to talk here—is there anywhere we can go—one of those stone huts?'

I said sedately, 'Yes, we can go into a net-house. We'll be out of the wind in one of them, and it'll be less noisy than if we take shelter against the sea-wall.' I walked away as formally as if I was leading him up a ward. I had to be formal; it was my last defence.

There was some hay in the corner of the net-house, left by a thoughtful shepherd for stray sheep. It was musty but fairly dry. I sat down in silence, and he sat a yard or so away, leaning against the rough-stone wall. The building had a low roof and no windows, and the light tilted through the open doorway.

I wanted so much to say something brilliant and kind; I could not say a single word. I stared at him dumbly and waited for him to go on, or for myself to wake up.

He said at last, 'I have always felt in town that if you listened to me it was because you thought you had to listen to me. And had I asked you out I would not have been sure whether you had not come out with me for the same reason. Do you understand?'

'Yes.'

'The other night in Christian'—his voice was very deep—'I told you that at times I couldn't stand it. I didn't mind your knowing that, and I don't mind your knowing how much I have missed you this last week, and how I can't stand this much longer.' He picked up a piece of hay and methodically tucked it through the band of his hat, then took another piece and then another. 'I have'—he twisted the hat and began on the other side—'reached the point of no return where you are concerned. So I thought I had better come down and see you about it.'

'Where—I—am—concerned?'

He looked at me. 'Yes.'

I said carefully, 'Do I concern you?'

He nodded. 'Didn't you know?' He answered himself. 'How could you? And why should you bother to know? It was not important to you.'

I seemed incapable of doing anything but echo his words.

'Not important to me?'

He picked up another handful of straw and began sorting suitable pieces for his hat decorating.

'I'm sorry you've had this upset over Kier,' he said gently. 'I didn't mean to remind you of it—but now I am. Of course, what I felt about you has been unimportant to you—you have never been interested in any other man.' He dropped his hat as if it was hot. 'Perhaps I should not have come.' He looked round at me. 'No perhaps about it. I'll'—he heaved himself on to his knees—'I'll push off and leave you to your walk.'

I suddenly realised that I did not have to accept his going; that we were not in the hospital; that the barriers were down even though he was using his usual words.

I said sharply, 'No. Don't push off.'

He was standing, and bent nearly double because of that low ceiling. 'You want me to stay?'

'Yes.' I held out a hand. 'Please.'

He took my hand and dropped down on to the hay. 'Why?'

I said, 'Why have you come here today? Why today?'

He put my hand down on the straw as if it was a package and leant back against the wall.

He said, 'This visit is two years over-due. I have wanted to talk to you, to be alone with you, since I walked into Peter and Paul when I got back to the general side as S.S.O., and saw you rushing round with the lunch trays.' He looked round at me. 'I did not know your name—I discovered it very shortly —at the same time I discovered that you and Kier were considered inseparable. Hospital etiquette,' he said dryly, 'works both ways. You wouldn't even drink a cup of coffee with me the other night; how could I pester a second-year nurse, sixteen years younger than myself? You may not have wanted that coffee, but I have very much wanted to do more than that with you, for a long time.' Still he did not take his eyes from my face. 'A very long time,' he repeated. 'And why I chose today is that somehow I have seen so much more of you lately—Robert— O.P.s—and then there was last Saturday night in Christian. And seeing so much more of you only accentuated how much I was missing. I know you are still upset over Kier, I saw how stricken you looked that night after I found you standing on the fire-escape outside Susan—but I had to move in, now, before you left Joe's for good, or met someone else. That is why I came today. And now,' he said quietly, 'I've said what I came to say—would you like me to go?'

I said, 'Don't go.'

He did not answer. He sat very still.

'That night outside Susan,' I told him, 'it wasn't Peter that was wrong. I did feel stricken, but he wasn't the cause.'

He said, 'Did Carol Ash tell you she had taken that morphia?'

I stared at him. 'How on earth did you know?'

'I didn't. I just worked it out. Remember my once telling you I thought it had been pinched intentionally?' I nodded. 'Well, I felt she was the most likely person.'

'But—she was supposed to be my greatest friend. Everyone knew that.'

He said, 'I knew it too. I also,' he said deliberately, 'knew her father. He was once a patient of mine. He was a clever man—too clever. And he was quite ruthless when he wanted anything. His daughter always struck me as being very like him. Quite natural. And that was the kind of thing Ashton Ash would have done to someone who had something he wanted.' He was silent, then he added, 'He was a very bad patient.'

'I never knew he was a patient of yours. Carol never told me.'

'She may well not have known. This was some years ago, just after the war. I was R.S.O. in one of the provincial places. She and you were school children then. He came into the Private Wing.' He frowned, 'How did you find out?'

I hesitated, and he guessed why immediately.

'My good child, you don't seriously think I'm going to turn into an avenging angel? Don't tell me if you don't want to—but I won't do anything about it if you do. That's how you want it, isn't it?'

'Yes. No point in raking it up.'

He said mildly, 'And of course you wouldn't have left it lying about to be swiped a second time.'

I smiled slightly. 'No one'll swipe it now. It's in the Thames —or wherever it is the bath water drains into.'

He smiled back. 'I thought you were supposed to have learned hygiene? Since when has the Thames been a public drain?' Then his voice and his expression changed. 'You've had a rotten time over all this,' he said softly. 'And I can't tell you how sorry I am about Kier.'

He looked so miserable that I ceased to feel shy.

'It doesn't bother me any more.' I looked at him. 'Nothing bothers me, if you are there.'

'Do you mean that, Gill?' He was incredulous.

I nodded. And then I was in his arms, and he was kissing my face, my lips, my hair. I ceased to worry about the things I still did not understand; I forgot everything but the strange and wonderful security that I felt in his arms—the wonder of being there at all.

In a little while he raised his head, but he did not let me go.

'This isn't just a reaction, dearest? A rebound from Kier? I'm happy to have you on any terms, but you wouldn't be happy that way. You can't marry a man'—his lips twisted—'for his bed-side manner, my dear.'

His words reminded me not of Peter but of Frances Mack. I moved away and he let go of me instantly.

He said, 'Kier is still in the way?'

'No. He hasn't been in the way for quite a while. Honestly. But——' I stopped. Old habits die very hard with me, and it was not easy to break the habit of years and ask him to explain his behaviour.

'But what?' He smiled rather wearily. 'I don't bite. Never have—gave it up years ago. What's worrying you?'

'Well, what about you? Mightn't that same danger be there for you?'

He said, 'Are we discussing Frances Mack?' I nodded. 'I was afraid of this. What do you want to know?'

'I thought you were in love with her.'

He looked at me thoughtfully. 'Now do you see why I left you alone? I asked that young woman to one dance. One. Once I met her by chance and we had tea together. One of the patients had sent me a brace of tickets, and I passed them on to her. They were for that afternoon. If I'd met you first you'd have had 'em. She took her mother, and they asked me to tea at their flat, presumably to return the compliment. And that was all.' He raised one hand and dropped it by his side again. 'But I know the hospital had married us off before we had had the first dance of the evening, and she's a Sister, and technically Sisters are above gossip. Can you imagine what would have been said if I had been rushing round after a nurse—sixteen years younger than myself? A nurse who clearly wasn't interested? Can you conceive how you'd feel to be the object of all that talk? My God, there'd have been talk,' he added bitterly, 'because if one thing is certain at Joe's, it is that there'll be talk!'

I said, 'I never thought of that.' I felt very happy and then I remembered that night in O.P.s. My expression must have altered because he said gently, 'Now what's wrong?'

I told him. He stared at me, then roared with laughter.

'My darling child, I spend my entire life writing letters for Sisters! I have to write a letter about every single patient that passes through my hands. Surely you knew that?'

'I do,' I agreed. 'It's just something else I never thought of. But why were you always around O.P.s lately?'

He said simply, 'Because you were there.' Then he smiled. 'Anything else you want cleared up?'

I shook my head. 'Not a thing. Not one thing.'

He said, 'My turn now. I want to know something. When,' his voice shook, 'did I stop being something you had to take round and offer coffee to?'

I thought it over. 'I'm not sure.' He looked amused. 'Truly. Everything's been such a muddle lately, and then, when the muddle began to clear, you were there.'

The laughter left his eyes. 'Dearest—perhaps I'm not being fair. I'm so much older than you, and you're used to doing what I say—perhaps because I love you so much I'm forcing you to say more than you feel?'

His face was lined and worried, and the sight of his anxiety brought back all the courage I ever had and a great deal more. I raised myself on to my heels and twisted round so that I was facing him. I put my hands on his shoulders and shook him slightly.

'You are a very clever man,' I said firmly, 'and a good surgeon. You are also the kindest man I ever met and, quite apart from loving you, I respect you more than any man I've ever known. But you are talking a packet of rubbish, Mr Dexter, sir, and I wish to goodness you'd stop.' His eyes were alight with laughter and more than laughter. I knew I was scarlet in the face, I did not care if I was purple. 'I've been quite daft,' I went on quickly, 'about a lot of things. But the daftest thing I ever did was not seeing you as you really are until these last few weeks.'

He took my face in his hands. 'Shake me again, Gill. I like being shaken by you.' He kissed me. 'You'll have to marry me after that—won't you, please?'

'Will you report me to Matron if I don't?'

'Of course.' He kissed me again. 'Rank insubordination. So you will?'

'I'd love to.'

Suddenly he laughed, and his shoulders shook.

'What's the joke?'

He controlled himself. 'Now we are engaged,' he murmured, 'don't you think you could break down and call me John?'

I laughed too. 'I never realised I hadn't. I always do.'

He said, 'I grasped that. I mean to my face.'

Some time later we saw the winter afternoon was dying, and the sky was heavy with rain clouds. He said, 'I'll have to get back. I've got three hours' driving ahead. I must do my night round—and I've had to leave Henderson standing in, when officially he's off.'

We had four miles to walk, and we walked slowly. It was dark when we reached the Blacks' house. He would not come in.

'I've got to push off in a few minutes and I don't want to waste those minutes sharing you with other people. I've shared you long enough.'

I remembered we had had no tea.

'Tea?' he said vaguely. 'Is it tea-time?'

I asked if he had had any lunch?

'I wanted to get away,' he said apologetically, 'so I skipped it. I'm a little out of touch with the finer points of life. I haven't lived in a house for—let's see—not since I was a preclinical, nineteen years ago. I lived in digs, and since I qualified, either in or out of the army I've lived in hospitals. It will be so nice,' he said softly as he stroked my hair, 'to have a home, with you.'

His job as S.S.O. was due to finish in the coming April. After that he had been promised a Consultant's job at Joe's and could live where he liked. He said, 'One thing—do you mind my being so much older than you?'

I said, 'Do you mind my being so much younger?' And there was no more talk.

When he got into the car he said, 'The other night in Christian when we were discussing my hypothetical wife, I was thinking how wonderful it would be, if that was you.'

I told him I had thought the same. He smiled, a wonderful smile.

'I knew Henderson had been in. I wasn't doing a general round as I was off. But I had to come to Christian. I was very cut up about that poor girl. I felt useless and weary, and I needed the comfort of your presence. So I came to you.'

I thought, no woman could ask for any more.

I did not go into the house immediately he left. It must have rained for some time while we were in the net-house, because the bare branches of the trees were dripping with water. I walked under the empty apple trees and over the sodden ground, and wished I could tell my parents how wonderful he was and how still more wonderful it was that he should love me. I stayed out for a long time, thinking about him and about tomorrow, when I would see him again. And before I went in I saw the night sky had cleared. The marsh wind had blown the rain clouds out to sea, and the stars were all over the sky.

THE END

A HOUSE FOR SISTER MARY by LUCILLA ANDREWS

When Sister Mary retired everyone was delighted to hear that she had found a cottage – and everyone from St Barnabas came to her retirement party.

Anne Rowe – still nursing the wounds from her broken engagement – hadn't expected to enjoy the party – nor to be swept off her feet by Nick Dexter, the dynamic young architect who had designed the Observation Unit of Barny's. When she went to work in the unit she found her days exacting and absorbing, and her growing relationship with Nick proved to be a delightful one.

Only the growing dislike between herself and Doctor Robert Gordon seemed to be marring her life . . .

0 552 11384 0   75p

THE YOUNG DOCTORS DOWNSTAIRS
by LUCILLA ANDREWS

'You married?' I asked.
'Not yet. Just as well under the circumstances.'
He sat on the floor as I had the only chair in his fishing hut. It was the only occupied hut on the island that wild night.
'Mind if I call you Aphrodite?'
My name was Shelley Dexter, but I didn't mind.
He'd just saved my life.
I didn't mind either when I discovered he was a senior medical student at my hospital, St Barnabas, London.
For I was still in love with Alistair that night.
Extraordinary what a dousing in icy water can do to a girl . . .
And a man . . .

0 552 11386 7   75p

A SELECTED LIST OF CORGI ROMANCE
FOR YOUR READING PLEASURE

ORDER FORM

All these books are available at your bookshop or newsagent, or can be ordered direct from the publisher. Just tick the titles you want and fill in the form below.

CORGI BOOKS, Cash Sales Department, P.O. Box 11, Falmouth, Cornwall.

Please send cheque or postal order, no currency.

U.K. send 30p for first book plus 15p per copy for each additional book ordered to a maximum charge of £1.29 to cover the cost of postage and packing.

B.F.P.O. and Eire allow 30p for first book plus 15p per copy for the next eight books, thereafter 6p per book.

Overseas Customers. Please allow 50p for the first book and 15p per copy for each additional book.

NAME (block letters) ....

ADDRESS ....

....

While every effort is made to keep prices low, it is sometimes necessary to increase prices at short notice. Corgi books reserve the right to show new retail prices on covers which may differ from those previously advertised in the text or elsewhere.